QUICK!

MISCHIEF MAKERS,

SIGN HERE so everyone knows **this book** belongs

TO YOU.

ROALD DAHL was a spy, ace fighter pilot, chocolate historian and medical inventor. He was also the author of *Charlie and the Chocolate Factory*, *Matilda*, *The BFG* and many more brilliant stories. He remains **THE WORLD'S NUMBER ONE STORYTELLER.**

QUENTIN BLAKE has illustrated more than three hundred books and was Roald Dahl's favourite illustrator. In 1980 he won the prestigious Kate Greenaway Medal. In 1999 he became the first ever Children's Laureate and in 2013 he was knighted for services to illustration.

INTRODUCING . . .

Mr Fox

Mrs Fox

The Small Foxes

Badger

Boggis

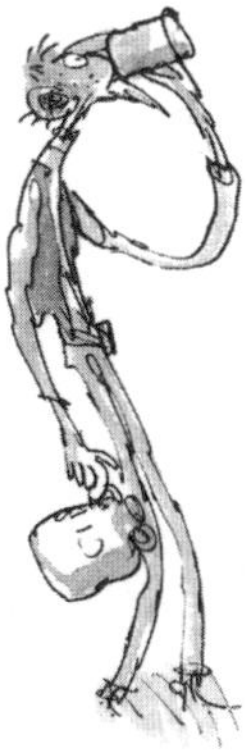

Bean

Bunce

Books by Roald Dahl

THE BFG
BOY: TALES OF CHILDHOOD
BOY *and* GOING SOLO
CHARLIE AND THE CHOCOLATE FACTORY
CHARLIE AND THE GREAT GLASS ELEVATOR
THE COMPLETE ADVENTURES OF CHARLIE AND MR WILLY WONKA
DANNY THE CHAMPION OF THE WORLD
THE ENORMOUS CROCODILE
ESIO TROT
FANTASTIC MR FOX
GEORGE'S MARVELLOUS MEDICINE
THE GIRAFFE AND THE PELLY AND ME
GOING SOLO
JAMES AND THE GIANT PEACH
MATILDA
THE MAGIC FINGER
THE TWITS
THE WITCHES

Picture books

DIRTY BEASTS
THE ENORMOUS CROCODILE
THE GIRAFFE AND THE PELLY AND ME
THE MINPINS
REVOLTING RHYMES

Plays

THE BFG: PLAYS FOR CHILDREN (*Adapted by David Wood*)
CHARLIE AND THE CHOCOLATE FACTORY: A PLAY (*Adapted by Richard George*)
DANNY THE CHAMPION OF THE WORLD: PLAYS FOR CHILDREN (*Adapted by David Wood*)
FANTASTIC MR FOX: A PLAY (*Adapted by Sally Reid*)
JAMES AND THE GIANT PEACH: A PLAY (*Adapted by Richard George*)
THE TWITS: PLAYS FOR CHILDREN (*Adapted by David Wood*)
THE WITCHES: PLAYS FOR CHILDREN (*Adapted by David Wood*)

Teenage fiction

THE GREAT AUTOMATIC GRAMMATIZATOR AND OTHER STORIES
RHYME STEW
SKIN AND OTHER STORIES
THE VICAR OF NIBBLESWICKE
THE WONDERFUL STORY OF HENRY SUGAR AND SIX MORE

Collections

THE ROALD DAHL TREASURY
SONGS AND VERSE

ROALD DAHL

FANTASTIC MR FOX

Illustrated by Quentin Blake

PUFFIN

Find out more about Roald Dahl by visiting the website at

roalddahl.com

PUFFIN BOOKS

UK | USA | Canada | Ireland | Australia
India | New Zealand | South Africa

Puffin Books is part of the Penguin Random House group of companies
whose addresses can be found at global.penguinrandomhouse.com.

puffinbooks.com

Penguin Random House UK

First published by George Allen & Unwin 1970
Published by Puffin Books 1974
Reissued with new artwork 1996
This edition published 2016

038

Set in Baskerville MT 14/17 pt by Palimpsest Book Produciton Limited, Falkirk, Stirlingshire
Printed in Great Britain by Clays Ltd, Elcograf S.p.A.

A CIP catalogue record for this book is available from the British Library

ISBN: 978-0-141-36544-2

www.greenpenguin.co.uk

FSC www.fsc.org MIX Paper from responsible sources FSC® C018179

Penguin Random House is committed to a sustainable future for our business, our readers and our planet. This book is made from Forest Stewardship Council® certified paper.

To Olivia

Contents

1

The Three Farmers

Down in the valley there were three farms. The owners of these farms had done well. They were rich men. They were also nasty men. All three of them were about as nasty and mean as any men you could meet. Their names were Farmer Boggis, Farmer Bunce and Farmer Bean.

Boggis was a chicken farmer. He kept thousands of chickens. He was enormously fat. This was because he ate three boiled chickens smothered with dumplings every day for breakfast, lunch and supper.

Bunce was a duck-and-goose farmer. He kept thousands of ducks and geese. He was a kind of pot-bellied dwarf. He was so short his chin would have been underwater in the shallow end of any swimming-pool in the world. His food was doughnuts and goose-livers. He mashed the livers into a disgusting paste and then stuffed the paste into the doughnuts. This diet gave him a tummy-ache and a beastly temper.

Bean was a turkey-and-apple farmer. He kept thousands of turkeys in an orchard full of apple trees. He never ate any food at all. Instead, he drank gallons of strong cider which he made from the apples in his orchard. He was as thin as a pencil and the cleverest of them all.

'Boggis and Bunce and Bean
One fat, one short, one lean.
These horrible crooks
So different in looks
Were none the less equally mean.'

That is what the children round about used to sing when they saw them.

2

Mr Fox

On a hill above the valley there was a wood.

In the wood there was a huge tree. Under the tree there was a hole.

In the hole lived Mr Fox and Mrs Fox and their four Small Foxes.

Every evening as soon as it got dark, Mr Fox would say to Mrs Fox, 'Well, my darling, what shall it be this time? A plump chicken from Boggis? A duck or a goose from Bunce? Or a nice turkey from Bean?' And when Mrs Fox had told him what she wanted, Mr Fox would creep down into the valley in the darkness of the night and help himself.

Boggis and Bunce and Bean knew very well what was going on, and it made them wild with rage. They were not men who liked to give anything away. Less still did they like anything to be stolen from them. So every night each of them would take his shotgun and hide in a dark place somewhere on his own farm, hoping to catch the robber.

But Mr Fox was too clever for them. He always approached a farm with the wind blowing in his face, and this meant that if any man were lurking in the shadows ahead, the wind would carry the smell of that man to Mr Fox's nose from far away. Thus, if Mr Boggis was hiding behind his Chicken House Number One, Mr Fox would smell him out from fifty yards off and quickly change direction, heading for Chicken House Number Four at the other end of the farm.

'Dang and blast that lousy beast!' cried Boggis.

'I'd like to rip his guts out!' said Bunce.

'He must be killed!' cried Bean.

'But how?' said Boggis. 'How on earth can we catch the blighter?'

Bean picked his nose delicately with a long finger. 'I have a plan,' he said.

'You've never had a decent plan yet,' said Bunce.

'Shut up and listen,' said Bean. 'Tomorrow night we will all hide just outside the hole where the fox lives. We will wait there until he comes out. Then . . . *Bang! Bang-bang-bang.*'

'Very clever,' said Bunce. 'But first we shall have to find the hole.'

'My dear Bunce, I've already found it,' said the crafty Bean. 'It's up in the wood on the hill. It's under a huge tree . . .'

3

The Shooting

'Well, my darling,' said Mr Fox. 'What shall it be tonight?'

'I think we'll have duck tonight,' said Mrs Fox. 'Bring us two fat ducks, if you please. One for you and me, and one for the children.'

'Ducks it shall be!' said Mr Fox. 'Bunce's best!'

'Now do be careful,' said Mrs Fox.

'My darling,' said Mr Fox, 'I can smell those goons a mile away. I can even smell one from the other. Boggis gives off a filthy stink of rotten chicken-skins. Bunce reeks of goose-livers, and as for Bean, the fumes of apple cider hang around him like poisonous gases.'

'Yes, but just don't get careless,' said Mrs Fox. 'You know they'll be waiting for you, all three of them.'

'Don't you worry about me,' said Mr Fox. 'I'll see you later.'

But Mr Fox would not have been quite so cocky had he known exactly *where* the three farmers were waiting at that moment. They were just outside the entrance to the hole, each one crouching behind a tree with his gun loaded. And what is more, they had chosen their positions very carefully, making sure that the wind was not blowing from them towards the fox's hole. In fact, it was blowing in the opposite direction. There was no chance of them being 'smelled out'.

Mr Fox crept up the dark tunnel to the mouth of his hole. He poked his long handsome face out into the night air and sniffed once.

He moved an inch or two forward and stopped. He sniffed again. He was always especially careful when coming out from his hole.

He inched forward a little more. The front half of his body was now in the open.

His black nose twitched from side to side, sniffing and sniffing for the scent of danger. He found none, and he was just about to go trotting forward into the wood when he heard or thought he heard a tiny noise, a soft rustling sound, as though someone had moved a foot ever so gently through a patch of dry leaves.

Mr Fox flattened his body against the ground and lay very still, his ears pricked. He waited a long time, but he heard nothing more.

'It must have been a field-mouse,' he told himself, 'or some other small animal.'

He crept a little further out of the hole . . . then further still. He was almost right out in the open now. He took a last careful look around. The wood was murky and very still. Somewhere in the sky the moon was shining.

Just then, his sharp night-eyes caught a glint of something bright behind a tree not far away. It was a small silver speck of moonlight shining on a polished surface. Mr Fox lay still, watching it. What on earth was it? Now it was moving. It was coming up and up . . . *Great heavens! It was the barrel of a gun!* Quick as a whip, Mr Fox jumped back into his hole and at that same instant the entire wood seemed to explode around him. *Bang-bang! Bang-bang! Bang-bang!*

The smoke from the three guns floated upward in the night air. Boggis and Bunce and Bean came out from behind their trees and walked towards the hole.

'Did we get him?' said Bean.

One of them shone a flashlight on the hole, and there on the ground, in the circle of light, half in and half out of the hole, lay the poor tattered bloodstained remains of . . . a fox's tail. Bean picked it up. 'We got the tail but we missed the fox,' he said, tossing the thing away.

'Dang and blast!' said Boggis. 'We shot too late. We should have let fly the moment he poked his head out.'

'He won't be poking it out again in a hurry,' Bunce said.

Bean pulled a flask from his pocket and took a swig of cider. Then he said, 'It'll take three days at least before he gets hungry enough to come out again. I'm not sitting around here waiting for that. Let's dig him out.'

'Ah,' said Boggis. 'Now you're talking sense. We can dig him out in a couple of hours. We know he's there.'

'I reckon there's a whole family of them down that hole,' Bunce said.

'Then we'll have the lot,' said Bean. 'Get the shovels!'

4

The Terrible Shovels

Down in the hole, Mrs Fox was tenderly licking the stump of Mr Fox's tail to stop the bleeding. 'It was the finest tail for miles around,' she said between licks.

'It hurts,' said Mr Fox.

'I know it does, sweetheart. But it'll soon get better.'

'And it will soon grow again, Dad,' said one of the Small Foxes.

'It will never grow again,' said Mr Fox. 'I shall be tail-less for the rest of my life.' He looked very glum.

There was no food for the foxes that night, and soon the children dozed off. Then Mrs Fox dozed off. But Mr Fox couldn't sleep because of the pain in the stump of his tail. 'Well,' he thought, 'I suppose I'm lucky to be alive at all. And now they've found our hole, we're going to have to move out as soon as possible. We'll never get any peace if we . . . What was *that*?' He turned his head sharply and listened. The noise he heard now was the most frightening noise a fox can ever hear – the scrape-scrape-scraping of shovels digging into the soil.

'Wake up!' he shouted. 'They're digging us out!'

Mrs Fox was wide awake in one second. She sat up, quivering all over. 'Are you sure that's it?' she whispered.

'I'm positive! Listen!'

'They'll kill my children!' cried Mrs Fox.

'Never!' said Mr Fox.

'But, darling, they will!' sobbed Mrs Fox. 'You know they will!'

Scrunch, scrunch, scrunch went the shovels above their heads. Small stones and bits of earth began falling from the roof of the tunnel.

'How will they kill us, Mummy?' asked one of the Small Foxes. His round black eyes were huge with fright. 'Will there be dogs?' he said.

Mrs Fox began to cry. She gathered her four children close to her and held them tight.

Suddenly there was an especially loud crunch above their heads and the sharp end of a shovel came right through the ceiling. The sight of this

awful thing seemed to have an electric effect upon Mr Fox. He jumped up and shouted, 'I've got it! Come on! There's not a moment to lose! Why didn't I think of it before!'

'Think of what, Dad?'

'A fox can dig quicker than a man!' shouted Mr Fox, beginning to dig. 'Nobody in the world can dig as quick as a fox!'

The soil began to fly out furiously behind Mr Fox as he started to dig for dear life with his front feet. Mrs Fox ran forward to help him. So did the four children.

'Go downwards!' ordered Mr Fox. 'We've got to go deep! As deep as we possibly can!'

The tunnel began to grow longer and longer. It sloped steeply downward. Deeper and deeper below the surface of the ground it went. The mother and the father and all four of the children were digging together. Their front legs were moving so fast you couldn't see them. And gradually the scrunching and scraping of the shovels became fainter and fainter.

After about an hour, Mr Fox stopped digging.

'Hold it!' he said. They all stopped. They turned and looked back up the long tunnel they had just dug. All was quiet. 'Phew!' said Mr Fox. 'I think we've done it! They'll never get as deep as this. Well done, everyone!'

They all sat down, panting for breath. And Mrs Fox said to her children, 'I should like you to know that if it wasn't for your father we should all be dead by now. Your father is a fantastic fox.'

Mr Fox looked at his wife and she smiled. He loved her more than ever when she said things like that.

5

The Terrible Tractors

As the sun rose the next morning, Boggis and Bunce and Bean were still digging. They had dug a hole so deep you could have put a house into it. But they had not yet come to the end of the foxes' tunnel. They were all very tired and cross.

'Dang and blast!' said Boggis. 'Whose rotten idea was this?'

'Bean's idea,' said Bunce.

Boggis and Bunce both stared at Bean. Bean took another swig of cider, then put the flask back into his pocket without offering it to the others. 'Listen,' he said angrily, 'I want that fox! I'm going to get that fox! I'm not giving in till I've strung him up over my front porch, dead as a dumpling!'

'We can't get him by digging, that's for sure,' said the fat Boggis. 'I've had enough of digging.'

Bunce, the little pot-bellied dwarf, looked up at Bean and said, 'Have you got any more stupid ideas, then?'

'What?' said Bean. 'I can't hear you.' Bean never took a bath. He never even washed. As a result, his earholes were clogged with all kinds of muck and

wax and bits of chewing-gum and dead flies and stuff like that. This made him deaf. 'Speak louder,' he said to Bunce, and Bunce shouted back, 'Got any more stupid ideas?'

Bean rubbed the back of his neck with a dirty finger. He had a boil coming there and it itched. 'What we need on this job,' he said, 'is machines . . . *mechanical* shovels. We'll have him out in five minutes with *mechanical* shovels.'

This was a pretty good idea and the other two had to admit it.

'All right then,' Bean said, taking charge. 'Boggis, you stay here and see the fox doesn't escape. Bunce and I will go and fetch our machinery. If he tries to get out, shoot him quick.'

The long, thin Bean walked away. The tiny Bunce trotted after him. The fat Boggis stayed where he was with his gun pointing at the fox-hole.

Soon, two enormous caterpillar tractors with mechanical shovels on their front ends came clanking into the wood. Bean was driving one, Bunce the other. The machines were both black. They were murderous, brutal-looking monsters.

'Here we go, then!' shouted Bean.

'Death to the fox!' shouted Bunce.

The machines went to work, biting huge mouthfuls of soil out of the hill. The big tree under which Mr Fox had dug his hole in the first place was toppled like a matchstick. On all sides, rocks were

sent flying and trees were falling and the noise was deafening.

Down in the tunnel the foxes crouched, listening to the terrible clanging and banging overhead.

'What's happening, Dad?' cried the Small Foxes. 'What are they doing?'

Mr Fox didn't know what was happening or what they were doing.

'It's an earthquake!' cried Mrs Fox.

'Look!' said one of the Small Foxes. 'Our tunnel's got shorter! I can see daylight!'

They all looked round, and yes, the mouth of the tunnel was only a few feet away from them now, and in the circle of daylight beyond they could see the two huge black tractors almost on top of them.

'Tractors!' shouted Mr Fox. 'And *mechanical* shovels! Dig for your lives! *Dig, dig, dig!*'

6

The Race

Now there began a desperate race, the machines against the foxes. In the beginning, the hill looked like this:

After about an hour, as the machines bit away more and more soil from the hilltop, it looked like this:

Sometimes the foxes would gain a little ground and the clanking noises would grow fainter and Mr Fox would say, 'We're going to make it! I'm sure we are!' But then a few moments later, the machines would come back at them and the crunch of the mighty shovels would get louder and louder. Once the foxes actually saw the sharp metal edge of one of the shovels as it scraped up the earth just behind them.

'Keep going, my darlings!' panted Mr Fox. 'Don't give up!'

'Keep going!' the fat Boggis shouted to Bunce and Bean. 'We'll get him any moment now!'

'Have you caught sight of him yet?' Bean called back.

'Not yet,' shouted Boggis. 'But I think you're close!'

'I'll pick him up with my bucket!' shouted Bunce. 'I'll chop him to pieces!'

But by lunchtime the machines were still at it. And so were the poor foxes. The hill now looked like this:

The farmers didn't stop for lunch; they were too keen to finish the job.

'Hey there, Mr Fox!' yelled Bunce, leaning out of his tractor. 'We're coming to get you now!'

'You've had your last chicken!' yelled Boggis. 'You'll never come prowling around *my* farm again!'

A sort of madness had taken hold of the three men. The tall skinny Bean and dwarfish pot-bellied Bunce were driving their machines like maniacs, racing the motors and making the shovels dig at a terrific speed. The fat Boggis was hopping about like a dervish and shouting, 'Faster! Faster!'

By five o'clock in the afternoon this is what had happened to the hill:

The hole the machines had dug was like the crater of a volcano. It was such an extraordinary sight that crowds of people came rushing out from the surrounding villages to have a look. They stood on the edge of the crater and stared down at Boggis and Bunce and Bean.

'Hey there, Boggis! What's going on?'

'We're after a fox!'

'You must be mad!'

The people jeered and laughed. But this only made the three farmers more furious and more obstinate and more determined than ever not to give up until they had caught the fox.

7

'We'll Never Let Him Go'

At six o'clock in the evening, Bean switched off the motor of his tractor and climbed down from the driver's seat. Bunce did the same. Both men had had enough. They were tired and stiff from driving the tractors all day. They were also hungry. Slowly they walked over to the small fox's hole in the bottom of the huge crater. Bean's face was purple with rage. Bunce was cursing the fox with dirty words that cannot be printed. Boggis came waddling up. 'Dang and blast that filthy stinking fox!' he said. 'What the heck do we do now?'

'I'll tell you what we *don't* do,' Bean said. 'We don't let him go!'

'We'll never let him go!' Bunce declared.

'Never never never!' cried Boggis.

'Did you hear that, Mr Fox!' yelled Bean, bending low and shouting down the hole. 'It's not over yet, Mr Fox! We're not going home till we've strung you up dead as a dingbat!' Whereupon the three men all shook hands with one another and swore a solemn oath that they would not go back to their farms until the fox was caught.

'What's the next move?' asked Bunce, the pot-bellied dwarf.

'We're sending you down the hole to fetch him up,' said Bean. 'Down you go, you miserable midget!'

'Not me!' screamed Bunce, running away.

Bean made a sickly smile. When he smiled you saw his scarlet gums. You saw more gums than teeth. 'Then there's only one thing to do,' he said. 'We starve him out. We camp here day and night watching the hole. He'll come out in the end. He'll have to.'

So Boggis and Bunce and Bean sent messages down to their farms asking for tents, sleeping-bags and supper.

8

The Foxes Begin to Starve

That evening three tents were put up in the crater on the hill – one for Boggis, one for Bunce and one for Bean. The tents surrounded Mr Fox's hole. And the three farmers sat outside their tents eating their supper. Boggis had three boiled chickens smothered in dumplings, Bunce had six doughnuts filled with disgusting goose-liver paste, and Bean had two gallons of cider. All three of them kept their guns beside them.

Boggis picked up a steaming chicken and held it close to the fox's hole. 'Can you smell this, Mr Fox?' he shouted. 'Lovely tender chicken! Why don't you come up and get it?'

The rich scent of chicken wafted down the tunnel to where the foxes were crouching.

'Oh, Dad,' said one of the Small Foxes, 'couldn't we just sneak up and snatch it out of his hand?'

'Don't you dare!' said Mrs Fox. 'That's just what they want you to do.'

'But we're so *hungry*!' they cried. 'How long will it be till we get something to eat?'

Their mother didn't answer them. Nor did their father. There was no answer to give.

As darkness fell, Bunce and Bean switched on the powerful headlamps of the two tractors and shone them on to the hole. 'Now,' said Bean, 'we'll take it in turn to keep watch. One watches while two sleep, and so on all through the night.'

Boggis said, 'What if the fox digs a hole right through the hill and comes out on the other side? You didn't think of that one, did you?'

'Of course I did,' said Bean, pretending he had.

'Go on, then, tell us the answer,' said Boggis.

Bean picked something small and black out of his ear and flicked it away. 'How many men have you got working on your farm?' he asked.

'Thirty-five,' Boggis said.

'I've got thirty-six,' Bunce said.

'And I've got thirty-seven,' Bean said. 'That makes one hundred and eight men altogether. We must order them to surround the hill. Each man will have a gun and a flashlight. There will be no escape then for Mr Fox.'

So the order went down to the farms, and that night one hundred and eight men formed a tight ring around the bottom of the hill. They were armed with sticks and guns and hatchets and pistols and all sorts of other horrible weapons. This made it quite impossible for a fox or indeed for any other animal to escape from the hill.

The next day, the watching and waiting went on. Boggis and Bunce and Bean sat upon small stools, staring at the fox's hole. They didn't talk much. They just sat there with their guns on their laps.

Every so often, Mr Fox would creep a little closer towards the mouth of the tunnel and take a sniff. Then he would creep back again and say, 'They're still there.'

'Are you quite sure?' Mrs Fox would ask.

'Positive,' said Mr Fox. 'I can smell that man Bean a mile away. He stinks.'

9

Mr Fox Has a Plan

For three days and three nights this waiting-game went on.

'How long can a fox go without food or water?' Boggis asked on the third day.

'Not much longer now,' Bean told him. 'He'll make a run for it soon. He'll have to.'

Bean was right. Down in the tunnel the foxes were slowly but surely starving to death.

'If only we could have just a tiny sip of water,' said one of the Small Foxes. 'Oh, Dad, can't you do *something*?'

'Couldn't we make a dash for it, Dad? We'd have a little bit of a chance, wouldn't we?'

'No chance at all,' snapped Mrs Fox. 'I refuse to let you go up there and face those guns. I'd sooner you stay down here and die in peace.'

Mr Fox had not spoken for a long time. He had been sitting quite still, his eyes closed, not even hearing what the others were saying. Mrs Fox knew that he was trying desperately to think of a way out. And now, as she looked at him, she saw him stir himself and get slowly to his feet. He looked back at his wife. There was a little spark of excitement dancing in his eyes.

'What is it, darling?' said Mrs Fox quickly.

'I've just had a bit of an idea,' Mr Fox said carefully.

'What?' they cried. 'Oh, Dad, what is it?'

'Come *on*!' said Mrs Fox. 'Tell us quickly!'

'Well . . .' said Mr Fox, then he stopped and sighed and sadly shook his head. He sat down again. 'It's no good,' he said. 'It won't work after all.'

'Why not, Dad?'

'Because it means more digging and we aren't any

of us strong enough for that after three days and nights without food.'

'Yes we are, Dad!' cried the Small Foxes, jumping up and running to their father. 'We can do it! You see if we can't! So can you!'

Mr Fox looked at the four Small Foxes and he smiled. What fine children I have, he thought. They are starving to death and they haven't had a drink for three days, but they are still undefeated. I must not let them down.

'I . . . I suppose we could give it a try,' he said.

'Let's go, Dad! Tell us what you want us to do!'

Slowly, Mrs Fox got to her feet. She was suffering more than any of them from the lack of food and water. She was very weak. 'I am so sorry,' she said, 'but I don't think I am going to be much help.'

'You stay right where you are, my darling,' said Mr Fox. 'We can handle this by ourselves.'

10

Boggis's Chicken House Number One

'This time we must go in a very special direction,' said Mr Fox, pointing sideways and downward.

So he and his four children started to dig once again. The work went much more slowly now. Yet they kept at it with great courage, and little by little the tunnel began to grow.

'Dad, I wish you would tell us *where* we are going,' said one of the children.

'I dare not do that,' said Mr Fox, 'because this place I am *hoping* to get to is so *marvellous* that if I described it to you now you would go crazy with excitement. And then, if we failed to get there (which is very possible), you would die of disappointment. I don't want to raise your hopes too much, my darlings.'

For a long long time they kept on digging. For how long they did not know, because there were no days and no nights down there in the murky tunnel. But at last Mr Fox gave the order to stop. 'I think,' he said, 'we had better take a peep upstairs now and see where we are. I know where I *want* to be, but I can't possibly be sure we're anywhere near it.'

Slowly, wearily, the foxes began to slope the tunnel up towards the surface. Up and up it went . . . until suddenly they came to something hard above their heads and they couldn't go up any further. Mr Fox reached up to examine this hard thing. 'It's wood!' he whispered. 'Wooden planks!'

'What does that mean, Dad?'

'It means, unless I am very much mistaken, that we are right underneath somebody's house,' whispered Mr Fox. 'Be very quiet now while I take a peek.'

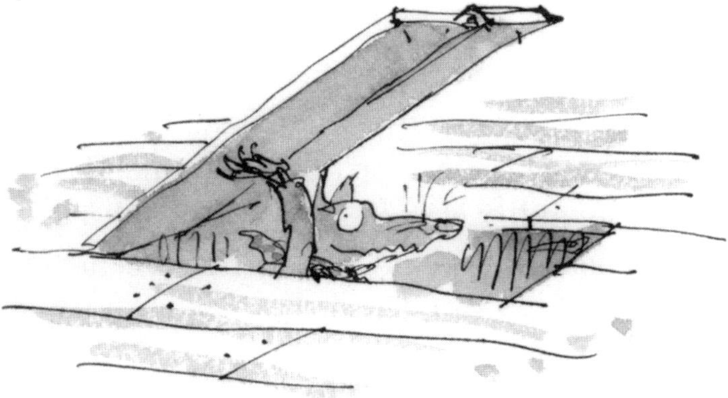

Carefully, Mr Fox began pushing up one of the floorboards. The board creaked most terribly and they all ducked down, waiting for something awful to happen. Nothing did. So Mr Fox pushed up a second board. And then, very very cautiously, he poked his head up through the gap. He let out a shriek of excitement.

'*I've done it!*' he yelled. 'I've done it *first time*! *I've done it! I've done it!*' He pulled himself up through the gap in the floor and started prancing and dancing with joy. 'Come on up!' he sang out. 'Come up and see where you are, my darlings! What a sight for a hungry fox! Hallelujah! Hooray! Hooray!'

The four Small Foxes scrambled up out of the tunnel and what a fantastic sight it was that now met their eyes! They were in a huge shed and the whole place was teeming with chickens. There were white chickens and brown chickens and black chickens by the thousand!

'Boggis's Chicken House Number One!' cried Mr Fox. 'It's exactly what I was aiming at! I hit it slap in the middle! First time! Isn't that fantastic! *And*, if I may say so, rather clever!'

The Small Foxes went wild with excitement. They started running around in all directions, chasing the stupid chickens.

'Wait!' ordered Mr Fox. 'Don't lose your heads! Stand back! Calm down! Let's do this properly! First of all, everyone have a drink of water!'

They all ran over to the chickens' drinking-trough and lapped up the lovely cool water. Then Mr Fox chose three of the plumpest hens, and with a clever flick of his jaws he killed them instantly.

'Back to the tunnel!' he ordered. 'Come on! No

fooling around! The quicker you move, the quicker you shall have something to eat!'

One after another, they climbed down through the hole in the floor and soon they were all standing once again in the dark tunnel. Mr Fox reached up and pulled the floorboards back into place. He did this with great care. He did it so that no one could tell they had ever been moved.

'My son,' he said, giving the three plump hens to the biggest of his four small children, 'run back with these to your mother. Tell her to prepare a feast. Tell her the rest of us will be along in a jiffy, as soon as we have made a few other little arrangements.'

11

A Surprise for Mrs Fox

The Small Fox ran back along the tunnel as fast as he could, carrying the three plump hens. He was exploding with joy. 'Just wait!' he kept thinking. 'Just wait till Mummy sees these!' He had a long way to run but he never stopped once on the way and he came bursting in upon Mrs Fox. 'Mummy!' he cried, out of breath. 'Look, Mummy, look! Wake up and see what I've brought you!'

Mrs Fox, who was weaker than ever now from lack of food, opened one eye and looked at the hens. 'I'm dreaming,' she murmured and closed the eye again.

'You're not dreaming, Mummy! They're real chickens! We're saved! We're not going to starve!'

Mrs Fox opened both eyes and sat up quickly. 'But, my *dear* child!' she cried. 'Where on earth . . .?'

'Boggis's Chicken House Number One!' spluttered the Small Fox. 'We tunnelled right up under the floor and you've never seen so many big fat hens in all your life! And Dad said to prepare a feast! They'll be back soon!'

The sight of food seemed to give new strength to Mrs Fox. 'A feast it shall be!' she said, standing up. 'Oh, what a fantastic fox your father is! Hurry up, child, and start plucking those chickens!'

Far away down in the tunnel, the fantastic Mr Fox was saying, 'Now for the next bit, my darlings! This one'll be as easy as pie! All we have to do is dig another little tunnel from *here* to there!'

'To where, Dad?'

'Don't ask so many questions. Start digging!'

12

Badger

Mr Fox and the three remaining Small Foxes dug fast and straight. They were all too excited now to feel tired or hungry. They knew they were going to have a whacking great feast before long and the fact that it was none other than Boggis's chickens they were going to eat made them churgle with laughter every time they thought of it. It was lovely to realize that while the fat farmer was sitting up there on the hill waiting for them to starve, he was also giving them their dinner without knowing it. 'Keep digging,' said Mr Fox. 'It's not much further.'

All of a sudden a deep voice above their heads said, '*Who goes there?*' The foxes jumped. They looked up quickly and they saw, peeking through a small hole in the roof of the tunnel, a long black pointed furry face.

'Badger!' cried Mr Fox.

'Foxy!' cried Badger. 'My goodness me, I'm glad I've found *someone* at last! I've been digging around in circles for three days and nights and I haven't the foggiest idea where I am!'

Badger made the hole in the ceiling bigger and dropped down beside the foxes. A Small Badger (his son) dropped down after him. 'Haven't you *heard* what's happening up on the hill?' Badger said excitedly. 'It's chaos! Half the wood has disappeared and there are men with guns all over the countryside! None of us can get out, even at night! We're all starving to death!'

'Who is *we*?' asked Mr Fox.

'All us diggers. That's me and Mole and Rabbit and all our wives and children. Even Weasel, who can usually sneak out of the tightest spots, is right now hiding down my hole with Mrs Weasel and six kids. What on earth are we going to do, Foxy? I think we're finished!'

Mr Fox looked at his three children and he smiled. The children smiled back at him, sharing his secret. 'My dear old Badger,' he said, 'this mess you're in is all my fault . . .'

'I know it's your fault!' said Badger furiously. 'And the farmers are not going to give up till they've got you. Unfortunately, that means *us* as well. It means everyone on the hill.' Badger sat down and put a paw around his small son. 'We're done for,' he said softly. 'My poor wife up there is so weak she can't dig another yard.'

'Nor can mine,' said Mr Fox. 'And yet at this very minute she is preparing for me and my children the most delicious feast of plump juicy chickens . . .'

'Stop!' cried Badger. 'Don't tease me! I can't stand it!'

'It's true!' cried the Small Foxes. 'Dad's not teasing! We've got chickens galore!'

'And because everything is entirely my fault,' said Mr Fox, 'I invite you to share the feast. I invite *everyone* to share it – you and Mole and Rabbit and Weasel and all your wives and children. There'll be plenty to go round, I can assure you.'

'You mean it?' cried Badger. 'You *really mean* it?'

Mr Fox pushed his face close to Badger's and whispered darkly, '*Do you know* where we've just been?'

'Where?'

'Right inside Boggis's Chicken House Number One!'

'No!'

'Yes! But that is nothing to where we are going now. You have come just at the right moment, my dear Badger. You can help us dig. And in the meanwhile, your small son can run back to Mrs Badger and all the others and spread the good news.' Mr Fox turned to the Small Badger and said, 'Tell them they are invited to a Fox's Feast. Then bring them all down here and follow this tunnel back until you find my home!'

'Yes, Mr Fox!' said the Small Badger. 'Yes, sir! Right away, sir! Oh, thank you, sir!' and he scrambled quickly back through the hole in the roof of the tunnel and disappeared.

13

Bunce's Giant Storehouse

'My dear Foxy!' cried Badger. 'What in the world has happened to your tail?'

'Don't talk about it, *please*,' said Mr Fox. 'It's a painful subject.'

They were digging the new tunnel. They dug on in silence. Badger was a great digger and the tunnel went forward at a terrific pace now that he was lending a paw. Soon they were crouching underneath yet another wooden floor.

Mr Fox grinned slyly, showing sharp white teeth. 'If I am not mistaken, my dear Badger,' he said, 'we are now underneath the farm which belongs to that nasty little pot-bellied dwarf, Bunce. We are, in

fact, directly underneath the most *interesting part* of that farm.'

'Ducks and geese!' cried the Small Foxes, licking their lips. 'Juicy tender ducks and big fat geese!'

'Ex-*actly*!' said Mr Fox.

'But how in the world can you know where we are?' asked Badger.

Mr Fox grinned again, showing even more white teeth. 'Look,' he said, 'I know my way around these farms blindfold. For me it's just as easy below ground as it is above it.' He reached high and pushed up one wooden floorboard, then another. He poked his head through the gap.

'Yes!' he shouted, jumping up into the room above. 'I've done it again! I've hit it smack on the nose! Right in the bull's-eye! Come and look!'

Quickly Badger and the three Small Foxes scrambled up after him. They stopped and stared. They stood and gaped. They were so overwhelmed they couldn't speak; for what they now saw was a kind of fox's dream, a badger's dream, a paradise for hungry animals.

'This, my dear old Badger,' proclaimed Mr Fox, 'is Bunce's Mighty Storehouse! All his finest stuff is stored in here before he sends it off to market.'

Against all the four walls of the great room, stacked in cupboards and piled upon shelves reaching from floor to ceiling, were thousands and thousands of the finest and fattest ducks and geese, plucked and ready for roasting! And up above, dangling from the rafters, there must have been at least a hundred smoked hams and fifty sides of bacon!

'Just feast your eyes on *that*!' cried Mr Fox, dancing up and down. 'What d'you think of it, eh? Pretty good grub!'

Suddenly, as though springs had been released in their legs, the three hungry Small Foxes and the ravenously hungry Badger sprang forward to grab the luscious food.

'Stop!' ordered Mr Fox. 'This is *my* party, so I shall do the choosing.' The others fell back, licking their chops. Mr Fox began prowling around the storehouse examining the glorious display with an expert eye. A thread of saliva slid down one side of his jaw and hung suspended in mid-air, then snapped.

'We mustn't overdo it,' he said. 'Mustn't give the game away. Mustn't let them know what we've been up to. We must be neat and tidy and take just a few of the choicest morsels. So, to start with we shall have four plump young ducks.' He took them from the shelf. 'Oh, how lovely and fat they are! No wonder Bunce gets a special price for them in the market! . . . All right, Badger, lend me a hand to get them down . . . You children can help as well . . . There we go . . . Goodness me, look how your mouths are watering . . . And now . . . I think we had better have a few geese . . . Three will be quite enough . . . We'll take the biggest . . . Oh my, oh my, you'll never see finer geese than these in a king's kitchen . . . Gently does it . . . that's the way . . . And what about a couple of nice smoked hams . . . I adore smoked ham, don't you, Badger? . . . Fetch me that step-ladder, will you please . . .'

Mr Fox climbed up the ladder and handed down three magnificent hams. 'And do you like bacon, Badger?'

'I'm mad about bacon!' cried Badger, dancing with excitement. 'Let's have a side of bacon! That big one up there!'

'And carrots, Dad!' said the smallest of the three Small Foxes. 'We must take some of those carrots.'

'Don't be a twerp,' said Mr Fox. 'You know we never eat things like that.'

'It's not for us, Dad. It's for the Rabbits. They only eat vegetables.'

'My goodness me, you're right!' cried Mr Fox. 'What a thoughtful little fellow you are! Take ten bunches of carrots!'

Soon, all this lovely loot was lying in a neat heap upon the floor. The Small Foxes crouched close, their noses twitching, their eyes shining like stars.

'And now,' said Mr Fox, 'we shall have to borrow from our friend Bunce two of those useful push-carts over in the corner.' He and Badger fetched the push-carts, and the ducks and geese and hams and bacon were loaded on to them. Quickly the push-carts were lowered through the hole in the floor. The animals slid down after them. Back in the tunnel, Mr Fox again pulled the floorboards very carefully into place so that no one could see they had been moved.

'My darlings,' he said, pointing to two of the three Small Foxes, 'take a cart each and run back as fast as you can to your mother. Give her my love and tell her we are having guests for dinner – the Badgers, the Moles, the Rabbits and the Weasels. Tell her it must be a truly great feast. And tell her the rest of us will be home as soon as we've done one more little job.'

'Yes, Dad! Right away, Dad!' they answered, and they grabbed a trolley each and went rushing off down the tunnel.

14

Badger Has Doubts

'Just one more visit!' cried Mr Fox.

'And I'll bet I know where that'll be,' said the only Small Fox now left. He was the Smallest Fox of them all.

'Where?' asked Badger.

'Well,' said the Smallest Fox. 'We've been to Boggis and we've been to Bunce but we haven't been to Bean. It must be Bean.'

'You are right,' said Mr Fox. 'But what you don't know is which *part* of Bean's place we are about to visit.'

'Which?' they said both together.

'Ah-ha,' said Mr Fox. 'Just you wait and see.' They were digging as they talked. The tunnel was going forward fast.

Suddenly Badger said, 'Doesn't this worry you just a tiny bit, Foxy?'

'Worry me?' said Mr Fox. 'What?'

'All this . . . this *stealing*.'

Mr Fox stopped digging and stared at Badger as though he had gone completely dotty. 'My dear old furry frump,' he said, 'do you know anyone in the *whole world* who wouldn't swipe a few chickens if his children were starving to death?'

There was a short silence while Badger thought deeply about this.

'You are far too respectable,' said Mr Fox.

'There's nothing wrong with being respectable,' Badger said.

'Look,' said Mr Fox, 'Boggis and Bunce and Bean are out to *kill* us. You realize that, I hope?'

'I do, Foxy, I do indeed,' said the gentle Badger.

'But *we're* not going to stoop to *their* level. We don't want to kill *them*.'

'I should hope not, indeed,' said Badger.

'We wouldn't dream of it,' said Mr Fox. 'We shall simply take a little food here and there to keep us and our families alive. Right?'

'I suppose we'll have to,' said Badger.

'If *they* want to be horrible, let them,' said Mr Fox. 'We down here are decent peace-loving people.'

Badger laid his head on one side and smiled at Mr Fox. 'Foxy,' he said, 'I love you.'

'Thank you,' said Mr Fox. 'And now let's get on with the digging.'

Five minutes later, Badger's front paws hit against something flat and hard. 'What on earth is this?' he said. 'It looks like a solid stone wall.' He and Mr Fox scraped away the soil. It *was* a wall. But it was built of bricks, not stones. The wall was right in front of them, blocking their way.

'Now who in the world would build a wall under the ground?' asked Badger.

'Very simple,' said Mr Fox. 'It's the wall of an underground room. And if I am not mistaken, it is exactly what I'm looking for.'

15

Bean's Secret Cider Cellar

Mr Fox examined the wall carefully. He saw that the cement between the bricks was old and crumbly, so he loosened a brick without much trouble and pulled it away. Suddenly, out from the hole where the brick had been, there popped a small sharp face with whiskers. 'Go away!' it snapped. 'You can't come in here! It's private!'

'Good Lord!' said Badger. 'It's Rat!'

'You saucy beast!' said Mr Fox. 'I should have guessed we'd find you down here somewhere.'

'Go away!' shrieked Rat. 'Go on, beat it! This is my private pitch!'

'Shut up,' said Mr Fox.

'I will not shut up!' shrieked Rat. 'This is *my* place! I got here first!'

Mr Fox gave a brilliant smile, flashing his white teeth. 'My dear Rat,' he said softly, 'I am a hungry

fellow and if you don't hop it quickly I shall eat-you-up-in-one-gulp!'

That did it. Rat popped back fast out of sight. Mr Fox laughed and began pulling more bricks out of the wall. When he had made a biggish hole, he crept through it. Badger and the Smallest Fox followed him in.

They found themselves in a vast, damp, gloomy cellar. 'This is it!' cried Mr Fox.

'This is *what*?' said Badger. 'The place is empty.'

'Where are the turkeys?' asked the Smallest Fox, staring into the gloom. 'I thought Bean was a turkey man.'

'He is a turkey man,' said Mr Fox. 'But we're not after turkeys now. We've got plenty of food.'

'Then what *do* we need, Dad?'

'Take a good look round,' said Mr Fox. 'Don't you see *anything* that interests you?'

Badger and the Smallest Fox peered into the half-darkness. As their eyes became accustomed to the gloom, they began to see what looked like a whole lot of big glass jars standing upon shelves around the walls. They went closer. They *were* jars. There were hundreds of them, and upon each one was written the word CIDER.

The Smallest Fox leaped high in the air. 'Oh, Dad!' he cried out. 'Look what we've found! It's cider!'

'Ex-*actly*,' said Mr Fox.

'Tremendous!' shouted Badger.

'Bean's Secret Cider Cellar,' said Mr Fox. 'But go carefully, my dears. Don't make a noise. This cellar is right underneath the farmhouse itself.'

'Cider,' said Badger, 'is especially good for Badgers. We take it as medicine – one large glass three times a day with meals and another at bedtime.'

'It will make the feast into a banquet,' said Mr Fox.

While they were talking, the Smallest Fox had sneaked a jar off the shelf and had taken a gulp. 'Wow!' he gasped. 'Wow-*ee*!'

You must understand this was not the ordinary weak fizzy cider one buys in a store. It was the real stuff, a home-brewed fiery liquor that burned in your throat and boiled in your stomach.

'Ah-h-h-h-h-h!' gasped the Smallest Fox. 'This is *some cider*!'

'That's quite enough of that,' said Mr Fox, grabbing the jar and putting it to his own lips. He took a tremendous gulp. 'It's miraculous!' he whispered, fighting for breath. 'It's fabulous! It's beautiful!'

'It's my turn,' said Badger, taking the jar and tilting his head well back. The cider gurgled and bubbled down his throat. 'It's . . . it's like melted gold!' he gasped. 'Oh, Foxy, it's . . . like drinking sunbeams and rainbows!'

'You're poaching!' shrieked Rat. 'Put that down at once! There'll be none left for me!' Rat was perched upon the highest shelf in the cellar, peering out from behind a huge jar. There was a small rubber tube inserted in the neck of the jar, and Rat was using this tube to suck out the cider.

'You're drunk!' said Mr Fox.

'Mind your own business!' shrieked Rat. 'And if you great clumsy brutes come messing about in here we'll all be caught! Get out and leave me to sip my cider in peace.'

At that moment they heard a woman's voice calling out in the house above them. 'Hurry up and get that cider, Mabel!' the voice called. 'You know Mr Bean doesn't like to be kept waiting! Especially when he's been out all night in a tent!'

The animals froze. They stayed absolutely still, their ears pricked, their bodies tense. Then they heard the sound of a door being opened. The door was at the top of a flight of stone steps leading down from the house to the cellar.

And now someone was starting to come down those steps.

16

The Woman

'Quick!' said Mr Fox. 'Hide!' He and Badger and the Smallest Fox jumped up on to a shelf and crouched behind a row of big cider jars. Peering around the jars, they saw a huge woman coming down into the cellar. At the foot of the steps, the woman paused, looking to right and left. Then she turned and headed straight for the place where Mr Fox and Badger and the Smallest Fox were hiding. She stopped right in front of them. The only thing between her and them was a row of cider jars. She was so close, Mr Fox could hear the sound of her breathing. Peeping through the crack between two bottles, he noticed that she carried a big rolling-pin in one hand.

'How many will he want this time, Mrs Bean?' the woman shouted. And from the top of the steps the other voice called back, 'Bring up two or three jars.'

'He drank four yesterday, Mrs Bean.'

'Yes, but he won't want that many today because he's not going to be up there more than a few hours longer. He says the fox is bound to make a run for it this morning. It can't possibly stay down that hole another day without food.'

The woman in the cellar reached out and lifted a jar of cider from the shelf. The jar she took was next but one to the jar behind which Mr Fox was crouching.

'I'll be glad when the rotten brute is killed and strung up on the front porch,' she called out. 'And by the way, Mrs Bean, your husband promised I could have the tail as a souvenir.'

'The tail's been all shot to pieces,' said the voice from upstairs. 'Didn't you know that?'

'You mean it's *ruined*?'

'Of course it's ruined. They shot the tail but missed the fox.'

'Oh heck!' said the big woman. 'I did so want that tail!'

'You can have the head instead, Mabel. You can get it stuffed and hang it on your bedroom wall. Hurry up now with that cider!'

'Yes, Ma'am, I'm coming,' said the big woman, and she took a second jar from the shelf.

If she takes one more, she'll see us, thought Mr Fox. He could feel the Smallest Fox's body pressed tightly against his own, quivering with excitement.

'Will two be enough, Mrs Bean, or shall I take three?'

'My goodness, Mabel, I don't care so long as you get a move on!'

'Then two it is,' said the huge woman, speaking to herself now. 'He drinks too much anyway.'

Carrying a jar in each hand and with the rolling-pin tucked under one arm, she walked away across the cellar. At the foot of the steps she paused and looked around, sniffing the air. 'There's rats down here again, Mrs Bean. I can smell 'em.'

'Then poison them, woman, poison them! You know where the poison's kept.'

'Yes, Ma'am,' Mabel said. She climbed slowly out of sight up the steps. The door slammed.

'Quick!' said Mr Fox. 'Grab a jar each and run for it!'

Rat stood on his high shelf and shrieked. 'What did I tell you! You nearly got nabbed, didn't you? You nearly gave the game away! You keep out of here from now on! I don't want you around! This is my place!'

'*You*,' said Mr Fox, 'are going to be poisoned.'

'Poppycock!' said Rat. 'I sit up here and watch her putting the stuff down. She'll never get *me*.'

Mr Fox and Badger and the Smallest Fox ran across the cellar clutching a gallon jar each. 'Goodbye, Rat!' they called out as they disappeared through the hole in the wall. 'Thanks for the lovely cider!'

'Thieves!' shrieked Rat. 'Robbers! Bandits! Burglars!'

17

The Great Feast

Back in the tunnel they paused so that Mr Fox could brick up the hole in the wall. He was humming to himself as he put the bricks back in place. 'I can still taste that glorious cider,' he said. 'What an impudent fellow Rat is.'

'He has bad manners,' Badger said. 'All rats have bad manners. I've never met a polite rat yet.'

'And he drinks too much,' said Mr Fox, putting the last brick in place. 'There we are. Now, home to the feast!'

They grabbed their jars of cider and off they went. Mr Fox was in front, the Smallest Fox came next and Badger last. Along the tunnel they flew . . . past the turning that led to Bunce's Mighty Storehouse . . .

past Boggis's Chicken House Number One and then up the long home stretch towards the place where they knew Mrs Fox would be waiting.

'Keep it up, my darlings!' shouted Mr Fox. 'We'll soon be there! Think what's waiting for us at the other end! And just think what we're bringing home with us in these jars! That ought to cheer up poor Mrs Fox.' Mr Fox sang a little song as he ran:

'Home again swiftly I glide,
Back to my beautiful bride.
She'll not feel so rotten
As soon as she's gotten
Some cider inside her inside.'

Then Badger joined in:

'Oh poor Mrs Badger, he cried,
So hungry she very near died.

But she'll not feel so hollow
If only she'll swallow
Some cider inside her inside.'

They were still singing as they rounded the final corner and burst in upon the most wonderful and amazing sight any of them had ever seen. The feast was just beginning. A large dining-room had been hollowed out of the earth, and in the middle

of it, seated around a huge table, were no less than twenty-nine animals. They were:

Mrs Fox and three Small Foxes.

Mrs Badger and three Small Badgers.

Mole and Mrs Mole and four Small Moles.

Rabbit and Mrs Rabbit and five Small Rabbits.

Weasel and Mrs Weasel and six Small Weasels.

The table was covered with chickens and ducks and geese and hams and bacon, and everyone was tucking into the lovely food.

'My darling!' cried Mrs Fox, jumping up and hugging Mr Fox. 'We couldn't wait! Please forgive us!' Then she hugged the Smallest Fox of all, and Mrs Badger hugged Badger, and everyone hugged everyone else. Amid shouts of joy, the great jars of cider were placed upon the table, and Mr Fox and Badger and the Smallest Fox sat down with the others.

You must remember no one had eaten a thing for several days. They were ravenous. So for a while there was no conversation at all. There was only the sound of crunching and chewing as the animals attacked the succulent food.

At last, Badger stood up. He raised his glass of cider and called out, 'A toast! I want you all to stand and drink a toast to our dear friend who has saved our lives this day – Mr Fox!'

'To Mr Fox!' they all shouted, standing up and raising their glasses. 'To Mr Fox! Long may he live!'

Then Mrs Fox got shyly to her feet and said, 'I don't want to make a speech. I just want to say one thing, and it is this: MY HUSBAND IS A FANTASTIC FOX.' Everyone clapped and cheered. Then Mr Fox himself stood up.

'This delicious meal . . .' he began, then he stopped. In the silence that followed, he let fly a tremendous belch. There was laughter and more clapping. 'This delicious meal, my friends,' he went on, 'is by courtesy of Messrs Boggis, Bunce and Bean.' (More cheering and laughter.) 'And I hope you have enjoyed it as much as I have.' He let fly another colossal belch.

'Better out than in,' said Badger.

'Thank you,' said Mr Fox, grinning hugely. 'But now, my friends, let us be serious. Let us think of tomorrow and the next day and the days after that. If we go out, we will be killed. Right?'

'Right!' they shouted.

'We'll be shot before we've gone a yard,' said Badger.

'Ex-*actly*,' said Mr Fox. 'But who *wants* to go out, anyway; let me ask you that? We are all diggers, every one of us. We hate the outside. The outside is full of enemies. We only go out because we have to, to get food for our families. But now, my friends, we have an entirely new set-up. We have a safe tunnel leading to three of the finest stores in the world!'

'We do indeed!' said Badger. 'I've seen 'em!'

'And you know what this means?' said Mr Fox. '*It means that none of us need ever go out into the open again!*' There was a buzz of excitement around the table.

'I therefore invite you all,' Mr Fox went on, 'to stay here with me for ever.'

'For ever!' they cried. 'My goodness! How marvellous!' And Rabbit said to Mrs Rabbit, 'My dear, just think! We're never going to be shot at again in our lives!'

'We will make,' said Mr Fox, 'a little underground village, with streets and houses on each side – separate houses for Badgers and Moles and Rabbits and Weasels and Foxes. And every day I will go shopping for you all. And every day we will eat like kings.'

The cheering that followed this speech went on for many minutes.

18

Still Waiting

Outside the fox's hole, Boggis and Bunce and Bean sat beside their tents with their guns on their laps. It was beginning to rain. Water was trickling down the necks of the three men and into their shoes.

'He won't stay down there much longer now,' Boggis said.

'The brute must be famished,' Bunce said.

'That's right,' Bean said. 'He'll be making a dash for it any moment. Keep your guns handy.'

They sat there by the hole, waiting for the fox to come out.

And so far as I know, they are still waiting.

Let's find out how carefully you were reading . . .

1. What are the three farmers called?
    a) Boggis, Bean and Bunce
    b) Declan, Duncan and Daniel
    c) John, James and Jack

2. Where is the hole Mr Fox lives in?
    a) Under a bush
    b) Near the train station
    c) Under a tree

3. When the three farmers shoot at him, what does Mr Fox lose?
    a) His jacket
    b) His tail
    c) His eye

4. How many jars of cider does Mabel take from the cellar?
    a) Two
    b) Three
    c) Five

5. How many children does Mr Fox have?
    a) Two
    b) Three
    c) Four

Answers: 1. a) 2. c) 3. b) 4. a) 5. c)

Fantastic Mr Fox outwitted the farmers, but can the Ladderless Window-Cleaning Company outwit the jewel thief?

Let's meet them . . .

THE GIRAFFE AND THE PELLY AND ME

THE
FUR SAIL

Not far from where I live there is a queer old empty wooden house standing all by itself on the side of the road. I long to explore inside it but the door is always locked, and when I peer through a window all I can see is darkness and dust. I know the ground floor used once to be a shop because I can still read the faded lettering across the front which says THE GRUBBER. My mother has told me that in our part of the country in the olden days a grubber was another name for a sweet-shop, and now every time I look at it I think to myself what a lovely old sweet-shop it must have been.

On the shop-window itself somebody has painted in white the words FOR SAIL.

One morning, I noticed that FOR SAIL had been scraped off the shop-window and in its place somebody had painted SOLED. I stood there staring at the new writing and wishing like mad that it had been me who had bought it because then I would have been able to make it into a grubber all over again. I have always longed and longed to own a sweet-shop. The sweet-shop of my dreams would be loaded from top to bottom with Sherbet Suckers and Caramel Fudge and Russian Toffee and Sugar Snorters and Butter Gumballs and thousands and thousands of other glorious things like that. Oh boy, what I couldn't have done with that old Grubber shop if it had been mine!

On my next visit to The Grubber, I was standing across the road gazing at the wonderful old building when suddenly an enormous bathtub came sailing out through one of the second-floor windows and crashed right on to the middle of the road!

THE GRUBBER
SOLED

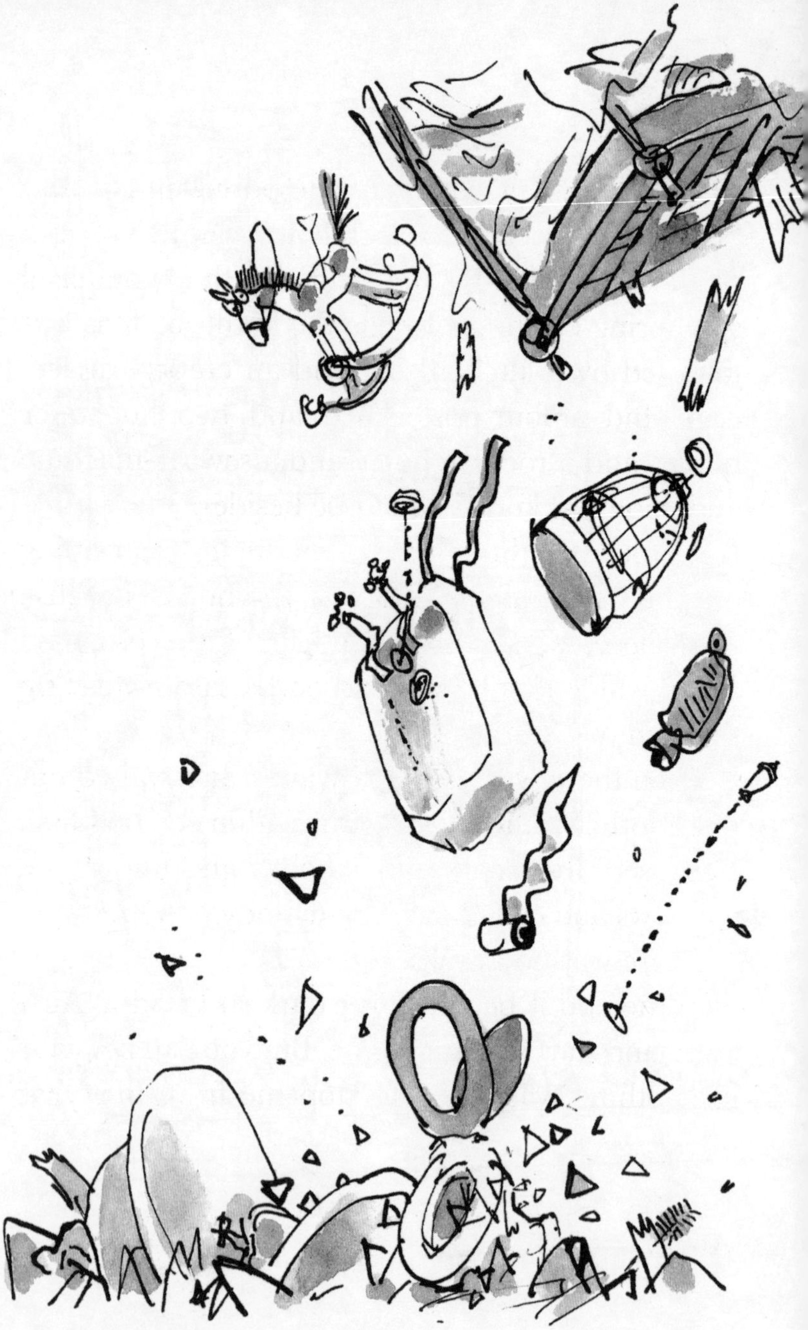

A few moments later, a white porcelain lavatory pan with the wooden seat still on it came flying out of the same window and landed with a wonderful splintering crash just beside the bathtub. This was followed by a kitchen sink and an empty canary-cage and a four-poster bed and two hot-water bottles and a rocking horse and a sewing-machine and goodness knows what else besides.

It looked as though some madman was ripping out the whole of the inside of the house, because now pieces of staircase and bits of the banisters and a whole lot of old floorboards came whistling through the windows.

Then there was silence. I waited and waited but not another sound came from within the building. I crossed the road and stood right under the windows and called out, 'Is anybody at home?'

There was no answer.

In the end it began to get dark so I had to turn away and start walking home. But you can bet your life nothing was going to stop me from hurrying

back there again tomorrow morning to see what the next surprise was going to be.

When I got back to The Grubber house the next morning, the first thing I noticed was the new door. The dirty old brown door had been taken out and in its place someone had fitted a brand-new red one. The new door was fantastic. It was twice as high as the other one had been and it looked ridiculous. I couldn't begin to imagine who would want a tremendous tall door like that in his house unless it was a giant.

As well as this, somebody had scraped away the SOLED notice on the shop-window and now there was a whole lot of different writing all over the glass. I stood there reading it and reading it and trying to figure out what on earth it all meant.

The LWC Co
THE LADDERLESS WINDOW-CLEANING COMPANY
Get your windows cleaned without a lot of dirty ladders leaning against your house.

I tried to catch some sign or sound of movement inside the house but there was none . . . until all of a sudden . . . out of the corner of my eye . . . I noticed that one of the windows on the top floor was slowly beginning to open outwards . . .

Then a HEAD appeared at the open window.

I stared at the head. The head stared back at me with big round dark eyes.

Suddenly, a second window was flung wide open and of all the crazy things a gigantic white bird hopped out and perched on the window-sill.

I knew what this one was because of its amazing beak, which was shaped like a huge orange-coloured basin. The Pelican looked down at me and sang out:

'Oh, how I wish
For a big fat fish!
I'm as hungry as ever could be!
A dish of fish is my only wish!
How far are we from the sea?'

'We are a long way from the sea,' I called back to him, 'but there is a fishmonger in the village not far away.'

'A fish *what*?'

'A fish*monger*.'

'Now what on earth would that be?' asked the Pelican. 'I have heard of a fish-*pie* and a fish-*cake* and a fish-*finger*, but I have never heard of a fish-*monger*. Are these mongers good to eat?'

This question baffled me a bit, so I said, 'Who is your friend in the next window?'

'She is the Giraffe!' the Pelican answered. 'Is she not wonderful? Her legs are on the ground floor and her head is looking out of the top window!'

As if all this wasn't enough, the window on the *first floor* was now flung wide open and out popped a Monkey!

The Monkey stood on the window-sill and did a jiggly little dance. He was so skinny he seemed to be made only out of furry bits of wire, but he danced wonderfully well, and I clapped and cheered and did a little dance myself in return.

That's it.
The end of the book.

HERE IS

one LAST **WORD**,

invented by **Roald Dahl**

HIMSELF.

Make sure you KEEP IT SAFE.

HIPSWITCH

Adverb: Doing something very quickly.

ROALD DAHL

QUICK!

MISCHIEF MAKERS,

SIGN HERE so everyone

knows **this book** belongs

TO YOU.

ROALD DAHL was a spy, ace fighter pilot, chocolate historian and medical inventor. He was also the author of *Charlie and the Chocolate Factory*, *Matilda*, *The BFG* and many more brilliant stories. He remains

THE WORLD'S NUMBER ONE STORYTELLER.

QUENTIN BLAKE has illustrated more than three hundred books and was Roald Dahl's favourite illustrator. In 1980 he won the prestigious Kate Greenaway Medal. In 1999 he became the first ever Children's Laureate and in 2013 he was knighted for services to illustration.

INTRODUCING . . .

Girl

Philip
Gregg

William
Gregg

Mr and Mrs
Gregg

Books by Roald Dahl

THE BFG
BOY: TALES OF CHILDHOOD
BOY *and* GOING SOLO
CHARLIE AND THE CHOCOLATE FACTORY
CHARLIE AND THE GREAT GLASS ELEVATOR
THE COMPLETE ADVENTURES OF CHARLIE AND MR WILLY WONKA
DANNY THE CHAMPION OF THE WORLD
THE ENORMOUS CROCODILE
ESIO TROT
FANTASTIC MR FOX
GEORGE'S MARVELLOUS MEDICINE
THE GIRAFFE AND THE PELLY AND ME
GOING SOLO
JAMES AND THE GIANT PEACH
MATILDA
THE MAGIC FINGER
THE TWITS
THE WITCHES

Picture books

DIRTY BEASTS
THE ENORMOUS CROCODILE
THE GIRAFFE AND THE PELLY AND ME
THE MINPINS
REVOLTING RHYMES

Plays

THE BFG: PLAYS FOR CHILDREN (*Adapted by David Wood*)
CHARLIE AND THE CHOCOLATE FACTORY: A PLAY (*Adapted by Richard George*)
DANNY THE CHAMPION OF THE WORLD: PLAYS FOR CHILDREN (*Adapted by David Wood*)
FANTASTIC MR FOX: A PLAY (*Adapted by Sally Reid*)
JAMES AND THE GIANT PEACH: A PLAY (*Adapted by Richard George*)
THE TWITS: PLAYS FOR CHILDREN (*Adapted by David Wood*)
THE WITCHES: PLAYS FOR CHILDREN (*Adapted by David Wood*)

Teenage fiction

THE GREAT AUTOMATIC GRAMMATIZATOR AND OTHER STORIES
RHYME STEW
SKIN AND OTHER STORIES
THE VICAR OF NIBBLESWICKE
THE WONDERFUL STORY OF HENRY SUGAR AND SIX MORE

Collections

THE ROALD DAHL TREASURY
SONGS AND VERSE

ROALD DAHL

THE MAGIC FINGER

Illustrated by Quentin Blake

PUFFIN

PUFFIN BOOKS

UK | USA | Canada | Ireland | Australia
India | New Zealand | South Africa

Puffin Books is part of the Penguin Random House group of companies
whose addresses can be found at global.penguinrandomhouse.com.

puffinbooks.com

Penguin
Random House
UK

First published in the USA by Harper & Row 1966
Published in Great Britain by George Allen & Unwin 1968
Published by Puffin Books 1974
Reissued with new illustrations 1995
This edition published 2016
029

Set in Baskerville MT 14/17pt by
Palimpsest Book Production Limited, Falkirk, Stirlingshire
Printed and bound in Great Britain by Clays Ltd, Elcograf S.p.A.

A CIP catalogue record for this book is available from the British Library

ISBN: 978–0–141–36540–4

This book is for Ophelia and Lucy

The farm next to ours is owned by Mr and Mrs Gregg. The Greggs have two children, both of them boys. Their names are Philip and William. Sometimes I go over to their farm to play with them.

I am a girl and I am eight years old.

Philip is also eight years old.

William is three years older. He is ten.

What?

Oh, all right, then.

He is eleven.

Last week, something very funny happened to the Gregg family. I am going to tell you about it as best I can.

Now the one thing that Mr Gregg and his two boys loved to do more than anything else was to go hunting. Every Saturday morning they would take their guns and go off into the woods to look for animals and birds to shoot. Even Philip, who was only eight years old, had a gun of his own.

I can't stand hunting. I just can't *stand* it. It doesn't seem right to me that men and boys should kill animals just for the fun they get out of it. So I used to try to stop Philip and William from doing it. Every time I went over to their farm I would do my best to talk them out of it, but they only laughed at me.

I even said something about it once to Mr Gregg, but he just walked on past me as if I weren't there.

Then, one Saturday morning, I saw Philip and William coming out of the woods with their father, and they were carrying a lovely young deer.

This made me so cross that I started shouting at them.

The boys laughed and made faces at me, and Mr Gregg told me to go home and mind my own P's and Q's.

Well, that did it!

I saw red.

And before I was able to stop myself, I did something I never meant to do.

I PUT THE MAGIC FINGER ON THEM ALL!

Oh, dear! Oh, dear! I even put it on Mrs Gregg, who wasn't there. I put it on the whole Gregg family.

For months I had been telling myself that I would never put the Magic Finger upon anyone again – not after what happened to my teacher, old Mrs Winter.

Poor old Mrs Winter.

One day we were in class, and she was teaching us spelling. 'Stand up,' she said to me, 'and spell cat.'

'That's an easy one,' I said. '*K-a-t.*'

'You are a stupid little girl!' Mrs Winter said.

'I am not a stupid little girl!' I cried. 'I am a very nice little girl!'

'Go and stand in the corner,' Mrs Winter said.

Then I got cross, and I saw red, and I put the Magic Finger on Mrs Winter good and strong, and almost at once . . .

Guess what?

Whiskers began growing out of her face! They were long black whiskers, just like the ones you see on a cat, only much bigger. And how fast they grew! Before we had time to think, they were out to her ears!

Of course the whole class started screaming with laughter, and then Mrs Winter said, 'Will you be so kind as to tell me what you find so madly funny, all of you?'

And when she turned around to write something on the blackboard we saw that she had grown a *tail* as well! It was a huge bushy tail!

I cannot begin to tell you what happened after that, but if any of you are wondering whether Mrs Winter is quite all right again now, the answer is No. And she never will be.

The Magic Finger is something I have been able to do all my life.

I can't tell you just *how* I do it, because I don't even know myself.

But it always happens when I get cross, when I see red . . .

Then I get very, very hot all over . . .

Then the tip of the forefinger of my right hand begins to tingle most terribly . . .

And suddenly a sort of flash comes out of me, a quick flash, like something electric.

It jumps out and touches the person who has made me cross . . .

And after that the Magic Finger is upon him or her, and things begin to happen . . .

Well, the Magic Finger was now upon the whole of the Gregg family, and there was no taking it off again.

I ran home and waited for things to happen.

They happened fast.

I shall now tell you what those things were. I got the whole story from Philip and William the next morning, after it was all over.

In the afternoon of the very same day that I put the Magic Finger on the Gregg family, Mr Gregg and Philip and William went out hunting once again. This time they were going after wild ducks, so they headed towards the lake.

In the first hour they got ten birds.

In the next hour they got another six.

'What a day!' cried Mr Gregg. 'This is the best yet!' He was beside himself with joy.

Just then four more wild ducks flew over their heads. They were flying very low. They were easy to hit.

BANG! BANG! BANG! BANG! went the guns.

The ducks flew on.

'We missed!' said Mr Gregg. 'That's funny.'

Then, to everyone's surprise, the four ducks turned around and came flying right back to the guns.

'Hey!' said Mr Gregg. 'What on earth are they doing? They are really asking for it this time!' He shot at them again. So did the boys. And again they all missed!

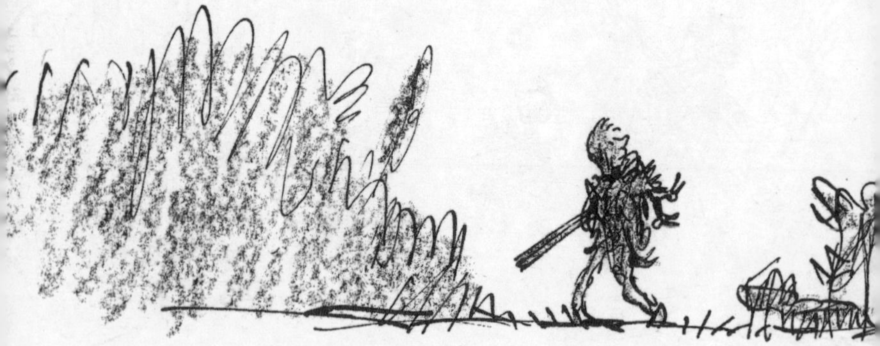

Mr Gregg got very red in the face. 'It's the light,' he said. 'It's getting too dark to see. Let's go home.'

So they started for home, carrying with them the sixteen birds they had shot before.

But the four ducks would not leave them alone. They now began flying around and around the hunters as they walked away.

Mr Gregg did not like it one bit. 'Be off!' he cried, and he shot at them many more times, but it was no good. He simply could not hit them. All the way home those four ducks flew around in the sky above their heads, and nothing would make them go away.

Late that night, after Philip and William had gone to bed, Mr Gregg went outside to get some wood for the fire.

He was crossing the yard when all at once he heard the call of a wild duck in the sky.

He stopped and looked up. The night was very still. There was a thin yellow moon over the trees on the hill, and the sky was filled with stars. Then Mr Gregg heard the noise of wings flying low over

his head, and he saw the four ducks, dark against the night sky, flying very close together. They were going around and around the house.

Mr Gregg forgot about the firewood, and hurried back indoors. He was now quite afraid. He did not like what was going on. But he said nothing about it to Mrs Gregg. All he said was, 'Come on, let's go to bed. I feel tired.'

So they went to bed and to sleep.

When morning came, Mr Gregg was the first to wake up.

He opened his eyes.

He was about to put out a hand for his watch, to see the time.

But his hand wouldn't come out.

'That's funny,' he said. 'Where is my hand?'

He lay still, wondering what was up.

Maybe he had hurt that hand in some way?

He tried the other hand.

That wouldn't come out either.

He sat up.

Then, for the first time, he saw what he looked like!

He gave a yell and jumped out of bed.

Mrs Gregg woke up. And when she saw Mr Gregg standing there on the floor, *she* gave a yell, too.

For he was now a tiny little man!

He was maybe as tall as the seat of a chair, but no taller.

And where his arms had been, he had a pair of duck's wings instead!

'But . . . but . . . but . . .' cried Mrs Gregg, going purple in the face. 'My dear man, what's happened to you?'

'What's happened to both of us, you mean!' shouted Mr Gregg.

It was Mrs Gregg's turn now to jump out of bed.

She ran to look at herself in the glass. But she was not tall enough to see into it. She was even smaller than Mr Gregg, and she, too, had got wings instead of arms.

'Oh! Oh! Oh! Oh!' sobbed Mrs Gregg.

'This is witches' work!' cried Mr Gregg. And both of them started running around the room, flapping their wings.

A minute later Philip and William burst in. The same thing had happened to them. They had wings and no arms. And they were *really* tiny. They were about as big as robins.

'Mama! Mama! Mama!' chirruped Philip. 'Look, Mama, we can fly!' And they flew up into the air.

'Come down at once!' said Mrs Gregg.'You're much too high!' But before she could say another word, Philip and William had flown right out the window.

Mr and Mrs Gregg ran to the window and looked out. The two tiny boys were now high up in the sky.

Then Mrs Gregg said to Mr Gregg, 'Do you think *we* could do that, my dear?'

'I don't see why not,' Mr Gregg said. 'Come on, let's try.'

Mr Gregg began to flap his wings hard, and all at once, up he went.

Then Mrs Gregg did the same.

'Help!' she cried as she started going up. 'Save me!'

'Come on,' said Mr Gregg. 'Don't be afraid.'

So out the window they flew, far up into the sky, and it did not take them long to catch up with Philip and William.

Soon the whole family was flying around and around together.

'Oh, isn't it lovely!' cried William. 'I've always wanted to know what it feels like to be a bird!'

'Your wings are not getting tired, are they, dear?' Mr Gregg asked Mrs Gregg.

'Not at all,' Mrs Gregg said. 'I could go on for ever!'

'Hey, look down there!' said Philip. 'Somebody is walking in our garden!'

They all looked down, and there below them, in their own garden, they saw four *enormous* wild ducks! The ducks were as big as men, and what is more, they had great long arms, like men, instead of wings.

The ducks were walking in a line to the door of the Greggs' house, swinging their arms and holding their beaks high in the air.

'Stop!' called the tiny Mr Gregg, flying down low over their heads. 'Go away! That's my house!'

The ducks looked up and quacked. The first one put out a hand and opened the door of the house and went in. The others went in after him. The door shut.

The Greggs flew down and sat on the wall near the door. Mrs Gregg began to cry.

'Oh, dear! Oh, dear!' she sobbed. 'They have taken our house. What *shall* we do? We have no place to go!'

Even the boys began to cry a bit now.

'We will be eaten by cats and foxes in the night!' said Philip.

'I want to sleep in my own bed!' said William.

'Now then,' said Mr Gregg. 'It isn't any good crying. That won't help us. Shall I tell you what we are going to do?'

'What?' they said.

Mr Gregg looked at them and smiled. 'We are going to build a nest.'

‘A nest!’ they said. ‘Can we do that?’

‘We *must* do it,’ said Mr Gregg. ‘We’ve got to have somewhere to sleep. Follow me.’

They flew off to a tall tree, and right at the top of it Mr Gregg chose the place for the nest.

'Now we want sticks,' he said. 'Lots and lots of little sticks. Off you go, all of you, and find them and bring them back here.'

'But we have no hands!' said Philip.

'Then use your mouths.'

Mrs Gregg and the children flew off. Soon they were back, carrying sticks in their mouths.

Mr Gregg took the sticks and started to build the nest.

'More,' he said. 'I want more and more and more sticks. Keep going.'

The nest began to grow. Mr Gregg was very good at making the sticks stick together.

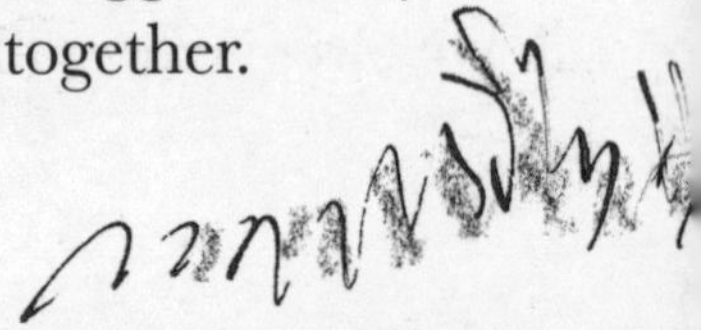

After a while he said, 'That's enough sticks. Now I want leaves and feathers and things like that to make the inside nice and soft.'

The building of the nest went on and on. It took a long time. But at last it was finished.

'Try it,' said Mr Gregg, hopping back. He was very pleased with his work.

'Oh, isn't it lovely!' cried Mrs Gregg, going into it and sitting down. 'I feel I might lay an egg any moment!'

The others all got in beside her.

'How warm it is!' said William.

'And what fun to be living so high up,' said Philip. 'We may be small, but nobody can hurt us up here.'

'But what about food?' said Mrs Gregg. 'We haven't had a thing to eat all day.'

'That's right,' Mr Gregg said. 'So we will now fly back to the house and go in by an open window and get the tin of biscuits when the ducks aren't looking.'

'Oh, we will be pecked to bits by those dirty great ducks!' cried Mrs Gregg.

'We shall be very careful, my love,' said Mr Gregg. And off they went.

But when they got to the house, they found all the windows and doors closed. There was no way in.

'Just look at that beastly duck cooking at my stove!' cried Mrs Gregg as she flew past the kitchen window. 'How dare she!'

'And look at *that* one holding my lovely gun!' shouted Mr Gregg.

'One of them is lying in my bed!' yelled William, looking into a top window.

'And one of them is playing with my electric train!' cried Philip.

'Oh, dear! Oh, dear!' said Mrs Gregg. 'They have taken over our whole house! We shall never get it back. And what *are* we going to eat?'

'I will *not* eat worms,' said Philip. 'I would rather die.'

'Or slugs,' said William.

Mrs Gregg took the two boys under her wings and hugged them. 'Don't worry,' she said. 'I can mince it all up very fine and you won't even know the difference. Lovely slugburgers. Delicious wormburgers.'

'Oh no!' cried William.

'Never!' said Philip.

'Disgusting!' said Mr Gregg. 'Just because we have wings, we don't have to eat bird food. We shall eat apples instead. Our trees are full of them. Come on!'

So they flew off to an apple tree.

But to eat an apple without holding it in your hands is not at all easy. Every time you try to get your teeth into it, it just pushes away. In the end, they were able to get a few small bites each. And then it began to get dark, so they all flew back to the nest and lay down to sleep.

It must have been at about this time that I, back in my own house, picked up the telephone and tried to call Philip. I wanted to see if the family was all right.

'Hello,' I said.

'Quack!' said a voice at the other end.

'Who is it?' I asked.

'Quack-quack!'

'Philip,' I said, 'is that you?'

'Quack-quack-quack-quack-quack!'

'Oh, stop it!' I said.

Then there came a very funny noise. It was like a bird laughing.

I put down the telephone quickly.

'Oh, that Magic Finger!' I cried. 'What *has* it done to my friends?'

That night, while Mr and Mrs Gregg and Philip and William were trying to get some sleep up in the high nest, a great wind began to blow. The tree rocked from side to side, and everyone, even Mr

Gregg, was afraid that the nest would fall down. Then came the rain. It rained and rained, and the water ran into the nest and they all got as wet as could be – and oh, it was a bad, bad night!

At last the morning came, and with it the warm sun.

'Well!' said Mrs Gregg. 'Thank goodness that's over! I never want to sleep in a nest again!' She got up and looked over the side . . .

'Help!' she cried. 'Look! Look down there!'

'What is it, my love?' said Mr Gregg. He stood up and peeped over the side.

He got the surprise of his life!

On the ground below them stood the four enormous ducks, as tall as men, and three of them were holding guns in their hands. One had Mr Gregg's gun, one had Philip's gun, and one had William's gun.

The guns were all pointing right up at the nest.

'No! No! No!' called out Mr and Mrs Gregg, both together. 'Don't shoot! Please don't shoot!'

'Why not?' said one of the ducks. It was the one who wasn't holding a gun. 'You are always shooting at *us*.'

'Oh, but that's not the same!' said Mr Gregg. 'We are *allowed* to shoot ducks!'

'Who allows you?' asked the duck.

'We allow each other,' said Mr Gregg.

'Very nice,' said the duck. 'And now *we* are going to allow each other to shoot you.'

(I would have loved to have seen Mr Gregg's face just then.)

'Oh, *please*!' cried Mrs Gregg. 'My two little children are up here with us! You wouldn't shoot my *children*!'

'Yesterday you shot *my* children,' said the duck. 'You shot all six of my children.'

'I'll never do it again!' cried Mr Gregg. 'Never, never, never!'

'Do you really mean that?' asked the duck.

'I *do* mean it!' said Mr Gregg. 'I'll never shoot another duck as long as I live!'

'That is not good enough,' said the duck. 'What about deer?'

'I'll do anything you say if you will only put down those guns!' cried Mr Gregg. 'I'll never shoot another duck or another deer or anything else again!'

'Will you give me your word on that?' said the duck.

'I will! I will!' said Mr Gregg.

'Will you throw away your guns?' asked the duck.

'I will break them into tiny bits!' said Mr Gregg. 'And never again need you be afraid of me or my family.'

'Very well,' said the duck. 'You may now come down. And by the way, may I congratulate you on the nest. For a first effort it's pretty good.'

Mr and Mrs Gregg and Philip and William hopped out of the nest and flew down.

Then all at once everything went black before their eyes, and they couldn't see. At the same time

a funny feeling came over them all, and they heard a great wind blowing in their ears.

Then the black that was before their eyes turned to blue, to green, to red, and then to gold, and suddenly, there they were, standing in lovely bright

sunshine in their own garden, near their own house, and everything was back to normal once again.

'Our wings have gone!' cried Mr Gregg. 'And our arms have come back!'

'And we are not tiny any more!' laughed Mrs Gregg. 'Oh, I am so glad!'

Philip and William began dancing about with joy.

Then, high above their heads, they heard the call of a wild duck. They all looked up, and they saw the four birds, lovely against the blue sky, flying very close together, heading back to the lake in the woods.

It must have been about half an hour later that I myself walked into the Greggs' garden. I had come to see how things were going, and I must admit I was expecting the worst. At the gate I stopped and stared. It was a queer sight.

In one corner Mr Gregg was smashing all three guns into tiny pieces with a huge hammer.

In another corner Mrs Gregg was placing beautiful flowers upon sixteen tiny mounds of soil which I learned later were the graves of the ducks that had been shot the day before.

And in the middle of the yard stood Philip and William, with a sack of their father's best barley beside them. They were surrounded by ducks, doves, pigeons, sparrows, robins, larks, and many other kinds that I did not know, and the birds were eating the barley that the boys were scattering by the handful.

'Good morning, Mr Gregg,' I said.

Mr Gregg lowered his hammer and looked at me. 'My name is not Gregg any more,' he said. 'In honour of my feathered friends, I have changed it from Gregg to Egg.'

'And I am Mrs Egg,' said Mrs Gregg.

'What happened?' I asked. They seemed to have gone completely dotty, all four of them.

Philip and William then began to tell me the whole story. When they had finished, William said, 'Look! There's the nest! Can you see it? Right up in the top of the tree! That's where we slept last night!'

'I built it *all* myself,' Mr Egg said proudly. 'Every stick of it.'

'If you don't believe us,' Mrs Egg said, 'just go into the house and take a look at the bathroom. It's a mess.'

'They filled the tub right up to the brim,' Philip said. 'They must have been swimming around in it all night! And feathers everywhere!'

'Ducks like water,' Mr Egg said. 'I'm glad they had a good time.'

Just then, from somewhere over by the lake, there came a loud BANG!

'Someone's shooting!' I cried.

'That'll be Jim Cooper,' Mr Egg said. 'Him and his three boys. They're shooting mad, those Coopers are, the whole family.'

Suddenly I started to see red . . .

Then I got very hot all over . . .

Then the tip of my finger began tingling most terribly. I could feel the power building up and up inside me . . .

I turned and started running towards the lake as fast as I could.

'Hey!' shouted Mr Egg. 'What's up? Where are you going?'

'To find the Coopers,' I called back.

'But why?'

'You wait and see!' I said. 'They'll be nesting in the trees tonight, every one of them!'

Are you ready to meet another little girl with an extraordinary gift? You are? Then here's a particularly tricky chapter from . . .

MATILDA

The Hat and the Superglue

The following morning, just before the father left for his beastly second-hand car garage, Matilda slipped into the cloakroom and got hold of the hat he wore each day to work. She had to stand on her toes and reach up as high as she could with a walking-stick in order to hook the hat off the peg, and even then she only just made it. The hat itself was one of those flat-topped pork-pie jobs with a jay's feather stuck in the hatband and Mr Wormwood was very proud of it. He thought it gave him a rakish daring look, especially when he wore it at an angle with his loud checked jacket and green tie.

Matilda, holding the hat in one hand and a thin tube of Superglue in the other, proceeded to squeeze a line of glue very neatly all round the inside rim of the hat. Then she carefully hooked the hat back on to the peg with the walking-stick. She timed this operation very carefully, applying the glue just as her father was getting up from the breakfast table.

Mr Wormwood didn't notice anything when he put the hat on, but when he arrived at the garage he couldn't get it off. Superglue is very powerful stuff, so powerful it will take your skin off if you pull too hard. Mr Wormwood didn't want to be scalped so he had to keep the hat on his head the whole day long, even when putting sawdust in gear-boxes and fiddling the

mileages of cars with his electric drill. In an effort to save face, he adopted a casual attitude hoping that his staff would think that he actually *meant* to keep his hat on all day long just for the heck of it, like gangsters do in the films.

When he got home that evening he still couldn't get the hat off. 'Don't be silly,' his wife said. 'Come here. I'll take it off for you.'

She gave the hat a sharp yank. Mr Wormwood let out a yell that rattled the window-panes. 'Ow-w-w!' he screamed. 'Don't do that! Let go! You'll take half the skin off my forehead!'

Matilda, nestling in her usual chair, was watching this performance over the rim of her book with some interest.

'What's the matter, Daddy?' she said. 'Has your head suddenly swollen or something?'

The father glared at his daughter with deep suspicion, but said nothing. How could he? Mrs Wormwood said to him, 'It *must* be Superglue. It couldn't be anything else. That'll teach you to go playing round with nasty stuff like that. I expect you were trying to stick another feather in your hat.'

'I haven't touched the flaming stuff!' Mr Wormwood shouted. He turned and looked again at Matilda, who looked back at him with large innocent brown eyes.

Mrs Wormwood said to him, 'You should read the label on the tube before you start messing with dangerous products. Always follow the instructions on the label.'

'What in heaven's name are you talking about, you stupid witch?' Mr Wormwood shouted, clutching the brim of his hat to stop anyone trying to pull it off again. 'D'you think I'm so stupid I'd glue this thing to my head on purpose?'

Matilda said, 'There's a boy down the road who got some Superglue on his finger without knowing it and then he put his finger to his nose.'

Mr Wormwood jumped. 'What happened to him?' he spluttered.

'The finger got stuck inside his nose,' Matilda said, 'and he had to go around like that for a week. People kept saying to him, "Stop picking your nose," and he couldn't do anything about it. He looked an awful fool.'

'Serve him right,' Mrs Wormwood said. 'He shouldn't have put his finger up there in the first place. It's a nasty habit. If all children had Superglue put on their fingers they'd soon stop doing it.'

Matilda said, 'Grown-ups do it too, Mummy. I saw you doing it yesterday in the kitchen.'

'That's quite enough from you,' Mrs Wormwood said, turning pink.

Mr Wormwood had to keep his hat on all through supper in front of the television. He looked ridiculous and he stayed very silent.

When he went up to bed he tried again to get the thing off, and so did his wife, but it wouldn't budge. 'How am I going to have my shower?' he demanded.

'You'll just have to do without it, won't you,' his wife told him. And later on, as she watched her skinny little husband skulking around the bedroom in his purple-striped pyjamas with a pork-pie hat on his head, she thought how stupid he looked. Hardly the kind of man a wife dreams about, she told herself.

Mr Wormwood discovered that the worst thing about having a permanent hat on his head was having to sleep in it. It was impossible to lie comfortably on the pillow. 'Now do stop fussing around,' his wife said to him after he had been tossing and turning for about an hour. 'I expect it will be loose by the morning and then it'll slip off easily.'

But it wasn't loose by the morning and it wouldn't slip off. So Mrs Wormwood took a pair of scissors and cut the thing off his head, bit by bit, first the top and then the brim. Where the inner band had stuck to the hair all around the sides and back, she had to chop the hair off right to the skin so that he finished up with a bald white ring round his head, like some sort of a monk. And in the front, where the band had stuck directly to the bare skin, there remained a whole lot of small patches of brown leathery stuff that no amount of washing would get off.

At breakfast Matilda said to him, 'You *must* try to get those bits off your forehead, Daddy. It looks as though you've got little brown insects crawling about all over you. People will think you've got lice.'

'Be quiet!' the father snapped. 'Just keep your nasty mouth shut, will you!'

All in all it was a most satisfactory exercise. But it was surely too much to hope that it had taught the father a permanent lesson.

STORIES ARE **GOOD** FOR **YOU.**

Roald Dahl said,
'If you have good thoughts, they will shine out of your face like sunbeams and you will always look lovely.'

We believe in doing good things.
That's why ten per cent of all Roald Dahl income* goes to our charity partners. We have supported causes including: specialist children's nurses, grants for families in need, and educational outreach programmes. Thank you for helping us to sustain this vital work.

Find out more at roalddahl.com

The Roald Dahl Charitable Trust is a registered UK charity (no. 1119330).
* All author payments and royalty income net of third-party commissions.

That's it.
The end of the book.

HERE IS
one LAST **WORD**,
invented by **Roald Dahl**
HIMSELF.

Make sure you KEEP IT SAFE.

BOOTBOGGLER

Noun: A foolish person.

ROALD DAHL

QUICK!

MISCHIEF MAKERS,

SIGN HERE so everyone

knows **this book** belongs

TO YOU.

ROALD DAHL was a spy, ace fighter pilot, chocolate historian and medical inventor. He was also the author of *Charlie and the Chocolate Factory*, *Matilda*, *The BFG* and many more brilliant stories. He remains **THE WORLD'S NUMBER ONE STORYTELLER.**

QUENTIN BLAKE has illustrated more than three hundred books and was Roald Dahl's favourite illustrator. In 1980 he won the prestigious Kate Greenaway Medal. In 1999 he became the first ever Children's Laureate and in 2013 he was knighted for services to illustration.

INTRODUCING . . .

Mr Hoppy

Alfie

Mrs Silver

The Pet-shop Owner

The Tortoise-catcher

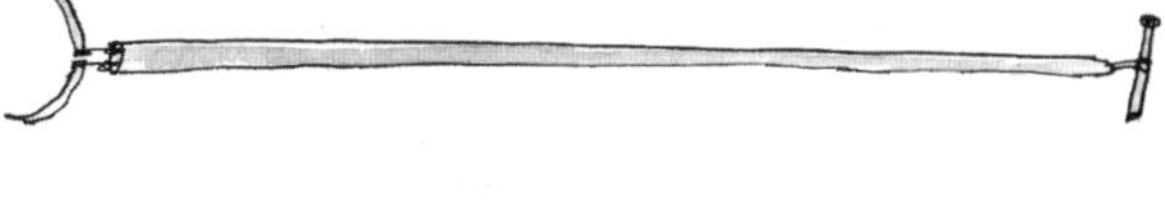

Books by Roald Dahl

THE BFG
BOY: TALES OF CHILDHOOD
BOY *and* GOING SOLO
CHARLIE AND THE CHOCOLATE FACTORY
CHARLIE AND THE GREAT GLASS ELEVATOR
THE COMPLETE ADVENTURES OF CHARLIE AND MR WILLY WONKA
DANNY THE CHAMPION OF THE WORLD
THE ENORMOUS CROCODILE
ESIO TROT
FANTASTIC MR FOX
GEORGE'S MARVELLOUS MEDICINE
THE GIRAFFE AND THE PELLY AND ME
GOING SOLO
JAMES AND THE GIANT PEACH
MATILDA
THE MAGIC FINGER
THE TWITS
THE WITCHES

Picture books

DIRTY BEASTS
THE ENORMOUS CROCODILE
THE GIRAFFE AND THE PELLY AND ME
THE MINPINS
REVOLTING RHYMES

Plays

THE BFG: PLAYS FOR CHILDREN (*Adapted by David Wood*)
CHARLIE AND THE CHOCOLATE FACTORY: A PLAY (*Adapted by Richard George*)
DANNY THE CHAMPION OF THE WORLD: PLAYS FOR CHILDREN (*Adapted by David Wood*)
FANTASTIC MR FOX: A PLAY (*Adapted by Sally Reid*)
JAMES AND THE GIANT PEACH: A PLAY (*Adapted by Richard George*)
THE TWITS: PLAYS FOR CHILDREN (*Adapted by David Wood*)
THE WITCHES: PLAYS FOR CHILDREN (*Adapted by David Wood*)

Teenage fiction

THE GREAT AUTOMATIC GRAMMATIZATOR AND OTHER STORIES
RHYME STEW
SKIN AND OTHER STORIES
THE VICAR OF NIBBLESWICKE
THE WONDERFUL STORY OF HENRY SUGAR AND SIX MORE

Collections

THE ROALD DAHL TREASURY
SONGS AND VERSE

ROALD DAHL

ESIO TROT

Illustrated by Quentin Blake

PUFFIN

PUFFIN BOOKS

UK | USA | Canada | Ireland | Australia
India | New Zealand | South Africa

Puffin Books is part of the Penguin Random House group of companies
whose addresses can be found at global.penguinrandomhouse.com.

puffinbooks.com

Penguin Random House UK

First published by Jonathan Cape 1990
Published by Puffin Books 1991
This edition published 2016
020

Set in Monotype Baskerville by Palimpsest Book Production Ltd, Falkirk, Stirlingshire
Printed in Great Britain by Clays Ltd, Elcograf S.p.A.

A CIP catalogue record for this book is available from the British Library

ISBN: 978–0–141–36548–0

www.greenpenguin.co.uk

MIX
Paper from
responsible sources
FSC® C018179
FSC www.fsc.org

Penguin Random House is committed to a sustainable future for our business, our readers and our planet. This book is made from Forest Stewardship Council® certified paper.

To Clover and Luke

Author's Note

Some years ago, when my own children were small, we usually kept a tortoise or two in the garden. In those days, a pet tortoise was a common sight crawling about on the family lawn or in the back yard. You could buy them quite cheaply in any pet-shop and they were probably the least troublesome of all childhood pets, and quite harmless.

Tortoises used to be brought into England by the thousand, packed in crates, and they came mostly from North Africa. But not many years ago a law was passed that made it illegal to bring any tortoises into the country. This was not done to protect us. The little tortoise was not a danger to anybody. It was done purely out of kindness to the tortoise itself. You see, the traders who brought them in used to cram hundreds of them tightly into the packing-crates without food or water and in such horrible conditions that a great many of them always died on the sea-journey over. So rather than allow this cruelty to go on, the Government stopped the whole business.

The things you are going to read about in this story all happened in the days when anyone could go out and buy a nice little tortoise from a pet-shop.

ESIO TROT

Mr Hoppy lived in a small flat high up in a tall concrete building. He lived alone. He had always been a lonely man and now that he was retired from work he was more lonely than ever.

There were two loves in Mr Hoppy's life. One was the flowers he grew on his balcony. They grew in pots and tubs and baskets, and in summer the little balcony became a riot of colour.

Mr Hoppy's second love was a secret he kept entirely to himself.

The balcony immediately below Mr Hoppy's jutted out a good bit further from the building than his own, so Mr Hoppy always had a fine view of what was going on down there. This balcony belonged to an attractive middle-aged lady called Mrs Silver. Mrs Silver was a widow who also lived alone. And although she didn't know it, it was she who was the object of Mr Hoppy's secret love. He had loved her from his balcony for many years, but he was a very shy man and he had never been able to bring himself to give her even the smallest hint of his love.

Every morning, Mr Hoppy and Mrs Silver exchanged polite conversation, the one looking down from above, the other looking up, but that was as far as it ever went. The distance between their balconies might not have been more than a few yards, but to Mr Hoppy it seemed like a million miles. He longed to invite Mrs Silver up for a cup of tea and a biscuit, but every time he was about to form the words on his lips, his courage failed him. As I said, he was a very very shy man.

Oh, if only, he kept telling himself, if only he could do something tremendous like saving her life or rescuing her from a gang of armed thugs, if only he could perform some great feat that would make him a hero in her eyes. If only . . .

The trouble with Mrs Silver was that she gave all her love to somebody else, and that somebody was a small tortoise called Alfie. Every day, when Mr Hoppy looked over his balcony and saw Mrs Silver whispering endearments to Alfie and stroking his shell, he felt absurdly jealous. He wouldn't even have minded becoming a tortoise himself if it meant Mrs Silver stroking his shell each morning and whispering endearments to him.

Alfie had been with Mrs Silver for years and he lived on her balcony summer and winter. Planks had been placed around the sides of the balcony so that Alfie could walk about without toppling over the edge, and in one corner there was a little house into which Alfie would crawl every night to keep warm.

When the colder weather came along in November, Mrs Silver would fill Alfie's house with dry hay, and the tortoise would crawl in there and bury himself deep under the hay and go to sleep for months on

end without food or water. This is called hibernating.

In early spring, when Alfie felt the warmer weather through his shell, he would wake up and crawl very slowly out of his house on to the balcony. And Mrs Silver would clap her hands with joy and cry out, 'Welcome back, my darling one! Oh, how I have missed you!'

It was at times like these that Mr Hoppy wished more than ever that he could change places with Alfie and become a tortoise.

Now we come to a certain bright morning in May when something happened that changed and indeed electrified Mr Hoppy's life. He was leaning over his balcony-rail watching Mrs Silver serving Alfie his breakfast.

'Here's the heart of the lettuce for you, my lovely,' she was saying. 'And here's a slice of fresh tomato and a piece of crispy celery.'

'Good morning, Mrs Silver,' Mr Hoppy said. 'Alfie's looking well this morning.'

'Isn't he gorgeous!' Mrs Silver said, looking up and beaming at him.

'Absolutely gorgeous,' Mr Hoppy said, not meaning it. And now, as he looked down at Mrs Silver's smiling face gazing up into his own, he thought for the thousandth time how pretty she was, how sweet and gentle and full of kindness, and his heart ached with love.

'I do so wish he would *grow* a little faster,' Mrs Silver was saying. 'Every spring, when he wakes up from his winter sleep, I weigh him on the kitchen scales. And do you know that in all the eleven years I've had him he's not gained more than *three ounces*! That's almost *nothing*!'

'What does he weigh now?' Mr Hoppy asked her.

'Just thirteen ounces,' Mrs Silver answered. 'About as much as a grapefruit.'

'Yes, well, tortoises are very slow growers,' Mr Hoppy said solemnly. 'But they can live for a hundred years.'

'I know that,' Mrs Silver said. 'But I do so wish he would grow just a little bit bigger. He's such a tiny wee fellow.'

'He seems just fine as he is,' Mr Hoppy said.

'No, he's *not* just fine!' Mrs Silver cried. 'Try to

think how miserable it must make him feel to be so titchy! Everyone wants to grow up.'

'You really *would* love him to grow bigger, wouldn't you?' Mr Hoppy said, and even as he said it his mind suddenly went *click* and an amazing idea came rushing into his head.

'Of course I would!' Mrs Silver cried. 'I'd give *anything* to make it happen! Why, I've seen pictures of giant tortoises that are so huge people can ride on their backs! If Alfie were to see those he'd turn green with envy!'

Mr Hoppy's mind was spinning like a fly-wheel. Here, surely, was his big chance! Grab it, he told himself. Grab it quick!

'Mrs Silver,' he said. 'I do actually happen to know how to make tortoises grow faster, if that's really what you want.'

'You do?' she cried. 'Oh, please tell me! Am I feeding him the wrong things?'

'I worked in North Africa once,' Mr Hoppy said. 'That's where all these tortoises in England come from, and a bedouin tribesman told me the secret.'

'Tell me!' cried Mrs Silver. 'I beg you to tell me, Mr Hoppy! I'll be your slave for life.'

When he heard the words *your slave for life*, a little shiver of excitement swept through Mr Hoppy. 'Wait there,' he said. 'I'll have to go in and write something down for you.'

In a couple of minutes Mr Hoppy was back on the balcony with a sheet of paper in his hand. 'I'm going to lower it to you on a bit of string,' he said, 'or it might blow away. Here it comes.'

Mrs Silver caught the paper and held it up in front of her. This is what she read:

ESIO TROT, ESIO TROT,
TEG REGGIB REGGIB!
EMOC NO, ESIO TROT,
WORG PU, FFUP PU, TOOHS PU!
GNIRPS PU, WOLB PU, LLEWS PU!
EGROG! ELZZUG! FFUTS! PLUG!
TUP NO TAF, ESIO TROT, TUP NO TAF!
TEG NO, TEG NO! ELBBOG DOOF!

'What *does* it mean?' she asked. 'Is it another language?'

'It's tortoise language,' Mr Hoppy said. 'Tortoises

are very backward creatures. Therefore they can only understand words that are written backwards. That's obvious, isn't it?'

'I suppose so,' Mrs Silver said, bewildered.

'Esio trot is simply tortoise spelled backwards,' Mr Hoppy said. 'Look at it.'

'So it is,' Mrs Silver said.

'The other words are spelled backwards, too,' Mr Hoppy said. 'If you turn them round into human language, they simply say:

TORTOISE, TORTOISE,
GET BIGGER BIGGER!
COME ON, TORTOISE,
GROW UP, PUFF UP, SHOOT UP!
SPRING UP, BLOW UP, SWELL UP!
GORGE! GUZZLE! STUFF! GULP!
PUT ON FAT, TORTOISE, PUT ON FAT!
GET ON, GET ON! GOBBLE FOOD!'

Mrs Silver examined the magic words on the paper more closely. 'I guess you're right,' she said. 'How clever. But there's an awful lot of poos in it. Are they something special?'

'Poo is a very strong word in any language,' Mr Hoppy said, 'especially with tortoises. Now what you have to do, Mrs Silver, is hold Alfie up to your face and whisper these words to him three times a day, morning, noon and night. Let me hear you practise them.'

Very slowly and stumbling a little over the strange words, Mrs Silver read the whole message out loud in tortoise language.

'Not bad,' Mr Hoppy said. 'But try to get a little more expression into it when you say it to Alfie. If you do it properly I'll bet you anything you like that in a few months' time he'll be twice as big as he is now.'

'I'll try it,' Mrs Silver said. 'I'll try anything. Of course I will. But I can't believe it'll work.'

'You wait and see,' Mr Hoppy said, smiling at her.

Back in his flat, Mr Hoppy was simply quivering all over with excitement. *Your slave for life*, he kept repeating to himself. What bliss!

But there was a lot of work to be done before that happened.

The only furniture in Mr Hoppy's small living-room was a table and two chairs. These he moved into his bedroom. Then he went out and bought a sheet of thick canvas and spread it over the entire living-room floor to protect his carpet.

Next, he got out the telephone-book and wrote down the address of every pet-shop in the city. There were fourteen of them altogether.

It took him two days to visit each pet-shop and choose his tortoises. He wanted a great many, at least one hundred, perhaps more. And he had to choose them very carefully.

To you and me there is not much difference between one tortoise and another. They differ only in their size and in the colour of their shells. Alfie had a darkish shell, so Mr Hoppy chose only the darker-shelled tortoises for his great collection.

Size, of course, was everything. Mr Hoppy chose all sorts of different sizes, some weighing only slightly more than Alfie's thirteen ounces, others a great deal more, but he didn't want any that weighed less.

'Feed them cabbage leaves,' the pet-shop owners told him. 'That's all they'll need. And a bowl of water.'

When he had finished, Mr Hoppy, in his enthusiasm, had bought no less than one hundred and forty tortoises and he carried them home in baskets, ten or fifteen at a time. He had to make a lot of trips and he was quite exhausted at the end of it all, but it was worth it. Boy, was it worth it! And what an amazing sight his living-room was when they were all in there together! The floor was swarming with tortoises of different sizes,

some walking slowly about and exploring, some munching cabbage leaves, others drinking water from a big shallow dish. They made just the faintest rustling sound as they moved over the canvas sheet, but that was all. Mr Hoppy had to pick his way carefully on his toes between this moving sea of brown shells whenever he walked across the room. But enough of that. He must get on with the job.

Before he retired Mr Hoppy had been a mechanic in a bus-garage. And now he went back to his old place of work and asked his mates if he might use his old bench for an hour or two.

What he had to do now was to make something that would reach down from his own balcony to Mrs Silver's balcony and pick up a tortoise. This was not difficult for a mechanic like Mr Hoppy.

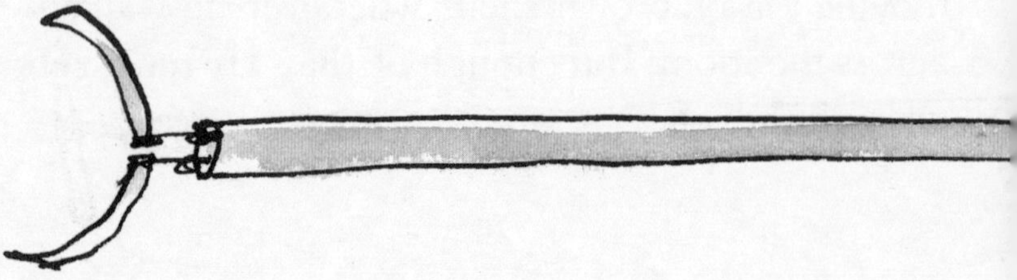

First he made two metal claws or fingers, and these he attached to the end of a long metal tube. He ran two stiff wires down inside the tube and connected them to the metal claws in such a way that when you pulled the wires, the claws closed, and when you pushed them, the claws opened. The wires were joined to a handle at the other end of the tube. It was all very simple.

Mr Hoppy was ready to begin.

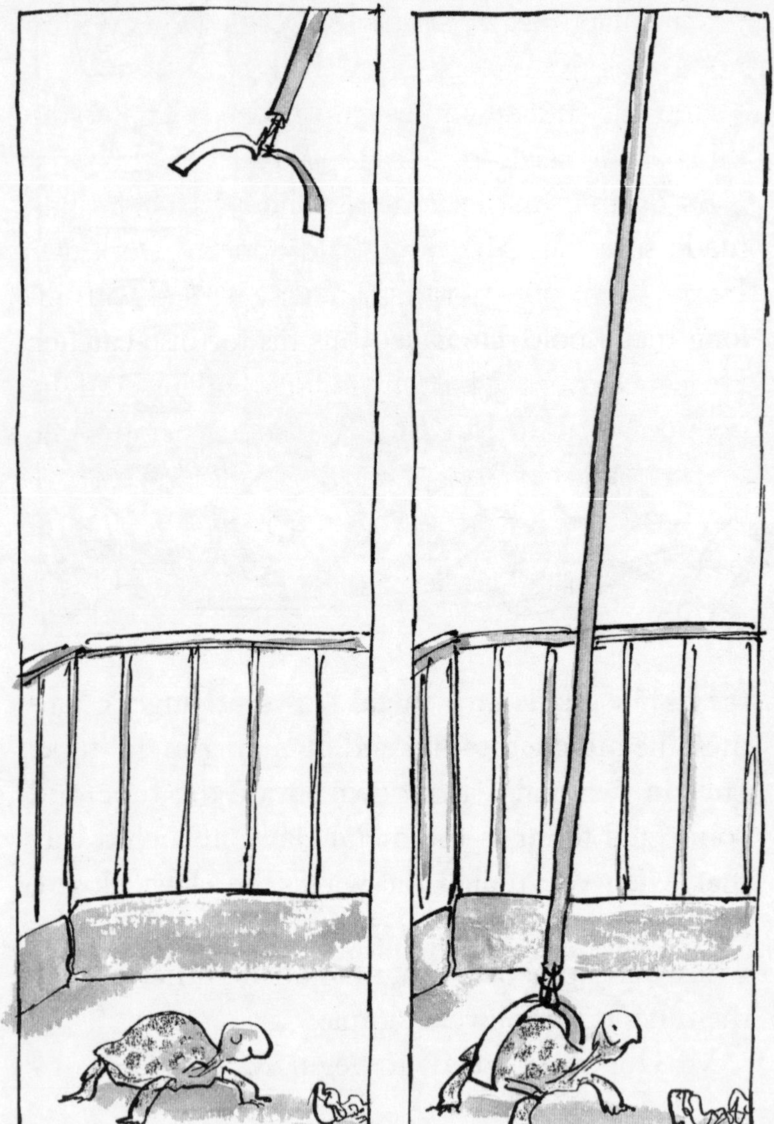

Mrs Silver had a part-time job. She worked from noon until five o'clock every weekday afternoon in a shop that sold newspapers and sweets. That made things a lot easier for Mr Hoppy.

So on that first exciting afternoon, after he had made sure that Mrs Silver had gone to work, Mr Hoppy went out on to his balcony armed with his long metal pole. He called this his tortoise-catcher. He leaned over the balcony railings and lowered the pole down on to Mrs Silver's balcony below. Alfie was basking in the pale sunlight over to one side.

'Hello, Alfie,' Mr Hoppy said. 'You are about to go for a little ride.'

He wiggled the tortoise-catcher till it was right above Alfie. He pushed the hand-lever so that the claws opened wide. Then he lowered the two claws neatly over Alfie's shell and pulled the lever. The claws closed tightly over the shell like two fingers of a hand. He hauled Alfie up on to his own balcony. It was easy.

Mr Hoppy weighed Alfie on his own kitchen scales just to make sure that Mrs Silver's figure of thirteen ounces was correct. It was.

Now, holding Alfie in one hand, he picked his way carefully through his huge collection of tortoises to find one that first of all had the same colour shell as Alfie's and secondly weighed *exactly two ounces more*.

Two ounces is not much. It is less than a smallish hen's egg weighs. But, you see, the important thing in Mr Hoppy's plan was to make sure that the new tortoise was bigger than Alfie but only a *tiny bit* bigger. The difference had to be so small that Mrs Silver wouldn't notice it.

From his vast collection, it was not difficult for Mr Hoppy to find just the tortoise he wanted. He wanted one that weighed fifteen ounces exactly on his kitchen scales, no more and no less. When he had got it, he put it on the kitchen table beside Alfie, and even he could hardly tell that one was bigger than the other. But it *was* bigger. It was bigger by two ounces. This was Tortoise Number 2.

Mr Hoppy took Tortoise Number 2 out on to the balcony and gripped it in the claws of his tortoise-catcher. Then he lowered it on to Mrs Silver's balcony, right beside a nice fresh lettuce.

Tortoise Number 2 had never eaten tender juicy lettuce leaves before. It had only had thick old cabbage leaves. It loved the lettuce and started chomping away at it with great gusto.

There followed a rather nervous two hours' wait for Mrs Silver to return from work.

Would she see any difference between the new tortoise and Alfie? It was going to be a tense moment.

Out on to her balcony swept Mrs Silver.

'Alfie, my darling!' she cried out. 'Mummy's back! Have you missed me?'

Mr Hoppy, peering over his railing, but well hidden between two huge potted plants, held his breath.

The new tortoise was still chomping away at the lettuce.

'My my, Alfie, you do seem hungry today,' Mrs Silver was saying. 'It must be Mr Hoppy's magic words I've been whispering to you.'

Mr Hoppy watched as Mrs Silver picked the tortoise up and stroked his shell. Then she fished Mr Hoppy's piece of paper out of her pocket, and holding the tortoise very close to her face, she whispered, reading from the paper:

'ESIO TROT, ESIO TROT,
TEG REGGIB REGGIB!
EMOC NO, ESIO TROT,
WORG PU, FFUP PU, TOOHS PU!
GNIRPS PU, WOLB PU, LLEWS PU!
EGROG! ELZZUG! FFUTS! PLUG!
TUP NO TAF, ESIO TROT, TUP NO TAF!
TEG NO, TEG NO! ELBBOG DOOF!'

Mr Hoppy popped his head out of the foliage and called out, 'Good evening, Mrs Silver. How is Alfie tonight?'

'Oh, he's lovely,' Mrs Silver said, looking up and beaming. 'And he's developing *such* an appetite! I've never seen him eat like this before! It must be the magic words.'

'You never know,' Mr Hoppy said darkly. 'You never know.'

Mr Hoppy waited seven whole days before he made his next move.

On the afternoon of the seventh day, when Mrs Silver was at work, he lifted Tortoise Number 2 from the balcony below and brought it into his living-room. Number 2 had weighed exactly *fifteen* ounces. He must now find one that weighed exactly *seventeen* ounces, two ounces more.

From his enormous collection, he easily found a seventeen-ounce tortoise and once again he made sure the shells matched in colour. Then he lowered Tortoise Number 3 on to Mrs Silver's balcony.

As you will have guessed by now, Mr Hoppy's secret was a very simple one. If a creature grows slowly enough – I mean very very slowly indeed – then you'll never notice that it has grown at all, especially if you see it every day.

It's the same with children. They are actually growing taller every week, but their mothers never notice it until they grow out of their clothes.

Slowly does it, Mr Hoppy told himself. Don't hurry it.

So this is how things went over the next eight weeks.

In the beginning

ALFIE weight 13 ounces

End of first week

TORTOISE NO. 2 weight 15 ounces

End of second week

TORTOISE NO. 3 weight 17 ounces

End of third week

TORTOISE NO. 4 weight 19 ounces

End of fourth week

TORTOISE NO. 5 weight 21 ounces

End of fifth week

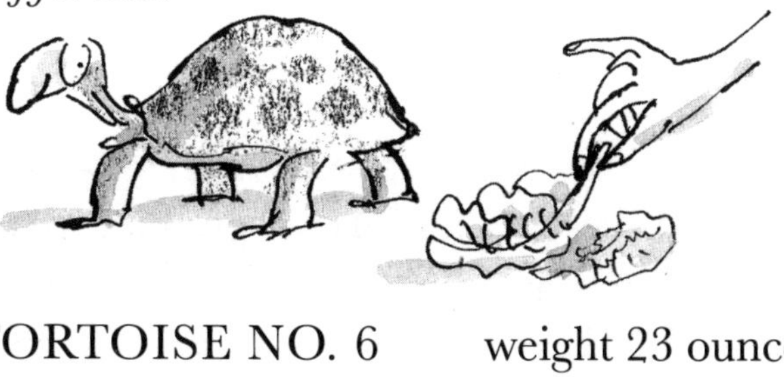

TORTOISE NO. 6 weight 23 ounces

End of sixth week

TORTOISE NO. 7 weight 25 ounces

End of seventh week

TORTOISE NO. 8 weight 27 ounces

Alfie's weight was thirteen ounces. Tortoise Number 8 was twenty-seven ounces. Very slowly, over seven weeks, Mrs Silver's pet had more than doubled in size and the good lady hadn't noticed a thing.

Even to Mr Hoppy, peering down over his railing, Tortoise Number 8 looked pretty big. It was amazing that Mrs Silver had hardly noticed anything at all during the great operation. Only once had she looked up and said, 'You know, Mr Hoppy, I do believe he's getting a bit bigger. What do you think?'

'I can't see a lot of difference myself,' Mr Hoppy had answered casually.

But now perhaps it was time to call a halt, and that evening Mr Hoppy was just about to go out and suggest to Mrs Silver that she ought to weigh Alfie when a startled cry from the balcony below brought him outside fast.

'Look!' Mrs Silver was shouting. 'Alfie's too big to get through the door of his little house! He must have grown enormously!'

'Weigh him,' Mr Hoppy ordered. 'Take him in and weigh him quick.'

Mrs Silver did just that, and in half a minute she was back holding the tortoise in both hands and waving it above her head and shouting, 'Guess what, Mr Hoppy! Guess what! He weighs twenty-seven ounces! He's twice as big as he was before! Oh, you darling!' she cried, stroking the tortoise. 'Oh, you great big wonderful boy! Just look what clever Mr Hoppy has done for you!'

Mr Hoppy suddenly felt very brave. 'Mrs Silver,' he said. 'Do you think I could pop down to your balcony and hold Alfie myself?'

'Why, of course you can!' Mrs Silver cried. 'Come down at once.'

Mr Hoppy rushed down the stairs and Mrs Silver opened the door to him. Together they went out on to the balcony. 'Just look at him!' Mrs Silver said proudly. 'Isn't he grand!'

'He's a big good-sized tortoise now,' Mr Hoppy said.

'And *you* did it!' Mrs Silver cried. 'You're a miracle-man, you are indeed!'

'But what *am* I going to do about his house?' Mrs Silver said. 'He must have a house to go into at night, but now he can't get through the door.'

They were standing on the balcony looking at the tortoise, who was trying to push his way into his house. But he was too big.

'I shall have to enlarge the door,' Mrs Silver said.

'Don't do that,' Mr Hoppy said. 'You mustn't go chopping up such a pretty little house. After all, he only needs to be just a tiny bit smaller and he could get in easily.'

'How can he possibly get smaller?' Mrs Silver asked.

'That's simple,' Mr Hoppy said. 'Change the magic words. Instead of telling him to get bigger and bigger, tell him to get a bit smaller. But in tortoise language of course.'

'Will that work?'

'Of course it'll work.'

'Tell me exactly what I have to say, Mr Hoppy.'

Mr Hoppy got out a piece of paper and a pencil and wrote:

ESIO TROT, ESIO TROT,

TEG A TIB RELLAMS, A TIB RELLAMS.

'That'll do it, Mrs Silver,' he said, handing her the paper.

'I don't mind trying it,' Mrs Silver said. 'But look here, I wouldn't want him to get titchy small all over again, Mr Hoppy.'

'He won't, dear lady, he won't,' Mr Hoppy said. 'Say it only tonight and tomorrow morning and then see what happens. We might be lucky.'

'If it works,' Mrs Silver said, touching him softly on the arm, 'then you are the cleverest man alive.'

The next afternoon, as soon as Mrs Silver had gone to work, Mr Hoppy lifted the tortoise up from her balcony and carried it inside. All he had to do now was to find one that was a shade smaller, so that it would just go through the door of the little house.

He chose one and lowered it down with his tortoise-catcher. Then, still gripping the tortoise, he tested it to see if it would go through the door. It wouldn't.

He chose another. Again he tested it. This one went through nicely. Good. He placed the tortoise in the middle of the balcony beside a nice piece of lettuce and went inside to await Mrs Silver's home-coming.

That evening, Mr Hoppy was watering his plants on the balcony when suddenly he heard Mrs Silver's shouts from below, shrill with excitement.

'Mr Hoppy! Mr Hoppy! Where are you?' she was shouting. 'Just look at this!'

Mr Hoppy popped his head over the railing and said, 'What's up?'

'Oh, Mr Hoppy, it's worked!' she was crying. 'Your magic words have worked again on Alfie! He can now get through the door of his little house! It's a miracle!'

'Can I come down and look?' Mr Hoppy shouted back.

'Come down at once, my dear man!' Mrs Silver answered. 'Come down and see the wonders you have worked upon my darling Alfie!'

Mr Hoppy turned and ran from the balcony into the living-room, jumping on tip-toe like a ballet-dancer between the sea of tortoises that covered the floor. He flung open his front door and flew down the stairs two at a time with the love-songs of a thousand cupids ringing in his ears. *This is it!* he whispered to himself under his breath. *The greatest moment of my life is coming up now! I mustn't bish it. I mustn't bosh it! I must keep very calm!* When he was three-quarters way down the stairs he caught sight of Mrs Silver already standing at the open door waiting to welcome him with a huge smile on her face. She flung her arms around him and cried out, 'You really are the most wonderful man I've ever met! You can do anything! Come in at once and let me make you a cup of tea. That's the very least you deserve!'

Seated in a comfortable armchair in Mrs Silver's parlour, sipping his tea, Mr Hoppy was all of a twitter. He looked at the lovely lady sitting opposite him and smiled at her. She smiled right back at him.

That smile of hers, so warm and friendly, suddenly gave him the courage he needed, and he said, 'Mrs Silver, please will you marry me?'

'Why, Mr Hoppy!' she cried. 'I didn't think you'd ever get round to asking me! Of course I'll marry you!'

Mr Hoppy got rid of his teacup and the two of them stood up and embraced warmly in the middle of the room.

'It's all due to Alfie,' Mrs Silver said, slightly breathless.

'Good old Alfie,' Mr Hoppy said. 'We'll keep him for ever.'

The next afternoon, Mr Hoppy took all his other tortoises back to the pet-shops and said they could have them for nothing. Then he cleaned up his living-room, leaving not a leaf of cabbage nor a trace of tortoise.

A few weeks later, Mrs Silver became Mrs Hoppy and the two of them lived very happily ever after.

P.S. I expect you are wondering what happened to little Alfie, the first of them all. Well, he was bought a week later from one of the pet-shops by a small girl called Roberta Squibb, and he settled down in Roberta's garden. Every day she fed him lettuce and tomato slices and crispy celery, and in the winters he hibernated in a box of dried leaves in the tool-shed.

That was a long time ago. Roberta has grown up and is now married and has two children of her own. She lives in another house, but Alfie is still with her, still the much-loved family pet, and Roberta reckons that by now he must be about thirty years old. It has taken him all that time to grow to twice the size he was when Mrs Silver had him. But he made it in the end.

If you could make magic happen, what would you do? A little girl is about to use her gift to teach her nasty neighbours a lesson . . .

THE MAGIC FINGER

The farm next to ours is owned by Mr and Mrs Gregg. The Greggs have two children, both of them boys. Their names are Philip and William. Sometimes I go over to their farm to play with them.

I am a girl and I am eight years old.

Philip is also eight years old.

William is three years older. He is ten.

What?

Oh, all right, then.

He is eleven.

Last week, something very funny happened to the Gregg family. I am going to tell you about it as best I can.

Now the one thing that Mr Gregg and his two boys loved to do more than anything else was to go hunting. Every Saturday morning they would take their guns and go off into the woods to look for animals and birds to shoot. Even Philip, who was only eight years old, had a gun of his own.

I can't stand hunting. I just can't *stand* it. It doesn't seem right to me that men and boys should kill animals just for the fun they get out of it. So I used to try to stop Philip and William from doing it. Every time I went over to their farm I would do my best to talk them out of it, but they only laughed at me.

I even said something about it once to Mr Gregg, but he just walked on past me as if I weren't there.

Then, one Saturday morning, I saw Philip and William coming out of the woods with their father, and they were carrying a lovely young deer.

This made me so cross that I started shouting at them.

The boys laughed and made faces at me, and Mr Gregg told me to go home and mind my own P's and Q's.

Well, that did it!

I saw red.

And before I was able to stop myself, I did something I never meant to do.

I PUT THE MAGIC FINGER ON THEM ALL!

Oh, dear! Oh, dear! I even put it on Mrs Gregg, who wasn't there. I put it on the whole Gregg family.

For months I had been telling myself that I would never put the Magic Finger upon anyone again – not after what happened to my teacher, old Mrs Winter.

Poor old Mrs Winter.

One day we were in class, and she was teaching us spelling. 'Stand up,' she said to me, 'and spell cat.'

'That's an easy one,' I said. '*K-a-t.*'

'You are a stupid little girl!' Mrs Winter said.

'I am not a stupid little girl!' I cried. 'I am a very nice little girl!'

'Go and stand in the corner,' Mrs Winter said.

Then I got cross, and I saw red, and I put the Magic Finger on Mrs Winter good and strong, and almost at once . . .

Guess what?

Whiskers began growing out of her face! They were long black whiskers, just like the ones you see on a cat, only much bigger. And how fast they grew! Before we had time to think, they were out to her ears!

Of course the whole class started screaming with laughter, and then Mrs Winter said, 'Will you be so kind as to tell me what you find so madly funny, all of you?'

And when she turned around to write something on the blackboard we saw that she had grown a *tail* as well! It was a huge bushy tail!

I cannot begin to tell you what happened after that, but if any of you are wondering whether Mrs Winter is quite all right again now, the answer is No. And she never will be.

The Magic Finger is something I have been able to do all my life.

I can't tell you just *how* I do it, because I don't even know myself.

But it always happens when I get cross, when I see red . . .

Then I get very, very hot all over . . .

Then the tip of the forefinger of my right hand begins to tingle most terribly . . .

And suddenly a sort of flash comes out of me, a quick flash, like something electric.

It jumps out and touches the person who has made me cross . . .

And after that the Magic Finger is upon him or her, and things begin to happen . . .

Well, the Magic Finger was now upon the whole of the Gregg family, and there was no taking it off again.

I ran home and waited for things to happen.

They happened fast.

I shall now tell you what those things were. I got the whole story from Philip and William the next morning, after it was all over.

That's it.
The end of the book.

HERE IS
one LAST **WORD**,
invented by **Roald Dahl**
HIMSELF.
Make sure you KEEP IT SAFE.

GLUBBAGE

Adjective: Rubbish.

ROALD
DAHL

QUICK!

MISCHIEF MAKERS,

SIGN HERE so everyone

knows **this book** belongs

TO YOU.

ROALD DAHL was a spy, ace fighter pilot, chocolate historian and medical inventor. He was also the author of *Charlie and the Chocolate Factory*, *Matilda*, *The BFG* and many more brilliant stories. He remains **THE WORLD'S NUMBER ONE STORYTELLER.**

QUENTIN BLAKE has illustrated more than three hundred books and was Roald Dahl's favourite illustrator. In 1980 he won the prestigious Kate Greenaway Medal. In 1999 he became the first ever Children's Laureate and in 2013 he was knighted for services to illustration.

INTRODUCING . . .

James
Henry
Trotter

Aunt Spiker and
Aunt Sponge

Old-Green-
Grasshopper

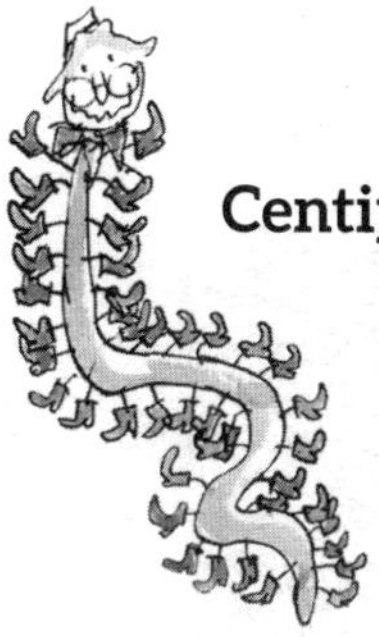

Centipede

Miss
Spider

Silkworm

Glow-worm

Earthworm

Ladybird

Books by Roald Dahl

THE BFG
BILLY AND THE MINPINS
BOY: TALES OF CHILDHOOD
BOY *and* GOING SOLO
CHARLIE AND THE CHOCOLATE FACTORY
CHARLIE AND THE GREAT GLASS ELEVATOR
THE COMPLETE ADVENTURES OF CHARLIE AND MR WILLY WONKA
DANNY THE CHAMPION OF THE WORLD
THE ENORMOUS CROCODILE
ESIO TROT
FANTASTIC MR FOX
GEORGE'S MARVELLOUS MEDICINE
THE GIRAFFE AND THE PELLY AND ME
GOING SOLO
JAMES AND THE GIANT PEACH
MATILDA
THE MAGIC FINGER
THE TWITS
THE WITCHES

Picture books

DIRTY BEASTS
THE ENORMOUS CROCODILE
THE GIRAFFE AND THE PELLY AND ME
THE MINPINS
REVOLTING RHYMES

Plays

THE BFG: THE PLAYS (*Adapted by David Wood*)
CHARLIE AND THE CHOCOLATE FACTORY: THE PLAY (*Adapted by Richard George*)
DANNY THE CHAMPION OF THE WORLD: THE PLAYS
(*Adapted by David Wood*)
FANTASTIC MR FOX: THE PLAY (*Adapted by Sally Reid*)
JAMES AND THE GIANT PEACH: THE PLAY (*Adapted by Richard George*)
THE TWITS: THE PLAYS (*Adapted by David Wood*)
THE WITCHES: THE PLAYS (*Adapted by David Wood*)

Teenage fiction

THE GREAT AUTOMATIC GRAMMATIZATOR AND OTHER STORIES
RHYME STEW
SKIN AND OTHER STORIES
THE VICAR OF NIBBLESWICKE
THE WONDERFUL STORY OF HENRY SUGAR AND SIX MORE

Collections

THE ROALD DAHL TREASURY
SONGS AND VERSE

ROALD DAHL

JAMES AND THE GIANT PEACH

Illustrated by Quentin Blake

PUFFIN

PUFFIN BOOKS

UK | USA | Canada | Ireland | Australia
India | New Zealand | South Africa

Puffin Books is part of the Penguin Random House group of companies
whose addresses can be found at global.penguinrandomhouse.com.

www.penguin.co.uk www.puffin.co.uk www.ladybird.co.uk

Penguin Random House UK

First published in the USA by Alfred A. Knopf, Inc., 1961
Published in Great Britain by George Allen & Unwin 1967
Published by Puffin Books 1973
Reissued with new illustrations 1995
This edition published 2016

012

Set in Monotype Baskerville 13/14 pt by Palimpsest Book Production Ltd, Falkirk, Stirlingshire
Printed in Great Britain by Clays Ltd, Elcograf S.p.A.

A CIP catalogue record for this book is available from the British Library

ISBN: 978–0–141–36545–9

All correspondence to:
Puffin Books, Penguin Random House Children's, 80 Strand, London WC2R 0RL

FSC www.fsc.org MIX Paper from responsible sources FSC® C018179

Penguin Random House is committed to a sustainable future for our business, our readers and our planet. This book is made from Forest Stewardship Council® certified paper.

This book
is for Olivia and Tessa

One

Until he was four years old, James Henry Trotter had a happy life. He lived peacefully with his mother and father in a beautiful house beside the sea. There were always plenty of other children for him to play with, and there was the sandy beach for him to run about on, and the ocean to paddle in. It was the perfect life for a small boy.

Then, one day, James's mother and father went to London to do some shopping, and there a terrible thing happened. Both of them suddenly got eaten up (in full daylight, mind you, and on a crowded street) by an enormous angry rhinoceros which had escaped from the London Zoo.

Now this, as you can well imagine, was a rather nasty experience for two such gentle parents. But in the long run it was far nastier for James than it was for them. *Their* troubles were all over in a jiffy. They were dead and gone in thirty-five seconds flat. Poor James, on the other hand, was still very much alive, and all at once he found himself alone and frightened in a vast unfriendly world. The lovely house by the seaside had to be sold immediately, and the little boy, carrying nothing but a small suitcase containing a pair of pyjamas and a toothbrush, was sent away to live with his two aunts.

Their names were Aunt Sponge and Aunt Spiker, and I am sorry to say that they were both really horrible people. They were selfish and lazy and cruel, and right from the beginning they started beating poor James for almost no reason at all. They never called him by his real name, but always referred to him as 'you disgusting little beast' or 'you filthy nuisance' or 'you miserable creature', and they certainly never gave him any toys to play with or any picture books to look at. His room was as bare as a prison cell.

They lived – Aunt Sponge, Aunt Spiker, and now James as well – in a queer ramshackle house on the top of a high hill in the south of England. The hill was so high that from almost anywhere in the garden James could look down and see for miles and miles across a marvellous landscape of woods and fields; and on a very clear day, if he looked in the right

direction, he could see a tiny grey dot far away on the horizon, which was the house that he used to live in with his beloved mother and father. And just beyond that, he could see the ocean itself – a long thin streak of blackish-blue, like a line of ink, beneath the rim of the sky.

But James was never allowed to go down off the top of that hill. Neither Aunt Sponge nor Aunt Spiker could ever be bothered to take him out herself, not even for a small walk or a picnic, and he certainly wasn't permitted to go alone. 'The nasty little beast will only get into mischief if he goes out of the garden,' Aunt Spiker had said. And terrible punishments were promised him, such as

being locked up in the cellar with the rats for a week, if he even so much as dared to climb over the fence.

The garden, which covered the whole of the top of the hill, was large and desolate, and the only tree in the entire place (apart from a clump of dirty old laurel bushes at the far end) was an ancient peach tree that never gave any peaches. There was no swing, no seesaw, no sand pit, and no other children were ever invited to come up the hill to play with poor James. There wasn't so much as a dog or a cat around to keep him company. And as time went on, he became sadder and sadder, and more and more lonely, and he used to spend hours every day standing at the bottom of the garden, gazing wistfully at the

lovely but forbidden world of woods and fields and ocean that was spread out below him like a magic carpet.

Two

After James Henry Trotter had been living with his aunts for three whole years there came a morning when something rather peculiar happened to him. And this thing, which as I say was only *rather* peculiar, soon caused a second thing to happen which was *very* peculiar. And then the *very* peculiar thing, in its own turn, caused a really *fantastically* peculiar thing to occur.

It all started on a blazing hot day in the middle of summer. Aunt Sponge, Aunt Spiker and James were all out in the garden. James had been put to work, as usual. This time he was chopping wood for the kitchen stove. Aunt Sponge and Aunt Spiker were sitting comfortably in deck-chairs near by, sipping tall glasses of fizzy lemonade and watching him to see that he didn't stop work for one moment.

Aunt Sponge was enormously fat and very short. She had small piggy eyes, a sunken mouth, and one of those white flabby faces that looked exactly as though it had been boiled. She was like a great white soggy overboiled cabbage. Aunt Spiker, on the other hand, was lean and tall and bony, and she wore steel-rimmed spectacles that fixed on to the end of her nose with a clip. She had a screeching voice and long wet narrow lips, and whenever she got angry or excited, little flecks of spit would come shooting out of her mouth as she talked. And there they sat, these two ghastly hags, sipping their drinks, and every now and again screaming at James to chop faster and faster. They also talked about themselves, each one saying how beautiful she thought she was.

Aunt Sponge had a long-handled mirror on her lap, and she kept picking it up and gazing at her own hideous face.

'I look and smell,' Aunt Sponge declared, 'as lovely as a rose!
Just feast your eyes upon my face, observe my shapely nose!
Behold my heavenly silky locks!
And if I take off both my socks
You'll see my dainty toes.'
'But don't forget,' Aunt Spiker cried, 'how much your tummy shows!'

Aunt Sponge went red. Aunt Spiker said, 'My sweet, you cannot win,
Behold MY gorgeous curvy shape, my teeth, my charming grin!
Oh, beauteous me! How I adore
My radiant looks! And please ignore
The pimple on my chin.'
'My dear old trout!' Aunt Sponge cried out. 'You're only bones and skin!'

'Such loveliness as I possess can only truly shine
In Hollywood!' Aunt Sponge declared: 'Oh, wouldn't that be fine!
I'd capture all the nations' hearts!
They'd give me all the leading parts!
The stars would all resign!'
'I think you'd make,' Aunt Spiker said, 'a lovely Frankenstein.'

Poor James was still slaving away at the chopping-block. The heat was terrible. He was sweating all over. His arm was aching. The chopper was a large blunt thing far too heavy for a small boy to use. And as he worked, James began thinking about all the other children in the world and what they might be doing at this moment. Some would be riding tricycles in their gardens. Some would be walking in cool woods and picking bunches of wild flowers. And all the little friends whom he used to know would be down by the seaside, playing in the wet sand and splashing around in the water . . .

Great tears began oozing out of James's eyes and rolling down his cheeks.

He stopped working and leaned against the chopping-block, overwhelmed by his own unhappiness.

'What's the matter with you?' Aunt Spiker screeched, glaring at him over the top of her steel spectacles.

James began to cry.

'Stop that immediately and get on with your work, you nasty little beast!' Aunt Sponge ordered.

'Oh, Auntie Sponge!' James cried out. 'And Auntie Spiker! Couldn't we all – *please* – just for once – go down to the seaside on the bus? It isn't very far – and I feel so hot and awful and lonely . . .'

'Why, you lazy good-for-nothing brute!' Aunt Spiker shouted.

'Beat him!' cried Aunt Sponge.

'I certainly will!' Aunt Spiker snapped. She glared at James, and James looked back at her with large frightened eyes. 'I shall beat you later on in the day when I don't feel so hot,' she said. 'And now get out of my sight, you disgusting little worm, and give me some peace!'

James turned and ran. He ran off as fast as he could to the far end of the garden and hid himself behind that clump of dirty old laurel bushes that we mentioned earlier on. Then he covered his face with his hands and began to cry and cry.

Three

It was at this point that the first thing of all, the *rather* peculiar thing that led to so many other *much* more peculiar things, happened to him.

For suddenly, just behind him, James heard a rustling of leaves, and he turned round and saw an old man in a funny dark-green suit emerging from the bushes. He was a very small old man, but he had a huge bald head and a face that was covered all over with bristly black whiskers. He stopped when he was about three yards away, and he stood there leaning on his stick and staring hard at James.

When he spoke, his voice was very slow and creaky. 'Come closer to me, little boy,' he said, beckoning to James with a finger. 'Come right up close to me and I will show you something *wonderful.*'

James was too frightened to move.

The old man hobbled a step or two nearer, and then he put a hand into the pocket of his jacket and took out a small white paper bag.

'You see this?' he whispered, waving the bag gently to and fro in front of James's face. 'You know what this is, my dear? You know what's inside this little bag?'

Then he came nearer still, leaning forward and pushing his face so close to James that James could feel breath blowing on his cheeks. The breath smelled

musty and stale and slightly mildewed, like air in an old cellar.

'Take a look, my dear,' he said, opening the bag and tilting it towards James. Inside it, James could see a mass of tiny green things that looked like little stones or crystals, each one about the size of a grain of rice. They were extraordinarily beautiful, and there was a strange brightness about them, a sort of luminous quality that made them glow and sparkle in the most wonderful way.

'Listen to them!' the old man whispered. 'Listen to them move!'

James stared into the bag, and sure enough there was a faint rustling sound coming up from inside it, and then he noticed that all the thousands of little green things were slowly, very very slowly stirring about and moving over each other as though they were alive.

'There's more power and magic in those things in there than in all the rest of the world put together,' the old man said softly.

'But – but – what *are* they?' James murmured, finding his voice at last. 'Where do they come from?'

'Ah-ha,' the old man whispered. 'You'd never guess that!' He was crouching a little now and pushing his face still closer and closer to James until the tip of his long nose was actually touching the skin on James's forehead. Then suddenly he jumped back and began waving his stick madly in the air. 'Crocodile tongues!' he cried. 'One thousand long slimy crocodile tongues boiled up in the skull of a dead witch for twenty days and nights with the eyeballs of a lizard! Add the fingers of a young monkey, the gizzard of a pig, the beak of a green parrot, the juice of a porcupine, and three spoonfuls of sugar. Stew for another week, and then let the moon do the rest!'

All at once, he pushed the white paper bag into

James's hands, and said, 'Here! You take it! It's yours!'

Four

James Henry Trotter stood there clutching the bag and staring at the old man.

'And now,' the old man said, 'all you've got to do is this. Take a large jug of water, and pour all the little green things into it. Then, very slowly, one by one, add ten hairs from your own head. That sets them off! It gets them going! In a couple of minutes the water will begin to froth and bubble furiously, and as soon as that happens you must quickly drink it all down, the whole jugful, in one gulp. And then, my dear, you will feel it churning and boiling in your stomach, and steam will start coming out of your mouth, and immediately after that, *marvellous* things will start happening to you, *fabulous, unbelievable* things – and you will never be miserable again in your life. Because you *are* miserable, aren't you? You needn't tell me! I know *all* about it! Now, off you go and do exactly as I say. And don't whisper a word of this to those two horrible aunts of yours! Not a word! And don't let those green things in there get away from you either! Because if they do escape, then they will be working their magic upon somebody else instead of upon *you*! And that isn't what you want at all, is it, my dear? *Whoever they meet first, be it bug, insect, animal, or tree, that will be the one who gets the full power of their magic!* So hold the bag tight! Don't tear the paper! Off you go! Hurry up! Don't wait! Now's the time! Hurry!'

With that, the old man turned away and disappeared into the bushes.

Five

The next moment, James was running back towards the house as fast as he could go. He would do it all in the kitchen, he told himself – if only he could get in there without Aunt Sponge and Aunt Spiker seeing him. He was terribly excited. He flew through the long grass and the stinging nettles, not caring whether he got stung or not on his bare knees, and in the distance he could see Aunt Sponge and Aunt Spiker sitting in their chairs with their backs towards him. He swerved away from them so as to go round the other side of the house, but then suddenly, just as he was passing underneath the old peach tree that stood in the middle of the garden, his foot slipped and he fell flat on his face in the grass. The paper bag burst open as it hit the ground and the thousands of tiny green things were scattered in all directions.

James immediately picked himself up on to his hands and knees and started searching around for

his precious treasures. *But what was this?* They were all sinking into the soil! He could actually see them wriggling and twisting as they burrowed their way downward into the hard earth, and at once he reached out a hand to pick some of them up before it was too late, but they disappeared right under his fingers. He went after some others, and the same thing happened! He began scrabbling around frantically in an effort to catch hold of those that were left, but they were too quick for him. Each time the tips of his fingers were just about to touch them, they vanished into the earth! And soon, in the space of only a few seconds, every single one of them had gone!

James felt like crying. He would never get them back now – they were lost, lost, lost forever.

But where had they gone to? And why in the world had they been so eager to push down into the earth like that? What were they after? There was nothing down *there*. Nothing except the roots of the old peach tree . . . and a whole lot of earthworms and centipedes and insects living in the soil.

But what was it that the old man had said? *Whoever they meet first, be it bug, insect, animal, or tree, that will be the one who gets the full power of their magic!*

Good heavens, thought James. What is going to happen in that case if they do meet an earthworm? Or a centipede? Or a spider? And what if they do go into the roots of the peach tree?

'Get up at once, you lazy little beast!' a voice was suddenly shouting in James's ear. James glanced up and saw Aunt Spiker standing over him, grim and tall and bony, glaring at him through her steel-rimmed spectacles. 'Get back over there immediately and finish chopping up those logs!' she ordered.

Aunt Sponge, fat and pulpy as a jellyfish, came waddling up behind her sister to see what was going on. 'Why don't we just lower the boy down the well in a bucket and leave him there for the night?' she suggested. 'That ought to teach him not to laze around like this the whole day long.'

'That's a very good wheeze, my dear Sponge. But let's make him finish chopping up the wood first. Be off with you at once, you hideous brat, and do some work!'

Slowly, sadly, poor James got up off the ground and went back to the woodpile. Oh, if only he hadn't slipped and fallen and dropped that precious bag. All hope of a happier life had gone completely now. Today and tomorrow and the next day and all the other days as well would be nothing but punishment and pain, unhappiness and despair.

He picked up the chopper and was just about to start chopping away again when he heard a shout behind him that made him stop and turn.

Six

'Sponge! Sponge! Come here at once and look at this!'

'At what?'

'It's a peach!' Aunt Spiker was shouting.

'A what?'

'A peach! Right up there on the highest branch! Can't you see it?'

'I think you must be mistaken, my dear Spiker. That miserable tree *never* has any peaches on it.'

'There's one on it now, Sponge! You look for yourself!'

'You're teasing me, Spiker. You're making my mouth water on purpose when there's nothing to put into it. Why, that tree's never even had a *blossom* on it, let alone a peach. Right up on the highest branch, you say? I can't see a thing. Very funny . . . Ha, ha . . . *Good gracious* me! Well, *I'll be blowed*! There really *is* a peach up there!'

'A nice big one, too!' Aunt Spiker said.

'A beauty, a beauty!' Aunt Sponge cried out.

At this point, James slowly put down his chopper and turned and looked across at the two women who were standing underneath the peach tree.

Something is about to happen, he told himself. *Something peculiar is about to happen any moment.* He hadn't the faintest idea what it might be, but he could feel it in his bones that something was going to happen soon. He could feel it in the air around him . . . in the sudden stillness that had fallen upon the garden . . .

James tiptoed a little closer to the tree. The aunts were not talking now. They were just standing there, staring at the peach. There was not a sound anywhere, not even a breath of wind, and overhead the sun blazed down upon them out of a deep blue sky.

'It looks ripe to me,' Aunt Spiker said, breaking the silence.

'Then why don't we eat it?' Aunt Sponge suggested, licking her thick lips. 'We can have half each. Hey, you! James! Come over here at once and climb this tree!'

James came running over.

'I want you to pick that peach up there on the highest branch,' Aunt Sponge went on. 'Can you see it?'

'Yes, Auntie Sponge, I can see it!'

'And don't you dare eat any of it yourself. Your Aunt Spiker and I are going to have it between us right here and now, half each. Get on with you! Up you go!'

James crossed over to the tree trunk.

'Stop!' Aunt Spiker said quickly. 'Hold everything!' She was staring up into the branches with her mouth wide open and her eyes bulging as though she had seen a ghost. '*Look!*' she said. '*Look*, Sponge, *look*!'

'What's the matter with you?' Aunt Sponge demanded.

'It's *growing*!' Aunt Spiker cried. 'It's getting bigger and bigger!'

'What is?'

'The peach, of course!'

'You're joking!'

'Well, look for yourself!'

'But my dear Spiker, that's perfectly ridiculous. That's impossible. That's – that's – that's – Now, wait *just* a minute – No – No – that can't be right – No – Yes – Great Scott! The thing really *is* growing!'

'It's nearly twice as big already!' Aunt Spiker shouted.

'It can't be true!'

'It is true!'

'It must be a miracle!'

'Watch it! Watch it!'

'I am watching it!'

'Great heavens alive!' Aunt Spiker yelled. 'I can actually see the thing bulging and swelling before my very eyes!'

Seven

The two women and the small boy stood absolutely still on the grass underneath the tree, gazing up at this extraordinary fruit. James's little face was glowing with excitement, his eyes were as big and bright as two stars. He could see the peach swelling larger and larger as clearly as if it were a balloon being blown up.

In half a minute, it was the size of a melon!

In another half-minute, it was *twice* as big again!

'Just *look* at it growing!' Aunt Spiker cried.

'Will it ever stop!' Aunt Sponge shouted, waving her fat arms and starting to dance around in circles.

And now it was so big it looked like an enormous butter-coloured pumpkin dangling from the top of the tree.

'Get away from that tree trunk, you stupid boy!' Aunt Spiker yelled. 'The slightest shake and I'm sure it'll fall off! It must weigh twenty or thirty pounds at least!'

The branch that the peach was growing upon was beginning to bend over further and further because of the weight.

'Stand back!' Aunt Sponge shouted. 'It's coming down! The branch is going to break!'

But the branch didn't break. It simply bent over more and more as the peach got heavier and heavier.

And still it went on growing.

In another minute, this mammoth fruit was as large and round and fat as Aunt Sponge herself, and probably just as heavy.

'It *has* to stop now!' Aunt Spiker yelled. 'It can't go on for ever!'

But it didn't stop.

Soon it was the size of a small car, and reached halfway to the ground.

Both aunts were now hopping round and round the tree, clapping their hands and shouting all sorts of silly things in their excitement.

'Hallelujah!' Aunt Spiker shouted. 'What a peach! What a peach!'

'Terrifico!' Aunt Sponge cried out. 'Magnifico! Splendifico! And what a meal!'

'It's still growing.'

'I know! I know!'

As for James, he was so spellbound by the whole thing that he could only stand and stare and murmur quietly to himself, 'Oh, isn't it beautiful. It's the most beautiful thing I've ever seen.'

'Shut up, you little twerp!' Aunt Spiker snapped, happening to overhear him. 'It's none of your business!'

'That's right,' Aunt Sponge declared. 'It's got nothing to do with you whatsoever! Keep out of it.'

'Look!' Aunt Spiker shouted. 'It's growing faster than ever now! It's speeding up!'

'I see it, Spiker! I do! I do!'

Bigger and bigger grew the peach, bigger and bigger and bigger.

Then at last, when it had become nearly as tall as the tree that it was growing on, as tall and wide, in fact, as a small house, the bottom part of it gently touched the ground – and there it rested.

'It can't fall off now!' Aunt Sponge shouted.

'It's stopped growing!' Aunt Spiker cried.

'No, it hasn't!'

'Yes, it has!'

'It's slowing down, Spiker, it's slowing down! But it hasn't stopped yet! You watch it!'

There was a pause.

'It has now!'

'I believe you're right.'

'Do you think it's safe to touch it?'

'I don't know. We'd better be careful.'

Aunt Sponge and Aunt Spiker began walking slowly round the peach, inspecting it very cautiously from all sides. They were like a couple of hunters who had just shot an elephant and were not quite sure whether it was dead or alive. And the massive round fruit towered over them so high that they looked like midgets from another world beside it.

The skin of the peach was very beautiful – a rich buttery yellow with patches of brilliant pink and red. Aunt Sponge advanced cautiously and touched it with the tip of one finger. 'It's ripe!' she cried. 'It's just perfect! Now, look here, Spiker. Why don't we go and get a shovel right away and dig out a great big chunk of it for you and me to eat?'

'No,' Aunt Spiker said. 'Not yet.'

'Why ever not?'

'Because I say so.'

'But I can't *wait* to eat some!' Aunt Sponge cried out. She was watering at the mouth now and a thin trickle of spit was running down one side of her chin.

'My dear Sponge,' Aunt Spiker said slowly, winking at her sister and smiling a sly, thin-lipped smile. 'There's a pile of money to be made out of this if only we can handle it right. You wait and see.'

Eight

The news that a peach almost as big as a house had suddenly appeared in someone's garden spread like wildfire across the countryside, and the next day a stream of people came scrambling up the steep hill to gaze upon this marvel.

Quickly, Aunt Sponge and Aunt Spiker called in carpenters and had them build a strong fence round the peach to save it from the crowd; and at the same time, these two crafty women stationed themselves at the front gate with a large bunch of tickets and started charging everyone for coming in.

'Roll up! Roll up!' Aunt Spiker yelled. 'Only one shilling to see the giant peach!'

'Half price for children under six weeks old!' Aunt Sponge shouted.

'One at a time, please! Don't push! Don't push! You're all going to get in!'

'Hey, you! Come back, there! You haven't paid!'

By lunchtime, the whole place was a seething mass of men, women, and children all pushing and shoving to get a glimpse of this miraculous fruit. Helicopters were landing like wasps all over the hill, and out of them poured swarms of newspaper reporters, cameramen, and men from the television companies.

'It'll cost you double to bring in a camera!' Aunt Spiker shouted.

'All right! All right!' they answered. 'We don't care!' And the money came rolling into the pockets of the two greedy aunts.

But while all this excitement was going on outside, poor James was forced to stay locked in his bedroom, peeping through the bars of his window at the crowds below.

'The disgusting little brute will only get in everyone's way if we let him wander about,' Aunt Spiker had said early that morning.

'Oh, *please*!' he had begged. 'I haven't met any other children for years and years and there are going to be lots of them down there for me to play with. And perhaps I could help you with the tickets.'

'Shut up!' Aunt Sponge had snapped. 'Your Aunt Spiker and I are about to become millionaires, and the last thing we want is the likes of you messing things up and getting in the way.'

Later, when the evening of the first day came and the people had all gone home, the aunts unlocked James's door and ordered him to go outside and pick up all the banana skins and orange peel and bits of paper that the crowd had left behind.

'Could I please have something to eat first?' he asked. 'I haven't had a thing all day.'

'No!' they shouted, kicking him out of the door. 'We're too busy to make food! We are counting our money!'

'But it's dark!' cried James.

'Get out!' they yelled. 'And stay out until you've cleaned up all the mess!' The door slammed. The key turned in the lock.

Nine

Hungry and trembling, James stood alone out in the open, wondering what to do. The night was all around him now, and high overhead a wild white moon was riding in the sky. There was not a sound, not a movement anywhere.

Most people – and especially small children – are often quite scared of being out of doors alone in the moonlight. Everything is so deadly quiet, and the shadows are so long and black, and they keep turning into strange shapes that seem to move as you look at them, and the slightest little snap of a twig makes you jump.

James felt exactly like that now. He stared straight ahead with large frightened eyes, hardly daring to breathe. Not far away, in the middle of the garden, he could see the giant peach towering over everything else. Surely it was even bigger tonight than ever before? And what a dazzling sight it was! The moonlight was shining and glinting on its great curving sides, turning them to crystal and silver. It looked like a tremendous silver ball lying there in the grass, silent, mysterious, and wonderful.

And then all at once, little shivers of excitement started running over the skin on James's back.

Something else, he told himself, *something stranger than ever this time, is about to happen to me again soon*. He was sure of it. He could feel it coming.

He looked around him, wondering what on earth it was going to be. The garden lay soft and silver in the moonlight. The grass was wet with dew and a million dewdrops were sparkling and twinkling like diamonds around his feet. And now suddenly, the whole place, the whole garden seemed to be *alive* with magic.

Almost without knowing what he was doing, as though drawn by some powerful magnet, James Henry Trotter started walking slowly towards the giant peach. He climbed over the fence that surrounded it, and stood directly beneath it, staring up at its great bulging sides. He put out a hand and touched it gently with the tip of one finger. It felt soft and warm and slightly furry, like the skin of a baby mouse. He moved a step closer and rubbed his cheek lightly against the soft skin. And then suddenly, while he was doing this, he happened to notice that right beside him and below him, close to the ground, there was a hole in the side of the peach.

Ten

It was quite a large hole, the sort of thing an animal about the size of a fox might have made.

James knelt down in front of it, and poked his head and shoulders inside.

He crawled in.

He kept on crawling.

This isn't a hole, he thought excitedly. *It's a tunnel!*

The tunnel was damp and murky, and all around him there was the curious bittersweet smell of fresh peach. The floor was soggy under his knees, the walls were wet and sticky, and peach juice was dripping from the ceiling. James opened his mouth and caught some of it on his tongue. It tasted delicious.

He was crawling uphill now, as though the tunnel were leading straight towards the very centre of the gigantic fruit. Every few seconds he paused and took a bite out of the wall. The peach flesh was sweet and juicy, and marvellously refreshing.

He crawled on for several more yards, and then suddenly – *bang* – the top of his head bumped into something extremely hard blocking his way. He glanced up. In front of him there was a solid wall that seemed at first as though it were made of wood. He touched it with his fingers. It certainly felt like wood, except that it was very jagged and full of deep grooves.

'Good heavens!' he said. 'I know what this is! I've come to the stone in the middle of the peach!'

Then he noticed that there was a small door cut into the face of the peach stone. He gave a push. It swung open. He crawled through it, and before he had time to glance up and see where he was, he heard a voice saying, '*Look* who's here!' And another one said, 'We've been *waiting* for you!'

James stopped and stared at the speakers, his face white with horror.

He started to stand up, but his knees were shaking so much he had to sit down again on the floor. He glanced behind him, thinking he could bolt back into the tunnel the way he had come, but the doorway had disappeared. There was now only a solid brown wall behind him.

Eleven

James's large frightened eyes travelled slowly round the room.

The creatures, some sitting on chairs, others reclining on a sofa, were all watching him intently.

Creatures?

Or were they insects?

An insect is usually something rather small, is it not? A grasshopper, for example, is an insect.

So what would you call it if you saw a grasshopper as large as a dog? As large as a *large* dog. You could hardly call *that* an insect, could you?

There was an Old-Green-Grasshopper as large as a large dog sitting directly across the room from James now.

And next to the Old-Green-Grasshopper, there was an enormous Spider.

And next to the Spider, there was a giant Ladybird with nine black spots on her scarlet shell.

Each of these three was squatting upon a magnificent chair.

On a sofa near by, reclining comfortably in curled-up positions, there were a Centipede and an Earthworm.

On the floor over in the far corner, there was something thick and white that looked as though it might be a Silkworm. But it was sleeping soundly and nobody was paying any attention to it.

Every one of these 'creatures' was at least as big as James himself, and in the strange greenish light that

shone down from somewhere in the ceiling, they were absolutely terrifying to behold.

'I'm hungry!' the Spider announced suddenly, staring hard at James.

'*I'm* famished!' the Old-Green-Grasshopper said.

'So am *I*!' the Ladybird cried.

The Centipede sat up a little straighter on the sofa. '*Everyone's* famished!' he said. 'We need food!'

Four pairs of round black glassy eyes were all fixed upon James.

The Centipede made a wriggling movement with his body as though he were about to glide off the sofa – but he didn't.

There was a long pause – and a long silence.

The Spider (who happened to be a female spider) opened her mouth and ran a long black tongue delicately over her lips. 'Aren't *you* hungry?' she asked suddenly, leaning forward and addressing herself to James.

Poor James was backed up against the far wall, shivering with fright and much too terrified to answer.

'What's the matter with you?' the Old-Green-Grasshopper asked. 'You look positively ill!'

'He looks as though he's going to faint any second,' the Centipede said.

'Oh, my goodness, the poor thing!' the Ladybird cried. 'I do believe he thinks it's *him* that we are wanting to eat!'

There was a roar of laughter from all sides.

'Oh dear, oh dear!' they said. 'What an awful thought!'

'You mustn't be frightened,' the Ladybird said kindly. 'We wouldn't *dream* of hurting you. You are one of *us* now, didn't you know that? You are one of the crew. We're all in the same boat.'

'We've been waiting for you all day long,' the Old-Green-Grasshopper said. 'We thought you were never going to turn up. I'm glad you made it.'

'So cheer up, my boy, cheer up!' the Centipede said. 'And meanwhile I wish you'd come over here and give me a hand with these boots. It takes me *hours* to get them all off by myself.'

Twelve

James decided that this was most certainly not a time to be disagreeable, so he crossed the room to where the Centipede was sitting and knelt down beside him.

'Thank you so much,' the Centipede said. 'You are very kind.'

'You have a lot of boots,' James murmured.

'I have a lot of legs,' the Centipede answered proudly. 'And a lot of feet. One hundred, to be exact.'

'*There* he goes again!' the Earthworm cried, speaking for the first time. 'He simply cannot stop telling lies about his legs! He doesn't have anything *like* a hundred of them! He's only got forty-two! The trouble is that most people don't bother to count them. They just take his word. And anyway, there is nothing *marvellous*, you know, Centipede, about having a lot of legs.'

'Poor fellow,' the Centipede said, whispering in James's ear. 'He's blind. He can't see how splendid I look.'

'In my opinion,' the Earthworm said, 'the *really* marvellous thing is to have no legs at all and to be able to walk just the same.'

'You call that *walking*!' cried the Centipede. 'You're a *slitherer*, that's all you are! You just *slither* along!'

'I glide,' said the Earthworm primly.

'You are a slimy beast,' answered the Centipede.

'I am *not* a slimy beast,' the Earthworm said. 'I am a useful and much loved creature. Ask any gardener you like. And as for you . . .'

'I am a pest!' the Centipede announced, grinning broadly and looking round the room for approval.

'He is *so* proud of that,' the Ladybird said, smiling at James. 'Though for the life of me I cannot understand why.'

'I am the only pest in this room!' cried the Centipede, still grinning away. 'Unless you count Old-Green-Grasshopper over there. But he is long past it now. He is too old to be a pest any more.'

The Old-Green-Grasshopper turned his huge black eyes upon the Centipede and gave him a withering look. 'Young fellow,' he said, speaking in a deep, slow, scornful voice, 'I have never been a pest in my life. I am a musician.'

'Hear, hear!' said the Ladybird.

'James,' the Centipede said. 'Your name *is* James, isn't it?'

'Yes.'

'Well, James, have you ever in your life seen such a marvellous colossal Centipede as me?'

'I certainly haven't,' James answered. 'How on earth did you get to be like that?'

'*Very* peculiar,' the Centipede said. '*Very, very* peculiar indeed. Let me tell you what happened. I was messing about in the garden under the old peach tree and suddenly a funny little green thing came wriggling past my nose. Bright green it was, and extraordinarily beautiful, and it looked like some kind of a tiny stone or crystal . . .'

'Oh, but I know what that was!' cried James.

'It happened to me, too!' said the Ladybird.

'And me!' Miss Spider said. 'Suddenly there were little green things everywhere! The soil was full of them!'

'I actually swallowed one!' the Earthworm declared proudly.

'So did I!' the Ladybird said.

'I swallowed three!' the Centipede cried. 'But who's telling this story anyway? Don't interrupt!'

'It's too late to tell stories now,' the Old-Green-Grasshopper announced. 'It's time to go to sleep.'

'I refuse to sleep in my boots!' the Centipede cried. 'How many more are there to come off, James?'

'I think I've done about twenty so far,' James told him.

'Then that leaves eighty to go,' the Centipede said.

'*Twenty-two*, not *eighty*!' shrieked the Earthworm. 'He's lying again.'

The Centipede roared with laughter.

'Stop pulling the Earthworm's leg,' the Ladybird said.

This sent the Centipede into hysterics. 'Pulling his *leg*!' he cried, wriggling with glee and pointing at the Earthworm. 'Which leg am I pulling? You tell me that!'

James decided that he rather liked the Centipede. He was obviously a rascal, but what a change it was to hear somebody laughing once in a while. He had never heard Aunt Sponge or Aunt Spiker laughing aloud in all the time he had been with them.

'We really *must* get some sleep,' the Old-Green-Grasshopper said. 'We've got a tough day ahead of us tomorrow. So would you be kind enough, Miss Spider, to make the beds?'

Thirteen

A few minutes later, Miss Spider had made the first bed. It was hanging from the ceiling, suspended by a rope of threads at either end so that actually it looked more like a hammock than a bed. But it was a magnificent affair, and the stuff that it was made of shimmered like silk in the pale light.

'I do hope you'll find it comfortable,' Miss Spider said to the Old-Green-Grasshopper. 'I made it as soft and silky as I possibly could. I spun it with gossamer. That's a much better quality thread than the one I use for my own web.'

'Thank you so much, my dear lady,' the Old-Green-Grasshopper said, climbing into the hammock. 'Ah, this is just what I needed. Good night, everybody. Good night.'

Then Miss Spider spun the next hammock, and the Ladybird got in.

After that, she spun a long one for the Centipede, and an even longer one for the Earthworm.

'And how do you like *your* bed?' she said to

James when it came to his turn. 'Hard or soft?'

'I like it soft, thank you very much,' James answered.

'For goodness' sake stop staring round the room and get on with my boots!' the Centipede said. 'You and I are never going to get any sleep at this rate! And kindly line them up neatly in pairs as you take them off. Don't just throw them over your shoulder.'

James worked away frantically on the Centipede's boots. Each one had laces that had to be untied and loosened before it could be pulled off, and to make matters worse, all the laces were tied up in the most terrible complicated knots that had to be unpicked with fingernails. It was just awful. It took about two hours. And by the time James had pulled off the last boot of all and had lined them up in a row on the floor – twenty-one pairs altogether – the Centipede was fast asleep.

'Wake up, Centipede,' whispered James, giving him a gentle dig in the stomach. 'It's time for bed.'

'Thank you, my dear child,' the Centipede said, opening his eyes. Then he got down off the sofa and ambled across the room and crawled into his hammock. James got into his own hammock – and oh, how soft and comfortable it was compared with the hard bare boards that his aunts had always made him sleep upon at home.

'Lights out,' said the Centipede drowsily.

Nothing happened.

'Turn out the light!' he called, raising his voice. James glanced round the room, wondering which of the others he might be talking to, but they were all asleep. The Old-Green-Grasshopper was snoring loudly through his nose. The Ladybird was making whistling noises as she breathed, and the Earthworm was coiled up like a spring at one end of his hammock, wheezing and blowing through his open mouth. As for Miss Spider, she had made a lovely web for herself across one corner of the room, and James could see her crouching right in the very centre of it, mumbling softly in her dreams.

'I said turn out the light!' shouted the Centipede angrily.

'Are you talking to me?' James asked him.

'Of course I'm not talking to you, you ass!' the Centipede answered. 'That crazy Glow-worm has gone to sleep with her light on!'

For the first time since entering the room, James glanced up at the ceiling – and there he saw a most extraordinary sight. Something that looked like a gigantic fly without wings (it was at least three feet long) was standing upside down upon its six legs in the middle of the ceiling, and the tail end of this creature seemed to be literally on fire. A brilliant greenish light as bright as the brightest electric bulb was shining out of its tail and lighting up the whole room.

'Is *that* a Glow-worm?' asked James, staring at the light. 'It doesn't look like a worm of any sort to me.'

'Of course it's a Glow-worm,' the Centipede answered. 'At least that's what *she* calls herself. Although actually you are quite right. She isn't really

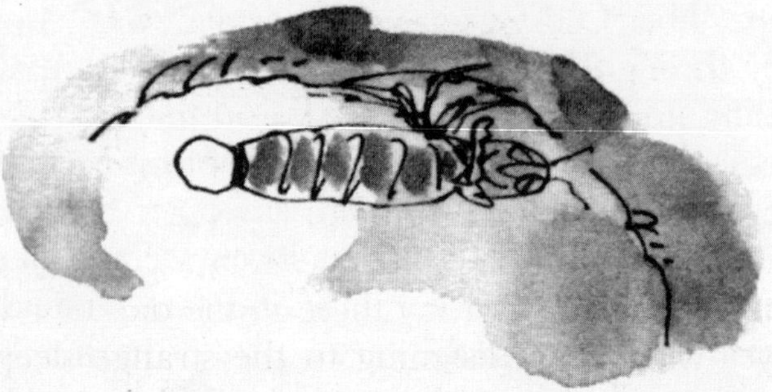

a worm at all. Glow-worms are never worms. They are simply lady fireflies without wings. Wake up, you lazy beast!'

But the Glow-worm didn't stir, so the Centipede reached out of his hammock and picked up one of his boots from the floor. 'Put out that wretched light!' he shouted, hurling the boot up at the ceiling.

The Glow-worm slowly opened one eye and stared at the Centipede. 'There is no need to be rude,' she said coldly. 'All in good time.'

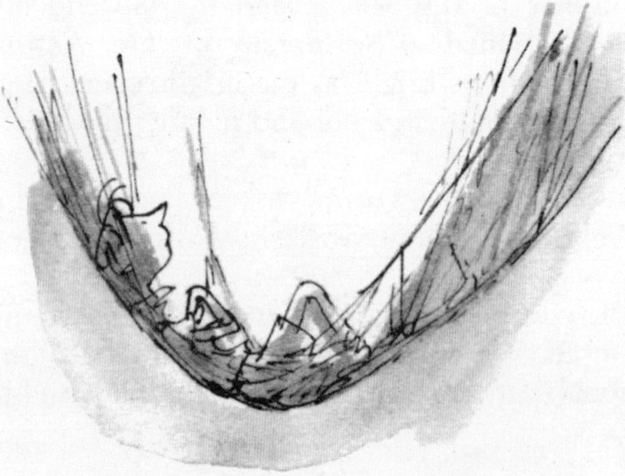

'Come on, come on, come on!' shouted the Centipede. 'Or I'll put it out for you!'

'Oh, hello, James!' the Glow-worm said, looking down and giving James a little wave and a smile. 'I didn't see you come in. Welcome, my dear boy, welcome – and good night!'

Then *click* – and out went the light.

James Henry Trotter lay there in the darkness with his eyes wide open, listening to the strange sleeping noises that the 'creatures' were making all around him, and wondering what on earth was going to happen to him in the morning. Already, he was beginning to like his new friends very much. They were not nearly as terrible as they looked. In fact they weren't really terrible at all. They seemed extremely kind and helpful in spite of all the shouting and arguing that went on between them.

'Good night, Old-Green-Grasshopper,' he whispered. 'Good night, Ladybird – Good night, Miss Spider –' But before he could go through them all, he had fallen fast asleep.

Fourteen

'We're off!' someone was shouting. 'We're off at last!'

James woke up with a jump and looked about him. The creatures were all out of their hammocks and moving excitedly around the room. Suddenly, the floor gave a great heave, as though an earthquake were taking place.

'Here we go!' shouted the Old-Green-Grasshopper, hopping up and down with excitement. 'Hold on tight!'

'What's happening?' cried James, leaping out of his hammock. 'What's going on?'

The Ladybird, who was obviously a kind and gentle creature, came over and stood beside him. 'In case you don't know it,' she said, 'we are about to depart for ever from the top of this ghastly hill that we've all been living on for so long. We are about to roll away inside this great big beautiful peach to a land of . . . of . . . of . . . to a land of –'

'Of what?' asked James.

'Never you mind,' said the Ladybird. 'But nothing could be worse than this desolate hilltop and those two repulsive aunts of yours –'

'Hear, hear!' they all shouted. 'Hear, hear!'

'You may not have noticed it,' the Ladybird went on, 'but the whole garden, even before it reaches the steep edge of the hill, happens to be on a steep slope. And therefore the only thing that has been stopping this peach from rolling away right from the beginning is the thick stem attaching it to the tree. Break the stem, and off we go.'

'Watch it!' cried Miss Spider, as the room gave another violent lurch. 'Here we go!'

'Not quite! Not quite!'

'At this moment,' continued the Ladybird, 'our Centipede, who has a pair of jaws as sharp as razors, is up there on top of the peach nibbling away at that stem. In fact, he must be nearly through it, as you can tell from the way we're lurching about. Would you like me to take you under my wing so that you won't fall over when we start rolling?'

'That's very kind of you,' said James, 'but I think I'll be all right.'

Just then, the Centipede stuck his grinning face through a hole in the ceiling and shouted, 'I've done it! We're off!'

'We're off!' the others cried. 'We're off!'

'The journey begins!' shouted the Centipede.

'And who knows where it will end,' muttered the Earthworm, 'if *you* have anything to do with it. It can only mean trouble.'

'Nonsense,' said the Ladybird. 'We are now about to visit the most marvellous places and see the most wonderful things! Isn't that so, Centipede?'

'There is no knowing what we shall see!' cried the Centipede.

'We may see a Creature with forty-nine heads
Who lives in the desolate snow,
And whenever he catches a cold (which he dreads)
He has forty-nine noses to blow.

'We may see the venomous Pink-Spotted Scrunch
Who can chew up a man with one bite.
It likes to eat five of them roasted for lunch
And eighteen for its supper at night.

'We may see a Dragon, and nobody knows
That we won't see a Unicorn there.
We may see a terrible Monster with toes
Growing out of the tufts of his hair.

'We may see the sweet little Biddy-Bright Hen
So playful, so kind and well-bred;
And such beautiful eggs! You just boil them and then
They explode and they blow off your head.

'A Gnu and a Gnocerous surely you'll see
And that gnormous and gnorrible Gnat
Whose sting when it stings you goes in at the knee
And comes out through the top of your hat.

'We may even get lost and be frozen by frost.
We may die in an earthquake or tremor.
Or nastier still, we may even be tossed
On the horns of a furious Dilemma.

'But who cares! Let us go from this horrible hill!
Let us roll! Let us bowl! Let us plunge!
Let's go rolling and bowling and spinning until
We're away from old Spiker and Sponge!'

One second later . . . slowly, insidiously, oh most gently, the great peach started to lean forward and steal into motion. The whole room began to tilt over and all the furniture went sliding across the floor, and crashed against the far wall. So did James and the Ladybird and the Old-Green-Grasshopper and Miss Spider and the Earthworm, and also the Centipede, who had just come slithering quickly down the wall.

Fifteen

Outside in the garden, at that very moment, Aunt Sponge and Aunt Spiker had just taken their places at the front gate, each with a bunch of tickets in her hand, and the first stream of early morning sightseers was visible in the distance climbing up the hill to view the peach.

'We shall make a fortune today,' Aunt Spiker was saying. 'Just look at all those people!'

'I wonder what became of that horrid little boy of ours last night,' Aunt Sponge said. 'He never did come back in, did he?'

'He probably fell down in the dark and broke his leg,' Aunt Spiker said.

'Or his neck, maybe,' Aunt Sponge said hopefully.

'Just *wait* till I get my hands on him,' Aunt Spiker said, waving her cane. 'He'll never want to stay out all night again by the time *I've* finished with him. Good gracious me! What's that awful noise?'

Both women swung round to look.

The noise, of course, had been caused by the giant peach crashing through the fence that surrounded it, and now, gathering speed every second, it came rolling across the garden towards the place where Aunt Sponge and Aunt Spiker were standing.

They gaped. They screamed. They started to run.

They panicked. They both got in each other's way. They began pushing and jostling, and each one of them was thinking only about saving herself. Aunt Sponge, the fat one, tripped over a box that she'd brought along to keep the money in, and fell flat on her face. Aunt Spiker immediately tripped over Aunt Sponge and came down on top of her. They both lay on the ground, fighting and clawing and yelling and struggling frantically to get up again, but before they could do this, the mighty peach was upon them.

There was a crunch.

And then there was silence.

The peach rolled on. And behind it, Aunt Sponge and Aunt Spiker lay ironed out upon the grass as flat and thin and lifeless as a couple of paper dolls cut out of a picture book.

Sixteen

And now the peach had broken out of the garden and was over the edge of the hill, rolling and bouncing down the steep slope at a terrific pace. Faster and faster and faster it went, and the crowds of people who were climbing up the hill suddenly caught sight of this terrible monster plunging down upon them and they screamed and scattered to right and left as it went hurtling by.

At the bottom of the hill it charged across the road,

knocking over a telegraph pole and flattening two parked cars as it went by.

Then it rushed madly across about twenty fields, breaking down all the fences and hedges in its path. It went right through the middle of a herd of fine Jersey cows, and then through a flock of sheep, and then through a paddock full of horses, and then through a yard full of pigs, and soon the whole countryside was a seething mass of panic-stricken animals stampeding in all directions.

The peach was still going at a tremendous speed with no sign of slowing down, and about a mile farther on it came to a village.

Down the main street of the village it rolled, with people leaping frantically out of its path right and left, and at the end of the street it went crashing right through the wall of an enormous building and out the other side, leaving two gaping round holes in the brickwork.

This building happened to be a famous factory where they made chocolate, and almost at once a great river of warm melted chocolate came pouring out of the holes in the factory wall. A minute later, this brown sticky mess was flowing through every street in the village, oozing under the doors of houses and into people's shops and gardens. Children were wading in it up to their knees, and some were even trying to swim in it and all of them were sucking it into their mouths in great greedy gulps and shrieking with joy.

But the peach rushed on across the countryside – on and on and on, leaving a trail of destruction in its wake. Cowsheds, stables, pigsties, barns, bungalows, hayricks, anything that got in its way went toppling over like a ninepin. An old man sitting quietly beside a stream had his fishing rod whisked out of his hands as it went dashing by, and a woman called Daisy Entwistle was standing so close to it as it passed that she had the skin taken off the tip of her long nose.

Would it ever stop?

Why should it? A round object will always keep on rolling as long as it is on a downhill slope, and in this case the land sloped downhill all the way until it reached the ocean – the same ocean that James had begged his aunts to be allowed to visit the day before.

Well, perhaps he was going to visit it now. The peach was rushing closer and closer to it every second, and closer also to the towering white cliffs that came first.

These cliffs are the most famous in the whole of England, and they are hundreds of feet high. Below them, the sea is deep and cold and hungry. Many ships have been swallowed up and lost for ever on this part of the coast, and all the men who were in them as well. The peach was now only a hundred yards away from the cliff – now fifty – now twenty – now ten – now five – and when it reached the edge of the cliff it seemed to leap up into the sky and hang there suspended for a few seconds, still turning over and over in the air.

Then it began to fall . . .

Down . . .

Down . . .
Down . . .
Down . . .
Down . . .

SMACK! It hit the water with a colossal splash and sank like a stone.

But a few seconds later, up it came again, and this time, up it stayed, floating serenely upon the surface of the water.

Seventeen

At this moment, the scene inside the peach itself was one of indescribable chaos. James Henry Trotter was lying bruised and battered on the floor of the room amongst a tangled mass of Centipede and Earthworm and Spider and Ladybird and Glow-worm and Old-Green-Grasshopper. In the whole history of the world, no travellers had ever had a more terrible journey than these unfortunate creatures. It had started out well, with much laughing and shouting, and for the first few seconds, as the peach had begun to roll slowly forward, nobody had minded being tumbled about a little bit. And when it went *BUMP!*, and the Centipede had shouted, '*That* was Aunt Sponge!' and then *BUMP!* again, and '*That* was Aunt Spiker!' there had been a tremendous burst of cheering all round.

But as soon as the peach rolled out of the garden

and began to go down the steep hill, rushing and plunging and bounding madly downward, then the whole thing became a nightmare. James found himself being flung up against the ceiling, then back on to the floor, then sideways against the wall, then up on to the ceiling again, and up and down and back and forth and round and round, and at the same time all the other creatures were flying through the air in every direction, and so were the chairs and the sofa, not to mention the forty-two boots belonging to the Centipede. Everything and all of them were being rattled around like peas inside an enormous rattle that was being rattled by a mad giant who refused to stop. To make it worse, something went wrong with the Glow-worm's lighting system, and the room was in pitchy darkness. There were screams and yells and curses and cries of pain, and everything kept going round and round, and once James made a frantic grab at some thick bars sticking out from the wall only to find that they were a couple of the Centipede's legs. 'Let go, you idiot!' shouted the Centipede, kicking himself free, and James was promptly flung across the room into the Old-Green-Grasshopper's horny lap. Twice he got tangled up in Miss Spider's legs (a horrid business), and towards the end, the poor Earthworm, who was cracking himself like a whip every time he flew through the air from one side of the room to the other, coiled himself around James's body in a panic and refused to unwind.

Oh, it was a frantic and terrible trip!

But it was all over now, and the room was suddenly

very still and quiet. Everybody was beginning slowly and painfully to disentangle himself from everybody else.

'Let's have some light!' shouted the Centipede.

'Yes!' they cried. 'Light! Give us some light!'

'I'm *trying*,' answered the poor Glow-worm. 'I'm doing my best. Please be patient.'

They all waited in silence.

Then a faint greenish light began to glimmer out of the Glow-worm's tail, and this gradually became stronger and stronger until it was anyway enough to see by.

'*Some great journey!*' the Centipede said, limping across the room.

'I shall *never* be the same again,' murmured the Earthworm.

'Nor I,' the Ladybird said. 'It's taken *years* off my life.'

'But my dear friends!' cried the Old-Green-Grasshopper, trying to be cheerful. 'We are *there*!'

'Where?' they asked. 'Where? Where is *there*?'

'I don't know,' the Old-Green-Grasshopper said. 'But I'll bet it's somewhere good.'

'We are probably at the bottom of a coal mine,' the Earthworm said gloomily. 'We certainly went down and down and down very suddenly at the last moment. I felt it in my stomach. I still feel it.'

'Perhaps we are in the middle of a beautiful country full of songs and music,' the Old-Green-Grasshopper said.

'Or near the seashore,' said James eagerly, 'with lots of other children down on the sand for me to play with!'

'Pardon me,' murmured the Ladybird, turning a trifle pale, 'but am I wrong in thinking that we seem to be bobbing up and down?'

'*Bobbing* up and down!' they cried. 'What on earth do you mean?'

'You're still giddy from the journey,' the Old-Green-Grasshopper told her. 'You'll get over it in a minute. Is everybody ready to go upstairs now and take a look round?'

'Yes, yes!' they chorused. 'Come on! Let's go!'

'I *refuse* to show myself out of doors in my bare feet,' the Centipede said. 'I *have* to get my boots on again first.'

'For heaven's sake, let's not go through all that nonsense again,' the Earthworm said.

'Let's *all* lend the Centipede a hand and get it over with,' the Ladybird said. 'Come on.'

So they did, all except Miss Spider, who set about weaving a long rope-ladder that would reach from the floor up to a hole in the ceiling. The Old-Green-Grasshopper had wisely said that they must not risk going out of the side entrance when they didn't know where they were, but must first of all go up on to the top of the peach and have a look round.

So half an hour later, when the rope-ladder had been finished and hung, and the forty-second boot had been laced neatly on to the Centipede's forty-second foot, they were all ready to go out. Amidst mounting excitement and shouts of 'Here we go, boys! The Promised Land! I can't wait to see it!' the whole company climbed up the ladder one by one and disappeared into a dark soggy tunnel in the ceiling that went steeply, almost vertically, upward.

Eighteen

A minute later, they were out in the open, standing on the very top of the peach, near the stem, blinking their eyes in the strong sunlight and peering nervously around.

'What happened?'

'Where are we?'

'But this is *impossible*!'

'Unbelievable!'

'Terrible!'

'I *told* you we were bobbing up and down,' the Ladybird said.

'We're in the middle of the sea!' cried James.

And indeed they were. A strong current and a high wind had carried the peach so quickly away from the shore that already the land was out of sight. All around them lay the vast black ocean, deep and hungry. Little waves were bibbling against the sides of the peach.

'But how did it happen?' they cried. 'Where are the fields? Where are the woods? Where is England?' Nobody, not even James, could understand how in the world a thing like this could have come about.

'Ladies and gentlemen,' the Old-Green-Grasshopper said, trying very hard to keep the fear and disappointment out of his voice, 'I am afraid that we find ourselves in a rather awkward situation.'

'Awkward!' cried the Earthworm. 'My dear Old Grasshopper, we are finished! Every one of us is about to perish! I may be blind, you know, but that much I can see quite clearly.'

'Off with my boots!' shouted the Centipede. 'I cannot swim with my boots on!'

'I can't swim at all!' cried the Ladybird.

'Nor can I,' wailed the Glow-worm.

'Nor I!' said Miss Spider. 'None of us three girls can swim a single stroke.'

'But you won't *have* to swim,' said James calmly. 'We are floating beautifully. And sooner or later a ship is bound to come along and pick us up.'

They all stared at him in amazement.

'Are you quite sure that we are not sinking?' the Ladybird asked.

'Of course I'm sure,' answered James. 'Go and look for yourselves.'

They all ran over to the side of the peach and peered down at the water below.

'The boy is quite right,' the Old-Green-Grasshopper said. 'We are floating beautifully. Now we must all sit down and keep perfectly calm. Everything will be all right in the end.'

'What absolute nonsense!' cried the Earthworm. 'Nothing is ever all right in the end, and well you know it!'

'Poor Earthworm,' the Ladybird said, whispering in James's ear. 'He loves to make everything into a disaster. He hates to be happy. He is only happy when he is gloomy. Now isn't that odd? But then, I suppose just *being* an Earthworm is enough to make a person pretty gloomy, don't you agree?'

'If this peach is not going to sink,' the Earthworm

was saying, 'and if we are not going to be drowned, then every one of us is going to *starve* to death instead. Do you realize that we haven't had a thing to eat since yesterday morning?'

'By golly, he's right!' cried the Centipede. 'For once, Earthworm is right!'

'Of course I'm right,' the Earthworm said. 'And we're not likely to find anything around here either. We shall get thinner and thinner and thirstier and thirstier, and we shall all die a slow and grisly death from starvation. I am dying already. I am slowly shrivelling up for want of food. Personally, I would rather drown.'

'But good heavens, you must be *blind*!' said James.

'You know very well I'm blind,' snapped the Earthworm. 'There's no need to rub it in.'

'I didn't mean that,' said James quickly. 'I'm sorry. But can't you *see* that –'

'See?' shouted the poor Earthworm. 'How can I see if I am blind?'

James took a deep, slow breath. 'Can't you *realize*,' he said patiently, 'that we have enough food here to last us for weeks and weeks?'

'Where?' they said. 'Where?'

'Why, the peach of course! Our whole ship is made of food!'

'Jumping Jehoshaphat!' they cried. 'We never thought of that!'

'My dear James,' said the Old-Green-Grasshopper, laying a front leg affectionately on James's shoulder, 'I don't know what we'd do without you. You are

so clever. Ladies and gentlemen – we are saved again!'

'We are most certainly not!' said the Earthworm. 'You must be crazy! You can't eat the ship! It's the only thing that is keeping us up!'

'We shall starve if we don't!' said the Centipede.

'And we shall drown if we do!' cried the Earthworm.

'Oh dear, oh dear,' said the Old-Green-Grasshopper. 'Now we're worse off than before!'

'Couldn't we just eat a *little* bit of it?' asked Miss Spider. 'I am so dreadfully hungry.'

'You can eat all you want,' James answered. 'It would take us weeks and weeks to make any sort of a dent in this enormous peach. Surely you can see that?'

'Good heavens, he's right again!' cried the Old-Green-Grasshopper, clapping his hands. 'It would take weeks and weeks! Of course it would! But let's not go making a lot of holes all over the deck. I think we'd better simply scoop it out of that tunnel over there – the one that we've just come up by.'

'An excellent idea,' said the Ladybird.

'What are you looking so worried about, Earthworm?' the Centipede asked. 'What's the problem?'

'The problem is . . .' the Earthworm said, 'the problem is . . . well, the problem is that there is no problem!'

Everyone burst out laughing. 'Cheer up, Earthworm!' they said. 'Come and eat!' And they all went over to the tunnel entrance and began scooping out great chunks of juicy, golden-coloured peach flesh.

'Oh, marvellous!' said the Centipede, stuffing it into his mouth.

'*Dee*-licious!' said the Old-Green-Grasshopper.

'Just fabulous!' said the Glow-worm.

'Oh my!' said the Ladybird primly. 'What a heavenly taste!' She looked up at James, and she smiled, and James smiled back at her. They sat down on the deck together, both of them chewing away happily. 'You know, James,' the Ladybird said, 'up until this moment, I have never in my life tasted anything except those tiny little green flies that live on rose-bushes. They have a perfectly delightful flavour. But this peach is even better.'

'Isn't it glorious!' Miss Spider said, coming over to join them. 'Personally, I had always thought that a big, juicy, caught-in-the-web bluebottle was the finest dinner in the world – until I tasted *this.*'

'*What* a flavour!' the Centipede cried. 'It's terrific! There's nothing like it! There never has been! And I should know because I personally have tasted all the finest foods in the world!' Whereupon, the Centipede, with his mouth full of peach and with juice running down all over his chin, suddenly burst into song:

'I've eaten many strange and scrumptious dishes in my
  time,
Like jellied gnats and dandyprats and earwigs cooked
  in slime,
And mice with rice – they're really nice
When roasted in their prime.
(But don't forget to sprinkle them with just a pinch of
grime.)

'I've eaten fresh mudburgers by the greatest cooks there are,
And scrambled dregs and stinkbugs' eggs and hornets stewed in tar,
And pails of snails and lizards' tails,
And beetles by the jar.
(A beetle is improved by just a splash of vinegar.)

'I often eat boiled slobbages. They're grand when served beside
Minced doodlebugs and curried slugs. And have you ever tried
Mosquitoes' toes and wampfish roes
Most delicately fried?
(The only trouble is they disagree with my inside.)

'I'm mad for crispy wasp-stings on a piece of buttered toast,
And pickled spines of porcupines. And then a gorgeous roast
Of dragon's flesh, well hung, not fresh –
It costs a pound at most.
(And comes to you in barrels if you order it by post.)

'I crave the tasty tentacles of octopi for tea
I like hot-dogs, I LOVE *hot-frogs, and surely you'll agree*
A plate of soil with engine oil's
A super recipe.
(I hardly need to mention that it's practically free.)

'For dinner on my birthday shall I tell you what
I chose:
Hot noodles made from poodles on a slice of
garden hose –
And a rather smelly jelly
Made of armadillo's toes.
(The jelly is delicious, but you have to hold your nose.)

'Now comes,' the Centipede declared, 'the burden of
my speech:
These foods are rare beyond compare – some are
right out of reach;
But there's no doubt I'd go without
A million plates of each
For one small mite,
One tiny bite,
Of this FANTASTIC PEACH*!'*

Everybody was feeling happy now. The sun was shining brightly out of a soft blue sky and the day was calm. The giant peach, with the sunlight glinting on its side, was like a massive golden ball sailing upon a silver sea.

Nineteen

'Look!' cried the Centipede just as they were finishing their meal. 'Look at that funny thin black thing gliding through the water over there!'

They all swung round to look.

'There are two of them,' said Miss Spider.

'There are *lots* of them!' said the Ladybird.

'What are they?' asked the Earthworm, getting worried.

'They must be some kind of fish,' said the Old-Green-Grasshopper. 'Perhaps they have come along to say hello.'

'They are sharks!' cried the Earthworm. 'I'll bet you anything you like that they are sharks and they have come along to eat us up!'

'What absolute rot!' the Centipede said, but his voice seemed suddenly to have become a little shaky, and he wasn't laughing.

'I am *positive* they are sharks!' said the Earthworm. 'I just *know* they are sharks!'

And so, in actual fact, did everybody else, but they were too frightened to admit it.

There was a short silence. They all peered down anxiously at the sharks who were cruising slowly round and round the peach.

'Just assuming that they *are* sharks,' the Centipede said, 'there still can't possibly be any danger if we stay up here.'

But even as he spoke, one of those thin black fins suddenly changed direction and came cutting swiftly through the water right up to the side of the peach itself. The shark paused and stared up at the company with small evil eyes.

'Go away!' they shouted. 'Go away, you filthy beast!'

Slowly, almost lazily, the shark opened his mouth

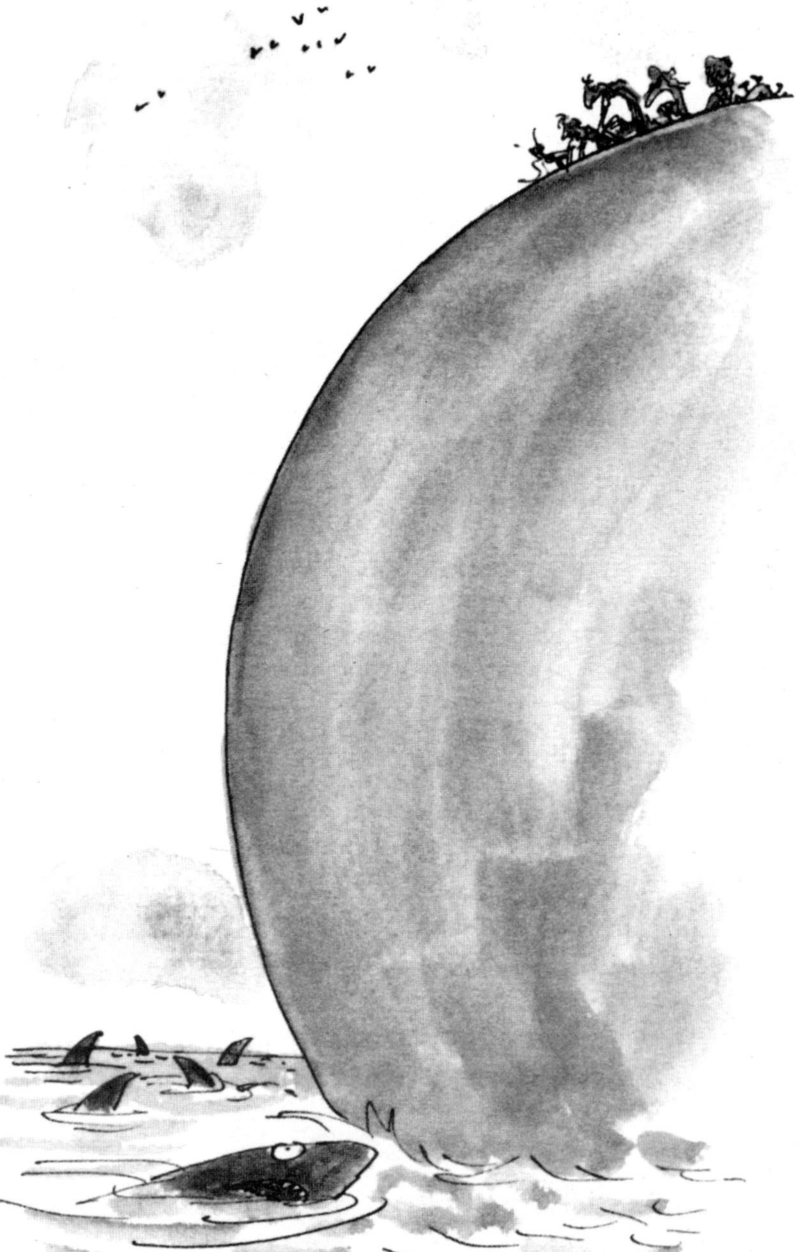

(which was big enough to have swallowed a perambulator) and made a lunge at the peach.

They all watched, aghast.

And now, as though at a signal from the leader, all the other sharks came swimming in towards the peach, and they clustered around it and began to attack it furiously. There must have been twenty or thirty of them at least, all pushing and fighting and lashing their tails and churning the water into a froth.

Panic and pandemonium broke out immediately on top of the peach.

'Oh, we are finished now!' cried Miss Spider, wringing her feet. 'They will eat up the whole peach and then there'll be nothing left for us to stand on and they'll start on us!'

'She is right!' shouted the Ladybird. 'We are lost for ever!'

'Oh, I don't want to be eaten!' wailed the Earthworm. 'But they will take me first of all because I am so fat and juicy and I have no bones!'

'Is there *nothing* we can do?' asked the Ladybird, appealing to James. 'Surely *you* can think of a way out of this.'

Suddenly they were all looking at James.

'Think!' begged Miss Spider. '*Think*, James, *think*!'

'Come on,' said the Centipede. 'Come on, James. There *must* be *something* we can do.'

Their eyes waited upon him, tense, anxious, pathetically hopeful.

Twenty

'There is *something* that I believe we might try,' James Henry Trotter said slowly. 'I'm not saying it'll work . . .'

'Tell us!' cried the Earthworm. 'Tell us quick!'

'We'll try anything you say!' said the Centipede. 'But hurry, hurry, hurry!'

'Be quiet and let the boy speak!' said the Ladybird. 'Go on, James.'

They all moved a little closer to him. There was a longish pause.

'Go *on*!' they cried frantically. '*Go on!*'

And all the time while they were waiting they could hear the sharks threshing around in the water below them. It was enough to make anyone frantic.

'Come on, James,' the Ladybird said, coaxing him.

'I . . . I . . . I'm afraid it's no good after all,' James murmured, shaking his head. 'I'm terribly sorry. I forgot. We don't have any string. We'd need hundreds of yards of string to make this work.'

'What sort of string?' asked the Old-Green-Grasshopper sharply.

'Any sort, just so long as it's strong.'

'But my dear boy, that's exactly what we do have! We've got all you want!'

'How? Where?'

'The Silkworm!' cried the Old-Green-Grasshopper. 'Didn't you ever notice the Silkworm? She's still downstairs! She never moves! She just lies there sleeping all day long, but we can easily wake her up and make her spin!'

'And what about me, may I ask?' said Miss Spider. 'I can spin just as well as any Silkworm. What's more, *I* can spin patterns.'

'Can you make enough between you?' asked James.

'As much as you want.'

'And quickly?'

'Of course! Of course!'

'And would it be strong?'

'The strongest there is! It's as thick as your finger! But why? What are you going to do?'

'I'm going to lift this peach clear out of the water!' James announced firmly.

'You're mad!' cried the Earthworm.

'It's our only chance.'

'The boy's crazy.'

'He's joking.'

'Go on, James,' the Ladybird said gently. 'How are you going to do it?'

'Skyhooks, I suppose,' jeered the Centipede.

'Seagulls,' James answered calmly. 'The place is full of them. Look up there!'

They all looked up and saw a great mass of seagulls wheeling round and round in the sky.

'I'm going to take a long silk string,' James went on, 'and I'm going to loop one end of it round a seagull's neck. And then I'm going to tie the other end to the stem of the peach.' He pointed to the peach stem, which was standing up like a short thick mast in the middle of the deck.

'Then I'm going to get another seagull and do the same thing again, then another and another –'

'Ridiculous!' they shouted.

'Absurd!'

'Poppycock!'

'Balderdash!'

'Madness!'

And the Old-Green-Grasshopper said, 'How can a few seagulls lift an enormous thing like this up into the air, and all of us as well? It would take hundreds . . . thousands . . .'

'There is no shortage of seagulls,' James answered. 'Look for yourself. We'll probably need four hundred, five hundred, six hundred . . . maybe even a thousand . . . I don't know . . . I shall simply go on hooking them up to the stem until we have enough to lift us. They'll be bound to lift us in the end. It's like balloons. You give someone enough balloons to hold, I mean *really* enough, then up he goes. And a seagull has far more lifting power than a balloon. If only we have the *time* to do it. If only we are not sunk first by those awful sharks . . .'

'You're absolutely off your head!' said the Earthworm.

'How on earth do you propose to get a loop of string round a seagull's neck? I suppose you're going to fly up there yourself and catch it!'

'The boy's dotty!' said the Centipede.

'Let him finish,' said the Ladybird. 'Go on, James. How *would* you do it?'

'With bait.'

'Bait! What sort of bait?'

'With a worm, of course. Seagulls love worms, didn't you know that? And luckily for us, we have here the biggest, fattest, pinkest, juiciest Earthworm in the world.'

'You can stop right there!' the Earthworm said sharply. 'That's quite enough!'

'Go on,' the others said, beginning to grow interested. 'Go on!'

'The seagulls have already spotted him,' James continued. 'That's why there are so many of them circling round. But they daren't come down to get him while all the rest of us are standing here. So this is what –'

'Stop!' cried the Earthworm. 'Stop, stop, stop! I won't have it! I refuse! I – I – I – I –'

'Be quiet!' said the Centipede. 'Mind your own business!'

'I *like* that!'

'My dear Earthworm, you're going to be eaten anyway, so what difference does it make whether it's sharks or seagulls?'

'I won't do it!'

'Why don't we hear what the plan is first?' said the Old-Green-Grasshopper.

'I don't give a hoot what the plan is!' cried the Earthworm. 'I am not going to be pecked to death by a bunch of seagulls!'

'You will be a martyr,' said the Centipede. 'I shall respect you for the rest of my life.'

'So will I,' said Miss Spider. 'And your name will

be in all the newspapers. Earthworm gives life to save friends . . .'

'But he won't *have* to give his life,' James told them. 'Now listen to me. This is what we'll do . . .'

Twenty-one

'Why, it's absolutely brilliant!' cried the Old-Green-Grasshopper when James had explained his plan.

'The boy's a genius!' the Centipede announced. 'Now I can keep my boots on after all.'

'Oh, I shall be pecked to death!' wailed the poor Earthworm.

'Of course you won't.'

'I will, I know I will! And I won't even be able to see them coming at me because I have no eyes!'

James went over and put an arm gently round the Earthworm's shoulders. 'I won't let them *touch* you,' he said. 'I promise I won't. But we've *got* to hurry! Look down there!'

There were more sharks than ever now around the peach. The water was boiling with them. There must have been ninety or a hundred at least. And to the travellers up on top, it certainly seemed as though the peach were sinking lower and lower into the water.

'Action stations!' James shouted. 'Jump to it! There's not a moment to lose!' He was the captain now, and

everyone knew it. They would do whatever he told them.

'All hands below deck except Earthworm!' he ordered.

'Yes, yes!' they said eagerly as they scuttled into the tunnel entrance. 'Come on! Let's hurry!'

'And you – Centipede!' James shouted. 'Hop

downstairs and get that Silkworm to work at once! Tell her to spin as she's never spun before! Our lives depend upon it! And the same applies to you, Miss Spider! Hurry on down! Start spinning.'

Twenty-two

In a few minutes everything was ready.

It was very quiet now on the top of the peach. There was nobody in sight – nobody except the Earthworm.

One half of the Earthworm, looking like a great, thick, juicy, pink sausage, lay innocently in the sun for all the seagulls to see.

The other half of him was dangling down the tunnel.

James was crouching close beside the Earthworm in the tunnel entrance, just below the surface, waiting for the first seagull. He had a loop of silk string in his hands.

The Old-Green-Grasshopper and the Ladybird were further down the tunnel, holding on to the Earthworm's tail, ready to pull him quickly in out of danger as soon as James gave the word.

And far below, in the great stone of the peach, the Glow-worm was lighting up the room so that the two spinners, the Silkworm and Miss Spider, could see what they were doing. The Centipede was down there too, exhorting them both frantically to greater efforts, and every now and again James could hear his voice coming up faintly from the depths, shouting, 'Spin, Silkworm, spin, you great fat lazy brute! Faster, faster, or we'll throw you to the sharks!'

'Here comes the first seagull!' whispered James. 'Keep still now, Earthworm. Keep still. The rest of you get ready to pull.'

'Please don't let it spike me,' begged the Earthworm.

'I won't, I won't. Ssshh . . .'

Out of the corner of one eye, James watched the seagull as it came swooping down towards the Earthworm. And then suddenly it was so close that he could see its small black eyes and its curved beak, and the beak was open, ready to grab a nice piece of flesh out of the Earthworm's back.

'Pull!' shouted James.

The Old-Green-Grasshopper and the Ladybird gave the Earthworm's tail an enormous tug, and like magic the Earthworm disappeared into the tunnel. At the same time, up went James's hand and the seagull flew right into the loop of silk that he was holding out. The loop, which had been cleverly made, tightened just the right amount (but not too much) around its neck, and the seagull was captured.

'Hooray!' shouted the Old-Green-Grasshopper, peering out of the tunnel. 'Well done, James!'

Up flew the seagull with James paying out the silk string as it went. He gave it about fifty yards and then tied the string to the stem of the peach.

'Next one!' he shouted, jumping back into the tunnel. 'Up you get again, Earthworm! Bring up some more silk, Centipede!'

'Oh, I don't like this at all,' wailed the Earthworm. 'It only just missed me! I even felt the wind on my back as it went swishing past!'

'Ssshh!' whispered James. 'Keep still! Here comes another one!'

So they did it again.

And again, and again, and again.

And the seagulls kept coming, and James caught them one after the other and tethered them to the peach stem.

'One hundred seagulls!' he shouted, wiping the sweat from his face.

'Keep going!' they cried. 'Keep going, James!'

'Two hundred seagulls!'

'Three hundred seagulls!'

'Four hundred seagulls!'

The sharks, as though sensing that they were in danger of losing their prey, were hurling themselves at the peach more furiously than ever, and the peach was sinking lower and lower still in the water.

'Five hundred seagulls!' James shouted.

'Silkworm says she's running out of silk!' yelled the Centipede from below. 'She says she can't keep it up much longer. Nor can Miss Spider!'

'Tell them they've *got* to!' James answered. 'They can't stop now!'

'We're lifting!' somebody shouted.

'No, we're not!'

'I felt it!'

'Put on another seagull, quick!'

'Quiet, everybody! Quiet! Here's one coming now!'

This was the five hundred and first seagull, and the moment that James caught it and tethered it to the stem with all the others, the whole enormous peach suddenly started rising up slowly out of the water.

'Look out! Here we go! Hold on, boys!'

But then it stopped.

And there it hung.

It hovered and swayed, but it went no higher.

The bottom of it was just touching the water. It was like a delicately balanced scale that needed only the tiniest push to tip it one way or the other.

'One more will do it!' shouted the Old-Green-Grasshopper, looking out of the tunnel. 'We're almost there!'

And now came the big moment. Quickly, the five hundred and second seagull was caught and harnessed to the peach-stem . . .

And then suddenly . . .

But slowly . . .

Majestically . . .

Like some fabulous golden balloon . . .

With all the seagulls straining at the strings above . . .

The giant peach rose up dripping out of the water and began climbing towards the heavens.

Twenty-three

In a flash, everybody was up on top.

'Oh, isn't it beautiful!' they cried.

'What a marvellous feeling!'

'Goodbye, sharks!'

'Oh, boy, this is the way to travel!'

Miss Spider, who was literally squealing with excitement, grabbed the Centipede by the waist and the two of them started dancing round and round the peach stem together. The Earthworm stood up on his tail and did a sort of wriggle of joy all by himself. The Old-Green-Grasshopper kept hopping higher and higher in the air. The Ladybird rushed over and shook James warmly by the hand. The Glow-worm, who at the best of times was a very shy and silent creature, sat glowing with pleasure near the tunnel entrance. Even the Silkworm, looking white and thin and completely exhausted, came creeping out of the tunnel to watch this miraculous ascent.

Up and up they went, and soon they were as high as the top of a church steeple above the ocean.

'I'm a bit worried about the peach,' James said to the others as soon as all the dancing and the shouting had stopped. 'I wonder how much damage those sharks have done to it underneath. It's quite impossible to tell from up here.'

'Why don't I go over the side and make an inspection?' Miss Spider said. 'It'll be no trouble at all, I

assure you.' And without waiting for an answer, she quickly produced a length of silk thread and attached the end of it to the peach stem. 'I'll be back in a jiffy,' she said, and then she walked calmly over to the edge of the peach and jumped off, paying out the thread behind her as she fell.

The others crowded anxiously around the place where she had gone over.

'Wouldn't it be dreadful if the thread broke,' the Ladybird said.

There was a rather long silence.

'Are you all right, Miss Spider?' shouted the Old-Green-Grasshopper.

'Yes, thank you!' her voice answered from below. 'I'm coming up now!' And up she came, climbing foot over foot up the silk thread, and at the same time tucking the thread back cleverly into her body as she climbed past it.

'Is it *awful*?' they asked her. 'Is it all eaten away? Are there great holes in it everywhere?'

Miss Spider clambered back on to the deck with a pleased but also a rather puzzled look on her face. 'You won't believe this,' she said, 'but actually there's hardly any damage down there at all! The peach is almost untouched! There are just a few tiny pieces out of it here and there, but nothing more.'

'You must be mistaken,' James told her.

'Of course she's mistaken!' the Centipede said.

'I promise you I'm not,' Miss Spider answered.

'But there were hundreds of sharks around us!'

'They churned the water into a froth!'

'We saw their great mouths opening and shutting!'

'I don't care what you saw,' Miss Spider answered. 'They certainly didn't do much damage to the peach.'

'Then why did we start sinking?' the Centipede asked.

'Perhaps we *didn't* start sinking,' the Old-Green-Grasshopper suggested. 'Perhaps we were all so frightened that we simply imagined it.'

This, in point of fact, was closer to the truth than any of them knew. A shark, you see, has an extremely long sharp nose, and its mouth is set very awkwardly underneath its face and a long way back. This makes it more or less impossible for it to get its teeth into a vast smooth curving surface such as the side of a peach. Even if the creature turns on to its back it still can't do it, because the nose always gets in the way. If you have ever seen a small dog trying to get its teeth into an enormous ball, then you will be able to imagine roughly how it was with the sharks and the peach.

'It must have been some kind of magic,' the Ladybird said. 'The holes must have healed up by themselves.'

'Oh, look! There's a ship below us!' shouted James.

Everybody rushed to the side and peered over. None of them had ever seen a ship before.

'It looks like a big one.'

'It's got three funnels.'

'You can even see the people on the decks!'

'Let's wave to them. Do you think they can see *us*?'

Neither James nor any of the others knew it, but the ship that was now passing beneath them was actually the *Queen Mary* sailing out of the English Channel on her way to America. And on the bridge of the *Queen Mary*, the astonished Captain was standing with a group of his officers, all of them gaping at the great round ball hovering overhead.

'I don't like it,' the Captain said.

'Nor do I,' said the First Officer.

'Do you think it's following us?' said the Second Officer.

'I tell you I don't like it,' muttered the Captain.

'It could be dangerous,' the First Officer said.

'That's it!' cried the Captain. 'It's a secret weapon! Holy cats! Send a message to the Queen at once! The country must be warned! And give me my telescope.'

The First Officer handed the telescope to the Captain. The Captain put it to his eye.

'There's birds everywhere!' he cried. 'The whole sky is teeming with birds! What in the world are *they* doing? And wait! Wait a second! There are *people* on it! I can see them moving! There's a – a – do I have this darned thing focused right? It looks like a little boy in short trousers! Yes, I can distinctly see a little boy in short trousers standing up there! And there's a – there's a – there's a – a – a – a sort of *giant ladybird*!'

'Now just a minute, Captain!' the First Officer said.

'And a *colossal green grasshopper*!'

'Captain!' the First Officer said sharply. 'Captain, please!'

'And a *mammoth spider*!'

'Oh dear, he's been at the whisky again,' whispered the Second Officer.

'And an *enormous – a simply enormous centipede*!' screamed the Captain.

'Call the Ship's Doctor,' the First Officer said. 'Our Captain is not well.'

A moment later, the great round ball disappeared into a cloud, and the people on the ship never saw it again.

Twenty-four

But up on the peach itself, everyone was still happy and excited.

'I wonder where we'll finish up this time,' the Earthworm said.

'Who cares?' they answered. 'Seagulls always go back to the land sooner or later.'

Up and up they went, high above the highest clouds, the peach swaying gently from side to side as it floated along.

'Wouldn't this be a perfect time for a little music?' the Ladybird asked. 'How about it, Old Grasshopper?'

'With pleasure, dear lady,' the Old-Green-Grasshopper answered, bowing from the waist.

'Oh, hooray! He's going to play for us!' they cried, and immediately the whole company sat themselves down in a circle around the Old Green Musician – and the concert began.

From the moment that the first note was struck, the audience became completely spellbound. And as for James, never had he heard such beautiful music as this! In the garden at home on summer evenings, he had listened many times to the sound of grasshoppers chirping in the grass, and he had always liked the noise that they made. But this was a different kind of noise altogether. This was real music – chords, harmonies, tunes, and all the rest of it.

And what a wonderful instrument the Old-Green-Grasshopper was playing upon. It was like a violin! It was almost exactly as though he were playing upon a violin!

The bow of the violin, the part that moved, was his back leg. The strings of the violin, the part that made the sound, was the edge of his wing.

He was using only the top of his back leg (the thigh), and he was stroking this up and down against the edge of his wing with incredible skill, sometimes slowly, sometimes fast, but always with the same easy flowing action. It was precisely the way a clever violinist would have used his bow; and the music came pouring out and filled the whole blue sky around them with magic melodies.

When the first part was finished, everyone clapped madly, and Miss Spider stood up and shouted, 'Bravo! Encore! Give us some more!'

'Did you like that, James?' the Old-Green-Grasshopper asked, smiling at the small boy.

'Oh, I loved it!' James answered. 'It was beautiful! It was as though you had a real violin in your hands!'

'A *real* violin!' the Old-Green-Grasshopper cried. 'Good heavens, I like that! My dear boy, I *am* a real violin! It is a part of my own body!'

'But do *all* grasshoppers play their music on violins, the same way as you do?' James asked him.

'No,' he answered, 'not all. If you want to know, I happen to be a "short-horned" grasshopper. I have two short feelers coming out of my head. Can you see them? There they are. They are quite short, aren't they? That's why they call me a "short-horn". And we "short-horns" are the only ones who play our music in the violin style, using a bow. My "long-horned" relatives, the ones who have long curvy feelers coming out of their heads, make their music simply by rubbing the edges of their two top wings together. They are not violinists, they are wing-rubbers. And a rather inferior noise these wing-rubbers produce, too, if I may say so. It sounds more like a banjo than a fiddle.'

'How fascinating this all is!' cried James. 'And to think that up until now I had never even *wondered* how a grasshopper made his sounds.'

'My dear young fellow,' the Old-Green-Grasshopper said gently, 'there are a whole lot of things in this world of ours that you haven't started wondering about yet. Where, for example, do you think that I keep my ears?'

'Your ears? Why, in your head, of course.'

Everyone burst out laughing.

'You mean you don't even know *that*?' cried the Centipede.

'Try again,' said the Old-Green-Grasshopper, smiling at James.

'You can't possibly keep them anywhere else?'

'Oh, can't I?'

'Well – I give up. Where *do* you keep them?'

'Right here,' the Old-Green-Grasshopper said. 'One on each side of my tummy.'

'It's not true!'

'Of course it's true. What's so peculiar about that? You ought to see where my cousins the crickets and the katydids keep theirs.'

'Where do they keep them?'

'In their legs. One in each front leg, just below the knee.'

'You mean you didn't know that either?' the Centipede said scornfully.

'You're joking,' James said. 'Nobody could possibly have his ears in his legs.'

'Why not?'

'Because . . . because it's ridiculous, that's why.'

'You know what I think is ridiculous?' the Centipede said, grinning away as usual. 'I don't mean to be rude, but *I* think it is ridiculous to have ears on the sides of one's head. It certainly *looks* ridiculous. You ought to take a peek in the mirror some day and see for yourself.'

'Pest!' cried the Earthworm. 'Why must you always be so rude and rambunctious to everyone? You ought to apologize to James at once.'

Twenty-five

James didn't want the Earthworm and the Centipede to get into another argument, so he said quickly to the Earthworm, 'Tell me, do *you* play any kind of music?'

'No, but I do *other* things, some of which are really quite *extraordinary*,' the Earthworm said, brightening.

'Such as what?' asked James.

'Well,' the Earthworm said. 'Next time you stand in a field or in a garden and look around you, then just remember this: that every grain of soil upon the surface of the land, every tiny little bit of soil that you can see has actually passed through the body of an Earthworm during the last few years! Isn't that wonderful?'

'It's not possible!' said James.

'My dear boy, it's a fact.'

'You mean you actually *swallow* soil?'

'Like mad,' the Earthworm said proudly. '*In* one end and *out* the other.'

'But what's the point?'

'What do you mean, what's the point?'

'Why do you do it?'

'We do it for the farmers. It makes the soil nice and light and crumbly so that things will grow well in it. If you really want to know, the farmers couldn't do without us. We are essential. We are vital. So it is only natural that the farmer should love us. He loves us even more, I believe, than he loves the Ladybird.'

'The Ladybird!' said James, turning to look at her. 'Do they love you, too?'

'I am told that they do,' the Ladybird answered modestly, blushing all over. 'In fact, I understand that in some places the farmers love us so much that they go out and buy live Ladybirds by the sackful and take them home and set them free in their fields. They are very pleased when they have lots of Ladybirds in their fields.'

'But why?' James asked.

'Because we gobble up all the nasty little insects that

are gobbling up all the farmer's crops. It helps enormously, and we ourselves don't charge a penny for our services.'

'I think you're wonderful,' James told her. 'Can I ask you one special question?'

'Please do.'

'Well, is it really true that I can tell how old a Ladybird is by counting her spots?'

'Oh no, that's just a children's story,' the Ladybird said. 'We never change our spots. Some of us, of course, are born with more spots than others, but we never change them. The number of spots that a Ladybird has is simply a way of showing which branch of the family she belongs to. I, for example, as you can see for yourself, am a Nine-Spotted Ladybird. I am very lucky. It is a fine thing to be.'

'It is, indeed,' said James, gazing at the beautiful scarlet shell with the nine black spots on it.

'On the other hand,' the Ladybird went on, 'some of my less fortunate relatives have no more than two spots altogether on their shells! Can you imagine that? They are called Two-Spotted Ladybirds, and very common and ill-mannered they are, I regret to say. And then, of course, you have the Five-Spotted Ladybirds as well. They are much nicer than the Two-Spotted ones, although I myself find them a trifle too saucy for my taste.'

'But they are all of them loved?' said James.

'Yes,' the Ladybird answered quietly. 'They are all of them loved.'

'It seems that almost *everyone* around here is loved!' said James. 'How nice this is!'

'Not me!' cried the Centipede happily. 'I am a pest and I'm proud of it! Oh, I am such a shocking dreadful pest!'

'Hear, hear,' the Earthworm said.

'But what about you, Miss Spider?' asked James. 'Aren't you also much loved in the world?'

'Alas, no,' Miss Spider answered, sighing long and loud. 'I am not loved at all. And yet I do nothing but good. All day long I catch flies and mosquitoes in my webs. I am a decent person.'

'I know you are,' said James.

'It is very unfair the way we Spiders are treated,' Miss Spider went on. 'Why, only last week your own horrible Aunt Sponge flushed my poor dear father down the plug-hole in the bathtub.'

'Oh, how awful!' cried James.

'I watched the whole thing from a corner up in the ceiling,' Miss Spider murmured. 'It was ghastly. We never saw him again.' A large tear rolled down her cheek and fell with a splash on the floor.

'But is it not very unlucky to kill a spider?' James inquired, looking around at the others.

'Of course it's unlucky to kill a spider!' shouted the Centipede. 'It's about the unluckiest thing anyone can do. Look what happened to Aunt Sponge after she'd done that! *Bump!* We all felt it, didn't we, as the peach went over her? Oh, what a lovely bump that must have been for you, Miss Spider!'

'It was very satisfactory,' Miss Spider answered. 'Will you sing us a song about it, please?'

So the Centipede did.

'Aunt Sponge was terrifically fat,
And tremendously flabby at that.
Her tummy and waist

Were as soggy as paste –
It was worse on the place where she sat!
So she said, "I must make myself flat.
I must make myself sleek as a cat.
I shall do without dinner
To make myself thinner."
But along came the peach!
Oh, the beautiful peach!
And made her far thinner than that!'

'That was very nice,' Miss Spider said. 'Now sing one about Aunt Spiker.'

'With pleasure,' the Centipede answered, grinning:

'Aunt Spiker was thin as a wire,
And dry as a bone, only drier.
She was so long and thin
If you carried her in
You could use her for poking the fire!

"I must do something quickly," she frowned.
"I want FAT. *I want pound upon pound!*
I must eat lots and lots
Of marshmallows and chocs
Till I start bulging out all around."

"Ah, yes," she announced, "I have sworn
That I'll alter my figure by dawn!"
Cried the peach with a snigger,
"I'LL *alter your figure –"*
And ironed her out on the lawn!'

Everybody clapped and called out for more songs from the Centipede, who at once launched into his favourite song of all:

'Once upon a time
When pigs were swine
And monkeys chewed tobacco
And hens took snuff
To make themselves tough
And the ducks said quack-quack-quacko,
And porcupines
Drank fiery wines
And goats ate tapioca
And Old Mother Hubbard
Got stuck in the c–'

'Look out, Centipede!' cried James. 'Look out!'

Twenty-six

The Centipede, who had begun dancing wildly round the deck during this song, had suddenly gone too close to the downward curving edge of the peach, and for three awful seconds he had stood teetering on the brink, swinging his legs frantically in circles in an effort to stop himself from falling over backward into space. But before anyone could reach him – down he went! He gave a shriek of terror as he fell, and the others, rushing to the side and peering over, saw his poor long body tumbling over and over through the air, getting smaller and smaller until it was out of sight.

'Silkworm!' yelled James. 'Quick! Start spinning!'

The Silkworm sighed, for she was still very tired from spinning all that silk for the seagulls, but she did as she was told.

'I'm going down after him!' cried James, grabbing the silk string as it started coming out of the Silkworm and tying the end of it around his waist. 'The rest of you hold on to Silkworm so I don't pull her over with me, and later on, if you feel three tugs on the string, start hauling me up again!'

He jumped, and he went tumbling down after the Centipede, down, down, down towards the sea below, and you can imagine how quickly the Silkworm had to spin to keep up with the speed of his fall.

'We'll never see either of them again!' cried the Ladybird. 'Oh dear! Oh dear! Just when we were all so happy, too!'

Miss Spider, the Glow-worm, and the Ladybird all began to cry. So did the Earthworm. 'I don't care a bit about the Centipede,' the Earthworm sobbed. 'But I really did love that little boy.'

Very softly, the Old-Green-Grasshopper started to play the Funeral March on his violin, and by the time he had finished, everyone, including himself, was in a flood of tears.

Suddenly, there came three sharp tugs on the rope.

'Pull!' shouted the Old-Green-Grasshopper. 'Everyone get behind me and pull!'

There was about a mile of string to be hauled in, but they all worked like mad, and in the end, over the side of the peach, there appeared a dripping-wet James with a dripping-wet Centipede clinging to him tightly with all forty-two of his legs.

'He saved me!' gasped the Centipede. 'He swam around in the middle of the Atlantic Ocean until he found me!'

'My dear boy,' the Old-Green-Grasshopper said, patting James on the back. 'I do congratulate you.'

'My boots!' cried the Centipede. 'Just look at my precious boots! They are ruined by the water!'

'Be quiet!' the Earthworm said. 'You are lucky to be alive.'

'Are we still going up and up?' asked James.

'We certainly are,' answered the Old-Green-Grasshopper. 'And it's beginning to get dark.'

'I know. It'll soon be night.'

'Why don't we all go down below and keep warm until tomorrow morning?' Miss Spider suggested.

'No,' the Old-Green-Grasshopper said. 'I think that would be very unwise. It will be safer if we all stay up here through the night and keep watch. Then, if anything happens, we shall anyway be ready for it.'

Twenty-seven

James Henry Trotter and his companions crouched close together on top of the peach as the night began closing in around them. Clouds like mountains towered high above their heads on all sides, mysterious, menacing, overwhelming. Gradually it grew darker and darker, and then a pale three-quarter moon came up over the tops of the clouds and cast an eerie light over the whole scene. The giant peach swayed gently from side to side as it floated along, and the hundreds of silky white strings going upward from its stem were beautiful in the moonlight. So also was the great flock of seagulls overhead.

There was not a sound anywhere. Travelling upon the peach was not in the least like travelling in an aeroplane. The aeroplane comes clattering and roaring through the sky, and whatever might be lurking secretly up there in the great cloud-mountains goes running for cover at its approach. That is why people who travel in aeroplanes never see anything.

But the peach . . . ah, yes . . . the peach was a soft, stealthy traveller, making no noise at all as it floated along. And several times during that long silent night ride high up over the middle of the ocean in the

moonlight, James and his friends saw things that no one had ever seen before.

Once, as they drifted silently past a massive white cloud, they saw on the top of it a group of strange, tall, wispy-looking things that were about twice the height of ordinary men. They were not easy to see at first because they were almost as white as the cloud itself, but as the peach sailed closer, it became obvious that these 'things' were actually living creatures – tall, wispy, wraithlike, shadowy, white creatures who looked as though they were made out of a mixture of cotton-wool and candyfloss and thin white hairs.

'Ooooooooooooh!' the Ladybird said. 'I don't like this at all!'

'Ssshh!' James whispered back. 'Don't let them hear you! They must be Cloud-Men!'

'*Cloud-Men!*' they murmured, huddling closer together for comfort. 'Oh dear, oh dear!'

'I'm glad I'm blind and can't see them,' the Earthworm said, 'or I would probably scream.'

'I hope they don't turn round and see *us*,' Miss Spider stammered.

'Do you think they would eat us?' the Earthworm asked.

'They would eat *you*,' the Centipede answered, grinning. 'They would cut you up like a salami and eat you in thin slices.'

The poor Earthworm began to quiver all over with fright.

'But what are they *doing*?' the Old-Green-Grasshopper whispered.

'I don't know,' James answered softly. 'Let's watch and see.'

The Cloud-Men were all standing in a group, and they were doing something peculiar with their hands. First, they would reach out (all of them at once) and grab handfuls of cloud. Then they would roll these handfuls of cloud in their fingers until they turned into what looked like large white marbles. Then they would toss the marbles to one side and quickly grab more bits of cloud and start over again.

It was all very silent and mysterious. The pile of marbles beside them kept growing larger and larger. Soon there was a truckload of them there at least.

'They must be absolutely mad!' the Centipede said. 'There's nothing to be afraid of here!'

'Be quiet, you pest!' the Earthworm whispered. 'We shall *all* be eaten if they see us!'

But the Cloud-Men were much too busy with what they were doing to have noticed the great peach floating silently up behind them.

Then the watchers on the peach saw one of the Cloud-Men raising his long wispy arms above his head and they heard him shouting, 'All right, boys! That's enough! Get the shovels!' And all the other

Cloud-Men immediately let out a strange high-pitched whoop of joy and started jumping up and down and waving their arms in the air. Then they picked up enormous shovels and rushed over to the pile of marbles and began shovelling them as fast as they could over the side of the cloud, into space. '*Down they go!*' they chanted as they worked.

'Down they go!
Hail and snow!
Freezes and sneezes and noses will blow!'

'It's *hailstones*!' whispered James excitedly. 'They've been making hailstones and now they are showering them down on to the people in the world below!'

'Hailstones?' the Centipede said. 'That's ridiculous! This is summertime. You don't have hailstones in summertime.'

'They are practising for the winter,' James told him.

'I don't believe it!' shouted the Centipede, raising his voice.

'Ssshh!' the others whispered. And James said softly, 'For heaven's sake, Centipede, don't make so much noise.'

The Centipede roared with laughter. 'Those imbeciles couldn't hear anything!' he cried. 'They're deaf as doorknobs! You watch!' And before anyone could stop him, he had cupped his front feet to his mouth and was yelling at the Cloud-Men as loud as he could. 'Idiots!' he yelled. 'Nincompoops! Half-wits!

Blunderheads! Asses! What on earth do you think you're doing over there!'

The effect was immediate. The Cloud-Men jumped round as if they had been stung by wasps. And when they saw the great golden peach floating past them not fifty yards away in the sky, they gave a yelp of surprise and dropped their shovels to the ground. And there they stood with the moonlight streaming down all over them, absolutely motionless, like a group of tall white hairy statues, staring and staring at the gigantic fruit as it went sailing by.

The passengers on the peach (all except the Centipede) sat frozen with terror, looking back at the Cloud-Men and wondering what was going to happen next.

'Now you've done it, you loathsome pest!' whispered the Earthworm to the Centipede.

'I'm not frightened of *them*!' shouted the Centipede, and to show everybody once again that he wasn't, he stood up to his full height and started dancing about and making insulting signs at the Cloud-Men with all forty-two of his legs.

This evidently infuriated the Cloud-Men beyond belief. All at once, they spun round and grabbed great handfuls of hailstones and rushed to the edge of the cloud and started throwing them at the peach, shrieking with fury all the time.

'Look out!' cried James. 'Quick! Lie down! Lie flat on the deck!'

It was lucky they did! A large hailstone can hurt you as much as a rock or a lump of lead if it is thrown hard enough – and my goodness, how those Cloud-Men could throw! The hailstones came whizzing through the air like bullets from a machine-gun, and James could hear them smashing against the sides of the peach and burying themselves in the peach flesh with horrible squelching noises – *plop! plop! plop! plop!* And then *ping! ping! ping!* as they bounced off the poor Ladybird's shell because she couldn't lie as flat as the others. And then *crack!* as one of them hit the Centipede right on the nose and *crack!* again as another one hit him somewhere else.

'Ow!' he cried. 'Ow! Stop! Stop! Stop!'

But the Cloud-Men had no intention of stopping. James could see them rushing about on the cloud like a lot of huge hairy ghosts, picking up hailstones from the pile, dashing to the edge of the cloud, hurling the hailstones at the peach, dashing back again to get more, and then, when the pile of stones was all gone, they simply grabbed handfuls of cloud and made as many more as they wanted, and much bigger ones now, some of them as large as cannon balls.

'Quickly!' cried James. 'Down the tunnel or we'll all be wiped out!'

There was a rush for the tunnel entrance, and half a minute later everybody was safely downstairs inside the stone of the peach, trembling with fright and listening to the noise of the hailstones as they came crashing against the side of the peach.

'I'm a wreck!' groaned the Centipede. 'I am wounded all over!'

'It serves you right,' said the Earthworm.

'Would somebody kindly look and see if my shell is cracked?' the Ladybird said.

'Give us some light!' shouted the Old-Green-Grasshopper.

'I can't!' wailed the Glow-worm. 'They've broken my bulb!'

'Then put in another one!' the Centipede said.

'Be quiet a moment,' said James. 'Listen! I do believe they're not hitting us any more!'

They all stopped talking and listened. Yes – the noise had ceased. The hailstones were no longer smashing against the peach.

'We've left them behind!'

'The seagulls must have pulled us away out of danger.'

'Hooray! Let's go up and see!'

Cautiously, with James going first, they all climbed back up the tunnel. James poked his head out and looked around. 'It's all clear!' he called. 'I can't see them anywhere!'

Twenty-eight

One by one, the travellers came out again on to the top of the peach and gazed carefully around. The moon was still shining as brightly as ever, and there were still plenty of huge shimmering cloud-mountains on all sides. But there were no Cloud-Men in sight now.

'The peach is leaking!' shouted the Old-Green-Grasshopper, peering over the side. 'It's full of holes and the juice is dripping out everywhere!'

'*That* does it!' cried the Earthworm. 'If the peach is leaking then we shall surely sink!'

'Don't be an ass!' the Centipede told him. 'We're not in the water now!'

'Oh, look!' shouted the Ladybird. 'Look, look, look! Over there!'

Everybody swung round to look.

In the distance and directly ahead of them, they now saw a most extraordinary sight. It was a kind of arch, a colossal curvy-shaped thing that reached high up into the sky and came down again at both ends. The ends were resting upon a huge flat cloud that was as big as a desert.

'Now what in the world is that?' asked James.

'It's a bridge!'

'It's an enormous hoop cut in half!'

'It's a giant horseshoe standing upside down!'

'Stop me if I'm wrong,' murmured the Centipede, going white in the face, 'but might those not be Cloud-Men climbing all over it?'

There was a dreadful silence. The peach floated closer and closer.

'They *are* Cloud-Men!'

'There are hundreds of them!'

'Thousands!'

'Millions!'

'I don't want to hear about it!' shrieked the poor

blind Earthworm. 'I'd rather be on the end of a fish hook and used as bait than come up against those terrible creatures again!'

'I'd rather be fried alive and eaten by a Mexican!' wailed the Old-Green-Grasshopper.

'Please keep quiet,' whispered James. 'It's our only hope.'

They crouched very still on top of the peach, staring at the Cloud-Men. The whole surface of the cloud was literally *swarming* with them, and there were hundreds more up above climbing about on that monstrous crazy arch.

'But what is that thing?' whispered the Ladybird. 'And what are they *doing* to it?'

'I don't care what they're doing to it!' the Centipede said, scuttling over to the tunnel entrance. 'I'm not staying up here! Goodbye!'

But the rest of them were too frightened or too hypnotized by the whole affair to make a move.

'Do you know what?' James whispered.

'*What?*' they said. '*What?*'

'That enormous arch – they seem to be *painting* it! They've got pots of paint and big brushes! You look!'

And he was quite right. The travellers were close enough now to see that this was exactly what the Cloud-Men were doing. They all had huge brushes in their hands and they were splashing the paint on to the great curvy arch in a frenzy of speed, so fast, in fact, that in a few minutes the whole of the arch became covered with the most glorious colours – reds, blues, greens, yellows, and purples.

'It's a rainbow!' everyone said at once. 'They are making a rainbow!'

'Oh, isn't it beautiful!'

'Just look at those colours!'

'Centipede!' they shouted. 'You *must* come up and see this!' They were so enthralled by the beauty and brilliance of the rainbow that they forgot to keep their voices low any longer. The Centipede poked his head cautiously out of the tunnel entrance.

'Well, well, well,' he said. 'I've *always* wondered how those things were made. But why all the ropes? What are they doing with those ropes?'

'Good heavens, they are pushing it off the cloud!' cried James. 'There it goes! They are lowering it down to the earth with ropes!'

'And I'll tell you something else,' the Centipede said sharply. 'If I'm not greatly mistaken, we ourselves are going to bump right into it!'

'Bless my soul, he's right!' the Old-Green-Grasshopper exclaimed.

The rainbow was now dangling in the air below the cloud. The peach was also just below the level of the cloud, and it was heading directly towards the rainbow, travelling rather fast.

'We are lost!' Miss Spider cried, wringing her feet again. 'The end has come!'

'I can't stand it!' wailed the Earthworm. 'Tell me what's happening!'

'We're going to miss it!' shouted the Ladybird.

'No, we're not!'

'Yes, we are!'

'Yes! – Yes! – No! – Oh, my heavens!'

'Hold on, everybody!' James called out, and suddenly there was a tremendous thud as the peach went crashing into the top of the rainbow. This was

followed by an awful splintering noise as the enormous rainbow snapped right across the middle and became two separate pieces.

The next thing that happened was extremely unfortunate. The ropes that the Cloud-Men had been using for lowering the rainbow got tangled up with the silk strings that went up from the peach to the seagulls! The peach was trapped! Panic and pandemonium broke out among the travellers, and James Henry Trotter, glancing up quickly, saw the faces of a thousand furious Cloud-Men peering down at him over the edge of the cloud. The faces had almost no shape at all because of the long white hairs that covered them. There were no noses, no mouths, no ears, no chins – only the eyes were visible in each face, two small black eyes glinting malevolently through the hairs.

Then came the most frightening thing of all. One Cloud-Man, a huge hairy creature who must have been fourteen feet tall at least, suddenly stood up and made a tremendous leap off the side of the cloud, trying to get to one of the silk strings above the peach. James and his friends saw him go flying through the air above them, his arms outstretched in front of him, reaching for the nearest string, and they saw him grab it and cling to it with his hands and legs. And then, very very slowly, hand over hand, he began to come down the string.

'Mercy! Help! Save us!' cried the Ladybird.

'He's coming down to eat us!' wailed the Old-Green-Grasshopper. 'Jump overboard!'

'Then eat the Earthworm first!' shouted the

Centipede. 'It's no good eating me, I'm full of bones like a kipper!'

'Centipede!' yelled James. 'Quickly! Bite through that string, the one he's coming down on!'

The Centipede rushed over to the stem of the peach and took the silk string in his teeth and bit through it with one snap of his jaws. Immediately, far above them, a single seagull was seen to come away from the rest of the flock and go flying off with a long string trailing from its neck. And clinging desperately to the end of the string, shouting and cursing with fury, was the huge hairy Cloud-Man. Up and up he went, swinging across the moonlit sky, and James Henry Trotter, watching him with delight, said, 'My goodness, he must weigh almost nothing at all for one seagull to be able to pull him up like that! He must be all hair and air!'

The rest of the Cloud-Men were so flabbergasted at seeing one of their company carried away in this manner that they let go the ropes they were holding and then of course down went the rainbow, both halves of it together, tumbling towards the earth below. This freed the peach, which at once began sailing away from that terrible cloud.

But the travellers were not in the clear yet. The infuriated Cloud-Men jumped up and ran after them along the cloud, pelting them mercilessly with all sorts of hard and horrible objects. Empty paint buckets, paint brushes, stepladders, stools, saucepans, frying-pans, rotten eggs, dead rats, bottles of hair-oil – anything those brutes could lay their hands on came raining down upon the peach. One Cloud-Man, taking very careful aim, tipped a gallon of thick purple paint over the edge of the cloud right on to the Centipede himself.

The Centipede screamed with anger. 'My legs!' he cried. 'They are all sticking together! I can't walk! And my eyelids won't open! I can't see! And my boots! My boots are ruined!'

But for the moment everyone was far too busy dodging the things that the Cloud-Men were throwing to pay any attention to the Centipede.

'The paint is drying!' he moaned. 'It's going hard! I can't move my legs! I can't move anything!'

'You can still move your mouth,' the Earthworm said. 'And that is a great pity.'

'James!' bawled the Centipede. 'Please help me! Wash off this paint! Scrape it off! Anything!'

Twenty-nine

It seemed like a long time before the seagulls were able to pull the peach away from that horrible rainbow-cloud. But they managed it at last, and then everybody gathered around the wretched Centipede and began arguing about the best way to get the paint off his body.

He really did look a sight. He was purple all over, and now that the paint was beginning to dry and harden, he was forced to sit very stiff and upright, as though he were encased in cement. And all forty-two of his legs were sticking out straight in front of him, like rods. He tried to say something, but his lips wouldn't move. All he could do now was to make gurgling noises in his throat.

The Old-Green-Grasshopper reached out and touched him carefully on the stomach. 'But how could it possibly have dried so quickly?' he asked.

'It's rainbow-paint,' James answered. 'Rainbow-paint dries very quick and very hard.'

'I detest paint,' Miss Spider announced. 'It frightens me. It reminds me of Aunt Spiker – the *late* Aunt Spiker, I mean – because the last time she painted her kitchen ceiling my poor darling grandmother stepped into it by mistake when it was still wet, and there she stuck. And all through the night we could hear her calling to us, saying "Help! help! help!" and it was heartbreaking to listen to her. But what could we do? Not a thing until the next day when the paint had dried, and then of course we all rushed over to her and calmed her down and gave her some food. Believe it or not, she lived for six months like that, upside down on the ceiling with her legs stuck permanently in the paint. She really did. We fed her every day. We brought her fresh flies straight from the web. But then on the twenty-sixth of April last, Aunt Sponge – the *late* Aunt Sponge, I mean – happened to glance up at the ceiling, and she spotted her. "A spider!" she cried. "A disgusting spider! Quick! Fetch me the mop with the long handle!" And then – Oh, it was so awful I can't bear to think of it . . .' Miss Spider wiped away a tear and looked sadly at the Centipede. 'You poor thing,' she murmured. 'I do feel sorry for you.'

'It'll never come off,' the Earthworm said brightly. 'Our Centipede will never move again. He will turn into a statue and we shall be able to put him in the middle of the lawn with a bird-bath on the top of his head.'

'We could try peeling him like a banana,' the Old-Green-Grasshopper suggested.

'Or rubbing him with sandpaper,' the Ladybird said.

'Now if he stuck out his tongue,' the Earthworm said, smiling a little for perhaps the first time in his life, 'if he stuck it out really far, then we could all catch hold of it and start pulling. And if we pulled hard enough, we could turn him inside out and he would have a new skin!'

There was a pause while the others considered this interesting proposal.

'I think,' James said slowly, 'I think that the best thing to do . . .' Then he stopped. 'What was *that*?' he asked quickly. 'I heard a voice! I heard someone shouting!'

Thirty

They all raised their heads, listening.

'Ssshh! There it is again!'

But the voice was too far away for them to hear what it was saying.

'It's a Cloud-Man!' Miss Spider cried. 'I just know it's a Cloud-Man! They're after us again!'

'It came from above!' the Earthworm said, and automatically everybody looked upward, everybody except the Centipede, who couldn't move.

'Ouch!' they said. 'Help! Mercy! We're going to catch it this time!' For what they now saw, swirling and twisting directly over their heads, was an immense black cloud, a terrible, dangerous, thundery-looking thing that began to rumble and roar even as they were staring at it. And then, from high up on the top of the cloud, the faraway voice came down to them once again, this time very loud and clear.

'*On with the faucets!*' it shouted. '*On with the faucets! On with the faucets!*'

Three seconds later, the whole underneath of the cloud seemed to split and burst open like a paper bag, and then – *out* came the water! They saw it coming. It was quite easy to see because it wasn't just raindrops. It wasn't raindrops at all. It was a great solid mass of water that might have been a lake or a whole ocean dropping out of the sky on top of them, and down it came, down and down and down, crashing first on to the seagulls and then on to the peach itself, while the poor travellers shrieked with

fear and groped around frantically for something to catch hold of – the peach stem, the silk strings, anything they could find – and all the time the water came pouring and roaring down upon them, bouncing and smashing and sloshing and slashing and swashing and swirling and surging and whirling and gurgling and gushing and rushing and rushing, and it was like being pinned down underneath the biggest waterfall in the world and not being able to get out. They couldn't speak. They couldn't see. They couldn't breathe. And James Henry Trotter, holding on madly to one of the silk strings above the peach stem, told himself that this must surely be the end of everything at last. But then, just as suddenly as it had started, the deluge stopped. They were out of it and it was all over. The wonderful seagulls had flown right through it and had come out safely on the other side. Once again the giant peach was sailing peacefully through the mysterious moonlit sky.

'I am drowned!' gasped the Old-Green-Grasshopper, spitting out water by the pint.

'It's gone right through my skin!' the Earthworm groaned. 'I always thought my skin was waterproof but it isn't and now I'm full of rain!'

'*Look at me, look at me!*' shouted the Centipede excitedly. 'It's washed me *clean*! The paint's all gone! I can move again!'

'That's the worst news I've had in a long time,' the Earthworm said.

The Centipede was dancing around the deck and turning somersaults in the air and singing at the top of his voice:

'Oh, hooray for the storm and the rain!
I can move! I don't feel any pain!
And now I'm a pest,
I'm the biggest and best,
The most marvellous pest once again!'

'Oh, do shut up,' the Old-Green-Grasshopper said.

'Look at me!' cried the Centipede.

'Look at ME*! I am freed! I am freed!*
Not a scratch nor a bruise nor a bleed!
To his grave this fine gent
They all thought they had sent
And I very near went!
Oh, I VERY *near went!*
But they cent quite the wrong Sentipede!'

Thirty-one

'How fast we are going all of a sudden,' the Ladybird said. 'I wonder why?'

'I don't think the seagulls like this place any better than we do,' James answered. 'I imagine they want to get out of it as soon as they can. They got a bad fright in that storm we've just been through.'

Faster and faster flew the seagulls, skimming across the sky at a tremendous pace, with the peach trailing out behind them. Cloud after cloud went by on either side, all of them ghostly white in the moonlight, and several more times during the night the travellers caught glimpses of Cloud-Men moving around on the tops of these clouds, working their sinister magic upon the world below.

Once they passed a snow machine in operation, with the Cloud-Men turning the handle and a blizzard of snowflakes blowing out of the great funnel above. They saw the huge drums that were used for making thunder, and the Cloud-Men beating them furiously with long hammers. They saw the frost factories and the wind producers and the places where cyclones and tornadoes were manufactured and sent spinning down towards the Earth, and once, deep in the hollow of a large billowy cloud, they spotted something that could only have been a Cloud-Men's city. There were caves everywhere running into the cloud, and at the entrances to the caves the Cloud-Men's wives were crouching over little stoves with frying-pans in their hands, frying snowballs for their husbands' suppers. And hundreds of Cloud-Men's children were frisking about all over the place and shrieking with laughter and sliding down the billows of the cloud on toboggans.

An hour later, just before dawn, the travellers heard a soft *whooshing* noise above their heads and they glanced up and saw an immense grey batlike creature swooping down towards them out of the dark. It circled round and round the peach, flapping its great wings slowly in the moonlight and staring at the travellers. Then it uttered a series of long deep melancholy cries and flew off again into the night.

'Oh, I do wish the morning would come!' Miss Spider said, shivering all over.

'It won't be long now,' James answered. 'Look, it's getting lighter over there already.'

They all sat in silence watching the sun as it came up slowly over the rim of the horizon for a new day.

Thirty-two

And when full daylight came at last, they all got to their feet and stretched their poor cramped bodies, and then the Centipede, who always seemed to see things first, shouted, 'Look! There's land below!'

'He's right!' they cried, running to the edge of the peach and peering over. 'Hooray! Hooray!'

'It looks like streets and houses!'

'But how enormous it all is!'

A vast city, glistening in the early morning sunshine, lay spread out three thousand feet below them. At that height, the cars were like little beetles crawling along the streets, and people walking on the pavements looked no larger than tiny grains of soot.

'But what tremendous tall buildings!' exclaimed the Ladybird. 'I've never seen anything like *them* before in England. Which town do you think it is?'

'This couldn't possibly be England,' said the Old-Green-Grasshopper.

'Then where is it?' asked Miss Spider.

'You know what those buildings are?' shouted James, jumping up and down with excitement. 'Those are skyscrapers! So this must be America! And that, my friends, means that we have crossed the Atlantic Ocean overnight!'

'You don't mean it!' they cried.

'It's not possible!'

'It's incredible! It's unbelievable!'

'Oh, I've always dreamed of going to America!' cried the Centipede. 'I had a friend once who –'

'Be quiet!' said the Earthworm. 'Who cares about your friend? The thing we've got to think about now is *how on earth are we going to get down to earth*?'

'Ask James,' said the Ladybird.

'I don't think that should be so very difficult,' James told them. 'All we'll have to do is to cut loose a few seagulls. Not too many, mind you, but just enough so that the others can't *quite* keep us up in the air. Then down we shall go, slowly and gently, until we reach the ground. Centipede will bite through the strings for us one at a time.'

Thirty-three

Far below them, in the City of New York, something like pandemonium was breaking out. A great round ball as big as a house had been sighted hovering high up in the sky over the very centre of Manhattan, and the cry had gone up that it was an enormous bomb sent over by another country to blow the whole city to smithereens. Air-raid sirens began wailing in every section. All radio and television programmes were interrupted with announcements that the population must go down into their cellars immediately. One million people walking in the streets on their way to work looked up into the sky and saw the monster hovering above them, and started running for the nearest subway entrance to take cover.

Generals grabbed hold of telephones and shouted orders to everyone they could think of. The Mayor of New York called up the President of the United States down in Washington, D.C., to ask him for help, and the President, who at that moment was having breakfast in his pyjamas, quickly pushed away his half-finished plate of Sugar Crisps and started pressing buttons right and left to summon his Admirals and his Generals. And all the way across the vast stretch of America, in all the fifty States from Alaska to Florida, from Pennsylvania to Hawaii, the alarm was sounded and the word went out that the biggest bomb in the history of the world was hovering over New York City, and that at any moment it might go off.

Thirty-four

'Come on, Centipede, bite through the first string,' James ordered.

The Centipede took one of the silk strings between his teeth and bit through it. And once again (but *not* with an angry Cloud-Man dangling from the end of the string this time) a single seagull came away from the rest of the flock and went flying off on its own.

'Bite another,' James ordered.

The Centipede bit through another string.

'Why aren't we sinking?'

'We are sinking!'

'No, we're not!'

'Don't forget the peach is a lot lighter now than when we started out,' James told them. 'It lost an awful lot of juice when all those hailstones hit it in the night. Cut away two more seagulls, Centipede!'

'Ah, that's better!'

'Here we go!'

'Now we really are sinking!'

'Yes, this is perfect! Don't bite any more, Centipede, or we'll sink too fast! Gently does it!'

Slowly the great peach began losing height, and the buildings and streets down below began coming closer and closer.

'Do you think we'll all get our pictures in the papers when we get down?' the Ladybird asked.

'My goodness, I've forgotten to polish my boots!' the Centipede said. 'Everyone must help me to polish my boots before we arrive.'

'Oh, for heaven's sake!' said the Earthworm. 'Can't you ever stop thinking about –'

But he never finished his sentence. For suddenly . . . *WHOOOSH!* . . . and they looked up and saw a huge four-engined plane come shooting out of a nearby cloud and go whizzing past them not more than twenty feet over their heads. This was actually the regular early morning passenger plane coming in to New York from Chicago, and as it went by, it sliced right through every single one of the silken strings, and immediately the seagulls broke away, and the enormous peach, having nothing to hold it up in the air any longer, went tumbling down towards the earth like a lump of lead.

'Help!' cried the Centipede.

'Save us!' cried Miss Spider.

'We are lost!' cried the Ladybird.

'This is the end!' cried the Old-Green-Grasshopper.

'James!' cried the Earthworm. 'Do something, James! Quickly, do something!'

'I can't!' cried James. 'I'm sorry! Goodbye! Shut your eyes, everybody! It won't be long now!'

Thirty-five

Round and round and upside down went the peach as it plummeted towards the earth, and they were all clinging desperately to the stem to save themselves from being flung into space.

Faster and faster it fell. Down and down and down, racing closer and closer to the houses and streets below, where it would surely smash into a million pieces when it hit. And all the way along Fifth Avenue and Madison Avenue, and along all the other streets in the City, people who had not yet reached the underground shelters looked up and saw it coming, and they stopped running and stood there staring in a sort of stupor at what they thought was the biggest bomb in all the world falling out of the sky on to their heads. A few women screamed. Others knelt down on the sidewalks and began praying aloud. Strong men turned to one another and said things like, 'I guess this is it, Joe,' and 'Goodbye, everybody, goodbye.' And for the next thirty seconds the whole City held its breath, waiting for the end to come.

Thirty-six

'Goodbye, Ladybird!' gasped James, clinging to the stem of the falling peach. 'Goodbye, Centipede. Goodbye, everybody!' There were only a few seconds to go now and it looked as though they were going to fall right in among all the tallest buildings. James could see the skyscrapers rushing up to meet them at the most awful speed, and most of them had square flat tops, but the very tallest of them all had a top that tapered off into a long sharp point – like an enormous silver needle sticking up into the sky.

And it was precisely on to the top of this needle that the peach fell!

There was a squelch. The needle went in deep. And suddenly – there was the giant peach, caught and spiked upon the very pinnacle of the Empire State Building.

Thirty-seven

It was really an amazing sight, and in two or three minutes, as soon as the people below realized that this now couldn't possibly be a bomb, they came pouring out of the shelters and the subways to gape at the marvel. The streets for half a mile around the building were jammed with men and women, and when the word spread that there were actually living things moving about on the top of the great round ball, then everyone went wild with excitement.

'It's a flying saucer!' they shouted.

'They are from Outer Space!'

'They are men from Mars!'

'Or maybe they came from the Moon!'

And a man who had a pair of binoculars to his eyes said, 'They look *pritt*-ty peculiar to me, I'll tell you that.'

Police cars and fire engines came screaming in from all over the city and pulled up outside the Empire State Building. Two hundred firemen and six hundred policemen swarmed into the building and went up in the elevators as high as they could go. Then they poured out on to the observation roof – which is the place where tourists stand – just at the bottom of the big spike.

All the policemen were holding their guns at the ready, with their fingers on the triggers, and the firemen were clutching their hatchets. But from where they stood, almost directly underneath the peach, they couldn't actually see the travellers up on top.

'Ahoy there!' shouted the Chief of Police. 'Come out and show yourselves!'

Suddenly, the great brown head of the Centipede appeared over the side of the peach. His black eyes, as large and round as two marbles, glared down at the policemen and the firemen below. Then his monstrous ugly face broke into a wide grin.

The policemen and the firemen all started shouting at once. 'Look out!' they cried. 'It's a Dragon!'

'It's not a Dragon! It's a Wampus!'

'It's a Gorgon!'

'It's a Sea-serpent!'

'It's a Prock!'

'It's a Manticore!'

Three firemen and five policemen fainted and had to be carried away.

'It's a Snozzwanger!' cried the Chief of Police.

'It's a Whangdoodle!' yelled the Head of the Fire Department.

The Centipede kept on grinning. He seemed to be enjoying enormously the commotion that he was causing.

'Now see here!' shouted the Chief of Police, cupping his hands to his mouth. 'You listen to me! I want you to tell me exactly where you've come from!'

'We've come from thousands of miles away!' the Centipede shouted back, grinning more broadly than ever and showing his brown teeth.

'There you are!' called the Chief of Police. 'I *told* you they came from Mars!'

'I guess you're right!' said the Head of the Fire Department.

At this point, the Old-Green-Grasshopper poked his huge green head over the side of the peach, alongside the Centipede's. Six more big strong men fainted when they saw him.

'That one's an Oinck!' screamed the Head of the Fire Department. 'I just *know* it's an Oinck!'

'Or a Cockatrice!' yelled the Chief of Police. 'Stand back, men! It may jump down on us any moment!'

'What on earth are they talking about?' the Old-Green-Grasshopper said to the Centipede.

'Search me,' the Centipede answered. 'But they seem to be in an awful stew about something.'

Then Miss Spider's large black murderous-looking head, which to a stranger was probably the most terrifying of all, appeared next to the Grasshopper's.

'Snakes and ladders!' yelled the Head of the Fire Department. 'We are finished now! It's a giant Scorpula!'

'It's worse than that!' cried the Chief of Police. 'It's a vermicious Knid! Oh, just look at its vermicious gruesome face!'

'Is that the kind that eats fully-grown men for breakfast?' the Head of the Fire Department asked, going white as a sheet.

'I'm afraid it is,' the Chief of Police answered.

'Oh, *please* why doesn't someone help us to get down from here?' Miss Spider called out. 'It's making me giddy.'

'This could be a trick!' said the Head of the Fire Department. 'Don't anyone make a move until I say!'

'They've probably got space guns!' muttered the Chief of Police.

'But we've *got* to do *something*!' the Head of the Fire Department announced grimly. 'About five million people are standing down there on the streets watching us.'

'Then why don't you put up a ladder?' the Chief

of Police asked him. 'I'll stand at the bottom and hold it steady for you while you go up and see what's happening.'

'Thanks very much!' snapped the Head of the Fire Department.

Soon there were no less than *seven* large fantastic faces peering down over the side of the peach – the Centipede's, the Old-Green-Grasshopper's, Miss Spider's, the Earthworm's, the Ladybird's, the Silkworm's, and the Glow-worm's. And a sort of panic was beginning to break out among the firemen and the policemen on the rooftop.

Then, all at once, the panic stopped and a great gasp of astonishment went up all round. For now, a small boy was seen to be standing up there beside the other creatures. His hair was blowing in the wind, and he was laughing and waving and calling out, 'Hello, everybody! Hello!'

For a few moments, the men below just stood and stared and gaped. They simply couldn't believe their eyes.

'*Bless* my soul!' cried the Head of the Fire Department, going red in the face. 'It really *is* a little boy, isn't it?'

'Don't be frightened of us, please!' James called out. 'We are so glad to be here!'

'What about those others beside you?' shouted the Chief of Police. 'Are any of them dangerous?'

'Of course they're not dangerous!' James answered. 'They're the nicest creatures in the world! Allow me to introduce them to you one by one and then I'm sure you will believe me.'

'My friends, this is the Centipede, and let me make it known
He is so sweet and gentle that (although he's overgrown)
The Queen of Spain, again and again, has summoned him by phone
To baby-sit and sing and knit and be a chaperone
When nurse is off and all the royal children are alone.'
('Small wonder,' said a fireman, 'they're no longer on the throne.')

'The Earthworm, on the other hand,'
Said James, beginning to expand,

'Is great for digging up the land
And making old soils newer.
Moreover, you should understand
He would be absolutely grand
For digging subway tunnels and
For making you a sewer.'
(The Earthworm blushed and beamed with pride.
Miss Spider clapped and cheered and cried,
'Could any words be truer?')

'And the Grasshopper, ladies and gents, is a boon
In millions and millions of ways.
You have only to ask him to give you a tune
And he plays and he plays and he plays.
As a toy for your children he's perfectly sweet;
There's nothing so good in the shops –
You've only to tickle the soles of his feet
And he hops and he hops and he hops.'
('He can't be very fierce!' exclaimed
The Head of all the Cops.)

'And now without excuse
I'd like to introduce
This charming Glow-worm, lover of simplicity.
She is easy to install
On your ceiling or your wall,
And although this smacks a bit of eccentricity,
It's really rather clever
For thereafter you will never
You will NEVER NEVER NEVER
Have the slightest need for using electricity.'
(At which, no less than fifty-two
Policemen cried, 'If this is true
That creature'll get some fabulous publicity!')

'And here we have Miss Spider
With a mile of thread inside her

Who has personally requested me to say
That she's NEVER *met Miss Muffet*
On her charming little tuffet –
If she had she'd NOT *have frightened her away.*
Should her looks sometimes alarm you
Then I don't think it would harm you
To repeat at least a hundred times a day:
"I must NEVER *kill a spider*
I must only help and guide her
And invite her in the nursery to play."'
(The police all nodded slightly,
And the firemen smiled politely,
And about a dozen people cried, 'Hooray!')

'And here's my darling Ladybird, so beautiful, so kind,
My greatest comfort since this trip began.
She has four hundred children and she's left them all behind,
But they're coming on the next peach if they can.'
(The cops cried, 'She's entrancing!'
All the firemen started dancing,
And the crowds all started cheering to a man!)

'And now, the Silkworm,' James went on,
'Whose silk will bear comparison
With all the greatest silks there are
In Rome and Philadelphia.
If you would search the whole world through
From Paraguay to Timbuctoo
I don't think you would find one bit
Of silk that could compare with it.
Even the shops in Singapore
Don't have the stuff. And what is more,
This Silkworm had, I'll have you know,
The honour, not so long ago,
To spin and weave and sew and press
The Queen of England's wedding dress.
And she's already made and sent
A waistcoat for your President.'
('Well, good for her!' the cops cried out,
And all at once a mighty shout
Went up around the Empire State,
'Let's get them down at once! Why WAIT?')

Thirty-eight

Five minutes later, they were all safely down, and James was excitedly telling his story to a group of flabbergasted officials.

And suddenly – everyone who had come over on the peach was a hero! They were all escorted to the steps of City Hall, where the Mayor of New York made a speech of welcome. And while he was doing this, one hundred steeplejacks, armed with ropes and ladders and pulleys, swarmed up to the top of the Empire State Building and lifted the giant peach off the spike and lowered it to the ground.

Then the Mayor shouted, 'We must now have a ticker-tape parade for our wonderful visitors!'

And so a procession was formed, and in the leading car (which was an enormous open limousine) sat James and all his friends.

Next came the giant peach itself. Men with cranes and hooks had quickly hoisted it on to a very large truck and there it now sat, looking just as huge and proud and brave as ever. There was, of course, a bit of a hole in the bottom of it where the spike of the Empire State Building had gone in, but who cared about that – or indeed about the peach juice that was dripping out of it on to the street?

Behind the peach, skidding about all over the place in the peach juice, came the Mayor's limousine, and behind the Mayor's limousine came about twenty other limousines carrying all the important people of the City.

And the crowds went wild with excitement. They lined the streets and they leaned out of the windows of the skyscrapers, cheering and yelling and screaming and clapping and throwing out bits of white paper and ticker-tape, and James and his friends stood up in their car and waved back at them as they went by.

Then a rather curious thing happened. The procession was moving slowly along Fifth Avenue when suddenly a little girl in a red dress ran out from the crowd and shouted, 'Oh, James, James! Could I *please* have just a tiny taste of your marvellous peach?'

'Help yourself!' James shouted back. 'Eat all you want! It won't keep for ever, anyway!'

No sooner had he said this than about fifty other children exploded out of the crowd and came running on to the street.

'Can *we* have some, too?' they cried.

'Of course you can!' James answered. 'Everyone can have some!'

The children jumped up on to the truck and swarmed like ants all over the giant peach, eating and eating to their hearts' content. And as the news of what was happening spread quickly from street to street, more and more boys and girls came running from all directions to join the feast. Soon, there was a trail of children a mile long chasing after the peach as it proceeded slowly up Fifth Avenue. Really, it was a fantastic sight. To some people it looked as though the Pied Piper of Hamelin had suddenly descended upon New York. And to James, who had never dreamed that there could be so many children as this in the world, it was the most marvellous thing that had ever happened.

By the time the procession was over, the whole gigantic fruit had been completely eaten up, and only the big brown stone in the middle, licked clean and shiny by ten thousand eager little tongues, was left standing on the truck.

Thirty-nine

And thus the journey ended. But the travellers lived on. Every one of them became rich and successful in the new country.

The Centipede was made Vice-President-in-Charge-of-Sales of a high-class firm of boot and shoe manufacturers.

The Earthworm, with his lovely pink skin, was employed by a company that made women's face creams to speak commercials on television.

The Silkworm and Miss Spider, after they had both been taught to make nylon thread instead of silk, set up a factory together and made ropes for tightrope walkers.

The Glow-worm became the light inside the torch on the Statue of Liberty, and thus saved a grateful City from having to pay a huge electricity bill every year.

The Old-Green-Grasshopper became a member of

the New York Symphony Orchestra, where his playing was greatly admired.

The Ladybird, who had been haunted all her life by the fear that her house was on fire and her children all gone, married the Head of the Fire Department and lived happily ever after.

And as for the enormous peach stone – it was set up permanently in a place of honour in Central Park and became a famous monument. But it was not *only* a famous monument. It was also a famous house. And inside the famous house there lived a famous person –

JAMES HENRY TROTTER

himself.

And all you had to do any day of the week was to go and knock upon the door, and the door would always be opened to you, and you would always be asked to come inside and see the famous room where James had first met his friends. And sometimes, if you were very lucky, you would find the Old-Green-Grasshopper in there as well, resting peacefully in a chair before the fire, or perhaps it would be the Ladybird who had dropped in for a cup of tea and a gossip, or the Centipede to show off a new batch of particularly elegant boots that he had just acquired.

Every day of the week, hundreds and hundreds of children from far and near came pouring into the City to see the marvellous peach stone in the Park. And James Henry Trotter, who once, if you remember, had

been the saddest and loneliest little boy that you could find, now had all the friends and playmates in the world. And because so many of them were always begging him to tell and tell again the story of his adventures on the peach, he thought it would be nice if one day he sat down and wrote it as a book.

So he did.

And *that* is what you have just finished reading.

Let's find out how carefully you were reading . . .

1. How did James Henry Trotter's parents die?
    a) They disappeared on a plane journey
    b) They ate a poisonous apple
    c) They were killed by an escaped rhino

2. What does Aunt Spiker look like?
    a) She is short and fat
    b) She is tall and thin
    c) She is strong and muscly

3. Which creatures attack the peach when it lands in the sea?
    a) Sharks
    b) Jelly fish
    c) Surfers

4. Upon which building is the peach impaled?
    a) The White House
    b) 10 Downing Street
    c) The Empire State Building

5. What happens to the Earthworm when he arrives in New York?
    a) He becomes a model for a skin-cream company
    b) He starts a worm farm
    c) He becomes a fisherman

Answers: 1. c) 2. b) 3. a) 4. c) 5. a)

© Miran Juršic

WILL BILLY BE YOUR NEW FAVOURITE ROALD DAHL HERO?

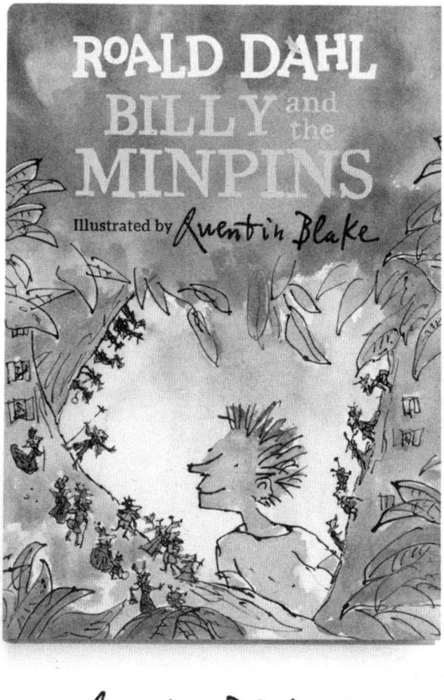

Illustrated by Quentin Blake for the first time

Read on for a sneak preview . . .

Being Good

Little Billy's mother was always telling him exactly what he was allowed to do and what he was not allowed to do.

All the things he was allowed to do were boring. All the things he was not allowed to do were exciting.

One of the things he was NEVER NEVER allowed to do, the most exciting of them all, was to go out through the garden gate all by himself and explore the world beyond.

On this sunny summer afternoon, Little Billy was kneeling on a chair in the living room, gazing out through the window at the wonderful world beyond. His mother was in the kitchen doing the ironing and although the door was open she couldn't see him.

Every now and again his mother would call out to him, saying, 'Little Billy, what are you up to in there?'

And Little Billy would always call back and say, 'I'm being good, Mummy.'

But Little Billy was awfully tired of being good.

Through the window, not so very far away, he could see the big black secret wood that was called The Forest of Sin. It was something he had always longed to explore.

His mother had told him that even grown-ups were frightened of going into The Forest of Sin.

She recited a poem to him that was well known in the district. It went like this:

Beware! Beware! The Forest of Sin!
None come out, but many go in!

'Why don't they come out?' Little Billy asked her. 'What happens to them in the wood?'

'That wood,' his mother said, 'is full of the most bloodthirsty wild beasts in the world.'

'You mean tigers and lions?' Little Billy asked.

'Much worse than that,' his mother said.

'What's worse than tigers and lions, Mummy?'

'Whangdoodles are worse,' his mother said, 'and Hornswogglers and Snozzwanglers and Vermicious Knids.

And worst of all is the Terrible Bloodsuckling Toothpluckling Stonechuckling Spittler. There's one of them in there, too.'

'A Spittler, Mummy?'

'Of course. And when the Spittler chases after you, he blows clouds of hot smoke out of his nose.'

'Would he eat me up?' Little Billy asked.

'In one gulp,' his mother said.

Little Billy did not believe a word of this. He guessed his mother was making it all up just to frighten him and stop him ever going out of the house alone.

And now Little Billy was kneeling on the chair, gazing with longing through the window at the famous Forest of Sin.

‘Little Billy,’ his mother called out from the kitchen. ‘What are you doing?’

‘I’m being good, Mummy,’ Little Billy called back.

Just then a funny thing happened. Little Billy began to hear somebody whispering in his ear. He knew exactly who it was. It was the Devil. The Devil always started whispering to him when he was especially bored.

‘It would be easy,’ the Devil was whispering, ‘to climb out through that window. No one would see you. And in a jiffy you would be in the garden, and in another jiffy you would be through the front gate, and in yet another jiffy you would be exploring the marvellous Forest of Sin all by yourself. It is a super place. Do not believe one word of what your mother says about Whangdoodles and Hornswogglers and Snozzwanglers and Vermicious Knids and the Terrible Bloodsuckling Toothpluckling Stonechuckling Spittler. There are no such things.'

'What *is* in there?' Little Billy whispered.

'Wild strawberries,' the Devil whispered back. 'The whole floor of the forest is carpeted with wild strawberries, every one of them luscious and red and juicy-ripe. Go and see for yourself.'

These were the words the Devil whispered softly into Little Billy's ear on that sunny summer afternoon.

The next moment, Little Billy had opened the window and was climbing out.

Have **YOU** PLAYED the **FANTASTICALLY** FUN **ROALD DAHL** apps?

www.roalddahl.com/apps

That's it.
The end of the book.

HERE IS
one LAST **WORD**,
invented by **Roald Dahl**
HIMSELF.
Make sure you KEEP IT SAFE.

FROTHBUNGLING

Adjective: Something that's ridiculous!

ROALD DAHL

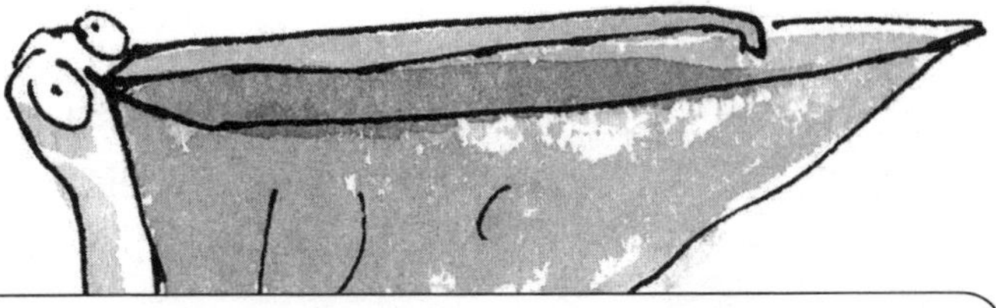

QUICK!

MISCHIEF MAKERS,

SIGN HERE so everyone knows **this book** belongs

TO YOU.

ROALD DAHL was a spy, ace fighter pilot, chocolate historian and medical inventor. He was also the author of *Charlie and the Chocolate Factory*, *Matilda*, *The BFG* and many more brilliant stories. He remains **THE WORLD'S NUMBER ONE STORYTELLER.**

QUENTIN BLAKE has illustrated more than three hundred books and was Roald Dahl's favourite illustrator. In 1980 he won the prestigious Kate Greenaway Medal. In 1999 he became the first ever Children's Laureate and in 2013 he was knighted for services to illustration.

INTRODUCING . . .

Billy

The Giraffe

The Pelly

The Duke of Hampshire

The Monkey

Books by Roald Dahl

THE BFG
BOY: TALES OF CHILDHOOD
BOY *and* GOING SOLO
CHARLIE AND THE CHOCOLATE FACTORY
CHARLIE AND THE GREAT GLASS ELEVATOR
THE COMPLETE ADVENTURES OF CHARLIE AND MR WILLY WONKA
DANNY THE CHAMPION OF THE WORLD
THE ENORMOUS CROCODILE
ESIO TROT
FANTASTIC MR FOX
GEORGE'S MARVELLOUS MEDICINE
THE GIRAFFE AND THE PELLY AND ME
GOING SOLO
JAMES AND THE GIANT PEACH
MATILDA
THE MAGIC FINGER
THE TWITS
THE WITCHES

Picture books

DIRTY BEASTS
THE ENORMOUS CROCODILE
THE GIRAFFE AND THE PELLY AND ME
THE MINPINS
REVOLTING RHYMES

Plays

THE BFG: PLAYS FOR CHILDREN (*Adapted by David Wood*)
CHARLIE AND THE CHOCOLATE FACTORY: A PLAY (*Adapted by Richard George*)
DANNY THE CHAMPION OF THE WORLD: PLAYS FOR CHILDREN (*Adapted by David Wood*)
FANTASTIC MR FOX: A PLAY (*Adapted by Sally Reid*)
JAMES AND THE GIANT PEACH: A PLAY (*Adapted by Richard George*)
THE TWITS: PLAYS FOR CHILDREN (*Adapted by David Wood*)
THE WITCHES: PLAYS FOR CHILDREN (*Adapted by David Wood*)

Teenage fiction

THE GREAT AUTOMATIC GRAMMATIZATOR AND OTHER STORIES
RHYME STEW
SKIN AND OTHER STORIES
THE VICAR OF NIBBLESWICKE
THE WONDERFUL STORY OF HENRY SUGAR AND SIX MORE

Collections

THE ROALD DAHL TREASURY
SONGS AND VERSE

ROALD DAHL

THE GIRAFFE AND THE PELLY AND ME

Illustrated by Quentin Blake

PUFFIN

PUFFIN BOOKS

UK | USA | Canada | Ireland | Australia
India | New Zealand | South Africa

Puffin Books is part of the Penguin Random House group of companies
whose addresses can be found at global.penguinrandomhouse.com.

puffinbooks.com

Penguin Random House UK

First published in the USA by Farrar, Straus and Giroux
and in Great Britain by Jonathan Cape 1985
Reissued by Jonathan Cape with new illustrations 1992
Published by Puffin Books 1993
This edition published 2016

022

Set in Baskerville MT 14/17 pt by Palimpsest Book Production Limited, Falkirk, Stirlingshire
Printed and bound in Great Britain by Clays Ltd, Elcograf S.p.A.

A CIP catalogue record for this book is available from the British Library

ISBN: 978–0–141–36543–5

www.greenpenguin.co.uk

MIX
Paper from
responsible sources
FSC® C018179
FSC
www.fsc.org

Penguin Random House is committed to a sustainable future for our business, our readers and our planet. This book is made from Forest Stewardship Council® certified paper.

For Neisha, Charlotte and Lorina

FUR SAIL

Not far from where I live there is a queer old empty wooden house standing all by itself on the side of the road. I long to explore inside it but the door is always locked, and when I peer through a window all I can see is darkness and dust. I know the ground floor used once to be a shop because I can still read the faded lettering across the front which says THE GRUBBER. My mother has told me that in our part of the country in the olden days a grubber was another name for a sweet-shop, and now every time I look at it I think to myself what a lovely old sweet-shop it must have been.

On the shop-window itself somebody has painted in white the words FOR SAIL.

One morning, I noticed that FOR SAIL had been scraped off the shop-window and in its place somebody had painted SOLED. I stood there staring at the new writing and wishing like mad that it had been me who had bought it because then I would have been able to make it into a grubber all over again. I have always longed and longed to own a sweet-shop. The sweet-shop of my dreams would be loaded from top to bottom with Sherbet Suckers and Caramel Fudge and Russian Toffee and Sugar Snorters and Butter Gumballs and thousands and thousands of other glorious things like that. Oh boy, what I couldn't have done with that old Grubber shop if it had been mine!

On my next visit to The Grubber, I was standing across the road gazing at the wonderful old building when suddenly an enormous bathtub came sailing out through one of the second-floor windows and crashed right on to the middle of the road!

THE GRUBBER
SOLED

A few moments later, a white porcelain lavatory pan with the wooden seat still on it came flying out of the same window and landed with a wonderful splintering crash just beside the bathtub. This was followed by a kitchen sink and an empty canary-cage and a four-poster bed and two hot-water bottles and a rocking horse and a sewing-machine and goodness knows what else besides.

It looked as though some madman was ripping out the whole of the inside of the house, because now pieces of staircase and bits of the banisters and a whole lot of old floorboards came whistling through the windows.

Then there was silence. I waited and waited but not another sound came from within the building. I crossed the road and stood right under the windows and called out, 'Is anybody at home?'

There was no answer.

In the end it began to get dark so I had to turn away and start walking home. But you can bet your life nothing was going to stop me from hurrying

back there again tomorrow morning to see what the next surprise was going to be.

When I got back to The Grubber house the next morning, the first thing I noticed was the new door. The dirty old brown door had been taken out and in its place someone had fitted a brand-new red one. The new door was fantastic. It was twice as high as the other one had been and it looked ridiculous. I couldn't begin to imagine who would want a tremendous tall door like that in his house unless it was a giant.

As well as this, somebody had scraped away the SOLED notice on the shop-window and now there was a whole lot of different writing all over the glass. I stood there reading it and reading it and trying to figure out what on earth it all meant.

The L W C Co
THE LADDERLESS WINDOW-CLEANING COMPANY
Get your windows cleaned without a lot of dirty ladders leaning against your house.

I tried to catch some sign or sound of movement inside the house but there was none . . . until all of a sudden . . . out of the corner of my eye . . . I noticed that one of the windows on the top floor was slowly beginning to open outwards . . .

Then a HEAD appeared at the open window.

I stared at the head. The head stared back at me with big round dark eyes.

Suddenly, a second window was flung wide open and of all the crazy things a gigantic white bird hopped out and perched on the window-sill.

I knew what this one was because of its amazing beak, which was shaped like a huge orange-coloured basin. The Pelican looked down at me and sang out:

'Oh, how I wish
For a big fat fish!
I'm as hungry as ever could be!
A dish of fish is my only wish!
How far are we from the sea?'

'We are a long way from the sea,' I called back to him, 'but there is a fishmonger in the village not far away.'

'A fish *what*?'

'A fish*monger*.'

'Now what on earth would that be?' asked the Pelican. 'I have heard of a fish-*pie* and a fish-*cake* and a fish-*finger*, but I have never heard of a fish-*monger*. Are these mongers good to eat?'

This question baffled me a bit, so I said, 'Who is your friend in the next window?'

'She is the Giraffe!' the Pelican answered. 'Is she not wonderful? Her legs are on the ground floor and her head is looking out of the top window!'

As if all this wasn't enough, the window on the *first floor* was now flung wide open and out popped a Monkey!

The Monkey stood on the window-sill and did a jiggly little dance. He was so skinny he seemed to be made only out of furry bits of wire, but he danced wonderfully well, and I clapped and cheered and did a little dance myself in return.

The L W C C
THE LADDERLESS
WINDOW-CLEANING
COMPANY
Get your windows
cleaned without
a lot of dirty
ladders leaning
against your
house.

'We are the Window-Cleaners!' sang out the Monkey.

'We will polish your glass
Till it's shining like brass
And it sparkles like sun on the sea!
We are quick and polite,
We will come day or night,
The Giraffe and the Pelly and me!

We're a fabulous crew,
We know just what to do,
And we never stop work to drink tea.
All your windows will glow
When we give them a go,
The Giraffe and the Pelly and me!

We use water and soap
Plus some kindness and hope,
But we never use ladders, not we.
Who needs ladders at all
When you're thirty feet tall?
Not Giraffe, and not Pelly! Not me!'

I stood there enthralled. Then I heard the Giraffe saying to the Pelican in the next window, 'Pelly, my dear, be so good as to fly down and bring that small person up here to talk to us.'

At once the Pelican spread his huge white wings and flew down on to the road beside me. 'Hop in,' he said, opening his enormous beak.

I stared at the great orange beak and backed away.

'Go ON!' the Monkey shouted from up in his window. 'The Pelly isn't going to *swallow* you! Climb IN!'

I said to the Pelican, 'I'll only get in if you promise not to shut your beak once I'm inside.'

'You have nothing to fear!' cried the Pelican,

'And let me tell you why.
I have a very special beak!
A special beak have I!
You'll never see a beak so fine,
I don't care where you go.
There's magic in this beak of mine!
Hop in and don't say NO!'

'I will *not* hop in,' I said, 'unless you swear on your honour you won't shut it once I'm inside. I don't like small dark places.'

'When I have done what I am just about to do,' said the Pelican, 'I won't be *able* to shut it. You don't seem to understand how my beak works.'

'Show me,' I said.

'Watch this!' cried the Pelican.

I watched in amazement as the top half of the Pelican's beak began to slide smoothly backwards into his head until the whole thing was almost out of sight.

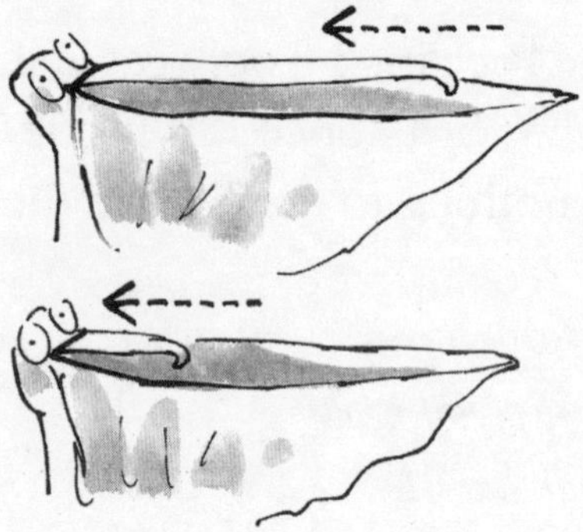

'It bends and goes down inside the back of my neck!' cried the Pelican. 'Is that not sensible? Is it not magical?'

'It's unbelievable,' I said. 'It's exactly like one of those metal tape-measures my father's got at home. When it's out, it's straight. When you slide it back in, it bends and disappears.'

'Precisely,' said the Pelican. 'You see, the top half is of no use to me unless I am chewing fish. The bottom half is what counts, my lad! The bottom half of this glorious beak of mine is the bucket in which we carry our window-cleaning water! So if I didn't slide the top half away I'd be standing around all day long holding it open!

'So I slide it away
For the rest of the day!
Even so, I'm still able to speak!
And wherever I've flown
It has always been known
As the Pelican's Patented Beak!

If I want to eat fish
(That's my favourite dish)
All I do is I give it a tweak!
In the blink of an eye
Out it pops! And they cry,
"It's the Pelican's Patented Beak!"'

'Stop showing off down there!' shouted the Monkey from the upstairs window. 'Hurry up and bring that small person up to us! The Giraffe is waiting!'

I climbed into the big orange beak, and with a swoosh of wings the Pelican carried me back to his perch on the window-sill.

The Giraffe looked out of her window at me and said, 'How do you do? What is your name?'

'Billy,' I told her.

'Well, Billy,' she said, 'we need your help and we

need it fast. We *must have* some windows to clean. We've spent every penny we had on buying this house and we've got to earn some more money quickly. The Pelly is starving, the Monkey is famished and I am perishing with hunger. The Pelly needs fish. The Monkey needs nuts and I am even more difficult to feed. I am a Geraneous Giraffe and a Geraneous Giraffe cannot eat anything except the pink and purple flowers of the tinkle-tinkle tree. But those, as I am sure you know, are hard to find and expensive to buy.'

The Pelican cried out, 'Right now I am so hungry I could eat a stale sardine!

'Has anyone seen a stale sardine
Or a bucket of rotten cod?
I'd eat the lot upon the spot,
I'm such a hungry bod!'

Every time the Pelican spoke, the beak I was standing in jiggled madly up and down, and the more excited he got, the more it jiggled.

The Monkey said, 'What Pelly's *really* crazy about is salmon!'

'Yes, yes!' cried the Pelican. 'Salmon! Oh, glorious salmon! I dream about it all day long but I never get any!'

'And *I* dream about walnuts!' shouted the Monkey. 'A walnut fresh from the tree is scrumptious-galumptious, so flavory-savory, so sweet to eat that it makes me all wobbly just thinking about it!'

At exactly that moment, a huge white Rolls-Royce pulled up right below us, and a chauffeur in a blue and gold uniform got out. He was carrying an envelope in one gloved hand.

'Good heavens!' I whispered. 'That's the Duke of Hampshire's car!'

'Who's he?' asked the Giraffe.

'He's the richest man in England!' I said.

The chauffeur knocked on the door of The Grubber.

He looked up and saw us. He saw the Giraffe, the Pelly, the Monkey and me all staring down at him from above, but not a muscle moved in his face, not an eyebrow was raised. The chauffeurs of very rich men are never surprised by anything they see. The chauffeur said, 'His Grace the Duke of Hampshire has instructed me to deliver this envelope to The Ladderless Window-Cleaning Company.'

'That's us!' cried the Monkey.

The Giraffe said, 'Be so good as to open the envelope and read us the letter.'

The chauffeur unfolded the letter and began to read, '"Dear Sirs, I saw your notice as I drove by this morning. I have been looking for a decent window-cleaner for the last fifty years but I have not found one yet. My house has six hundred and seventy-seven windows in it (not counting the greenhouse) and all of them are filthy. Kindly come and see me as soon as possible. Yours truly, Hampshire." That', added the chauffeur in a voice filled with awe and respect, 'was written by His Grace the Duke of Hampshire in his own hand.'

The Giraffe said to the chauffeur, 'Please tell His Grace the Duke that we will be with him as soon as possible.'

The chauffeur touched his cap and got back into the Rolls-Royce.

'Whoopee!' shouted the Monkey.

'Fantastic!' cried the Pelican. 'That must be the best window-cleaning job in the world!'

'Billy,' said the Giraffe, 'what is the house called and how do we get there?'

'It is called Hampshire House,' I said. 'It's just over the hill. I'll show you the way.'

'We're off!' cried the Monkey. 'We're off to see the Duke!'

The Giraffe stooped low and went out through the tall door. The Monkey jumped off the window-sill on to the Giraffe's back. The Pelican, with me in his beak hanging on for dear life, flew across and perched on the very top of the Giraffe's head. And away we went.

It wasn't long before we came to the gates of Hampshire House, and as the Giraffe moved slowly up the great wide driveway, we all began to feel just a little bit nervous.

'What's he like, this Duke?' the Giraffe asked me.

'I don't know,' I said. 'But he's very very famous and very rich. People say he has twenty-five gardeners just to look after his flower-beds.'

Soon the huge house itself came into view, and what a house it was! It was like a palace! It was bigger than a palace!

'Just look at those windows!' cried the Monkey. 'They'll keep us going for ever!'

Then suddenly we heard a man's voice a short distance away to the right. 'I want those big black ones at the top of the tree!' the man was shouting. 'Get me those great big black ones!'

We peered round the bushes and saw an oldish man with an immense white moustache standing under a tall cherry tree and pointing his walking-stick in the air. There was a ladder against the tree and another man, who was probably a gardener, was up the ladder.

'Get me those great big black juicy ones right at the very top!' the old man was shouting.

'I can't reach them, Your Grace,' the gardener called back. 'The ladder isn't long enough!'

'Damnation!' shouted the Duke. 'I *was* so looking forward to eating those big ones!'

'Here we go!' the Pelican whispered to me, and with a swish and a swoop he carried me up to the very top of the cherry tree and there he perched. 'Pick them, Billy!' he whispered. 'Pick them quickly and put them in my beak!'

The gardener got such a shock he fell off the ladder. Down below us, the Duke was shouting, 'My gun! Get me my gun! Some damnable monster of a bird is stealing my best cherries! Be off with you, sir! Go away! Those are *my* cherries, not yours! I'll have you shot for this, sir! Where *is* my gun?'

'Hurry, Billy!' whispered the Pelican. 'Hurry, hurry, hurry!'

'My gun!' the Duke was shouting to the gardener. 'Get me my gun, you idiot! I'll have that thieving bird for breakfast, you see if I don't.'

'I've picked them all,' I whispered to the Pelican.

At once the Pelly flew down and landed right beside the furious figure of the Duke of Hampshire, who was prancing about and waving his stick in the air!

'Your cherries, Your Grace!' I said as I leaned over the edge of the Pelican's beak and offered a handful to the Duke.

The Duke was staggered. He reeled back and his eyes popped nearly out of their sockets. 'Great Scott!' he gasped. 'Good Lord! What's this? Who are *you*?'

And now the Giraffe, with the Monkey dancing about on her back, emerged suddenly from the bushes. The Duke stared at them. He looked as though he was about to have a fit.

'*Who are these creatures?*' he bellowed. 'Has the whole world gone completely dotty?'

'We are the window-cleaners!' sang out the Monkey.

'We will polish your glass
Till it's shining like brass
And it sparkles like sun on the sea!
We will work for Your Grace
Till we're blue in the face,
The Giraffe and the Pelly and me!'

'You *asked* us to come and see you,' the Giraffe said.

The truth was at last beginning to dawn on the Duke. He put a cherry into his mouth and chewed it slowly. Then he spat out the stone. 'I like the way you picked these cherries for me,' he said. 'Could you also pick my apples in the autumn?'

'We could! We could! Of course we could!' we all shouted.

'And who are *you*?' the Duke said, pointing his stick at me.

'He is our Business Manager,' the Giraffe said. 'His name is Billy. We go nowhere without him.'

'Very well, very well,' the Duke muttered. 'Come along with me and let's see if you're any good at cleaning windows.'

I climbed out of the Pelican's beak and the kindly old Duke took me by the hand as we all walked towards the house. When we got there, the Duke said, 'What happens next?'

'It is all very simple, Your Grace,' the Giraffe replied. 'I am the ladder, the Pelly is the bucket and the Monkey is the cleaner. Watch us go!'

With that, the famous window-cleaning gang sprang into action. The Monkey jumped down from the Giraffe's back and turned on the garden tap. The Pelican held his great beak under the tap until it was full of water. Then, with a wonderful springy leap the Monkey leaped up once again on to the Giraffe's back. From there he scrambled, as easily as if he were climbing a tree, up the long long neck of the Giraffe until he stood balancing on the very top of her head. The Pelican remained standing on the ground beside us, looking up at the Giraffe.

'We'll do the top floor first!' the Giraffe shouted down. 'Bring the water up, please.'

The Duke called out, 'Don't worry about the two top floors. You can't reach them anyway.'

'Who says we can't reach them?' the Giraffe called back.

'I do,' the Duke said firmly, 'and I'm not having any of you risking your silly necks around here.'

If you wish to be friends with a Giraffe, never say anything bad about its neck. Its neck is its proudest possession.

'What's wrong with my neck?' snapped the Giraffe.

'Don't argue with me, you foolish creature!' cried the Duke. 'If you can't reach it, you can't reach it and that's the end of it! Now get on with your work!'

'Your Grace,' the Giraffe said, giving the Duke a small superior smile, 'there are no windows in the world I cannot reach with this magical neck of mine.'

The Monkey, who was dancing about most dangerously on top of the Giraffe's head, cried out, 'Show him, Giraffey! Go on and show him what you can do with your magical neck!'

The next moment, the Giraffe's neck, which heaven knows was long enough already, began to grow longer and LONGER

and LONGER

and LONGER

and HIGHER

and HIGHER

and HIGHER

until at last the Giraffe's head with the Monkey on top of it was level with the windows of the top floor.

The Giraffe looked down from her great height and said to the Duke, 'How's that?'

The Duke was speechless. So was I. It was the most magical thing I had ever seen, more magical even than the Pelican's Patented Beak.

Up above us, the Giraffe was beginning to sing a little song, but she sang so softly I could hardly catch the words. I think it went something like this:

'My neck can stretch terribly high,
Much higher than eagles can fly.
If I ventured to show
Just how high it would go
You'd lose sight of my head in
the sky!'

The Pelican, with his huge beak full of water, flew up and perched on one of the top-floor window-sills near the Monkey, and now the great window-cleaning business really began.

The speed with which the team worked was astonishing. As soon as one window was done, the Giraffe moved the Monkey over to the next one and the Pelican followed.

When all the fourth-floor windows on that side of the house were finished, the Giraffe simply drew in her magical neck until the Monkey was level with the third-floor windows and off they went again.

'Amazing!' cried the Duke. 'Astonishing! Remarkable! Incredible! I haven't seen out of any

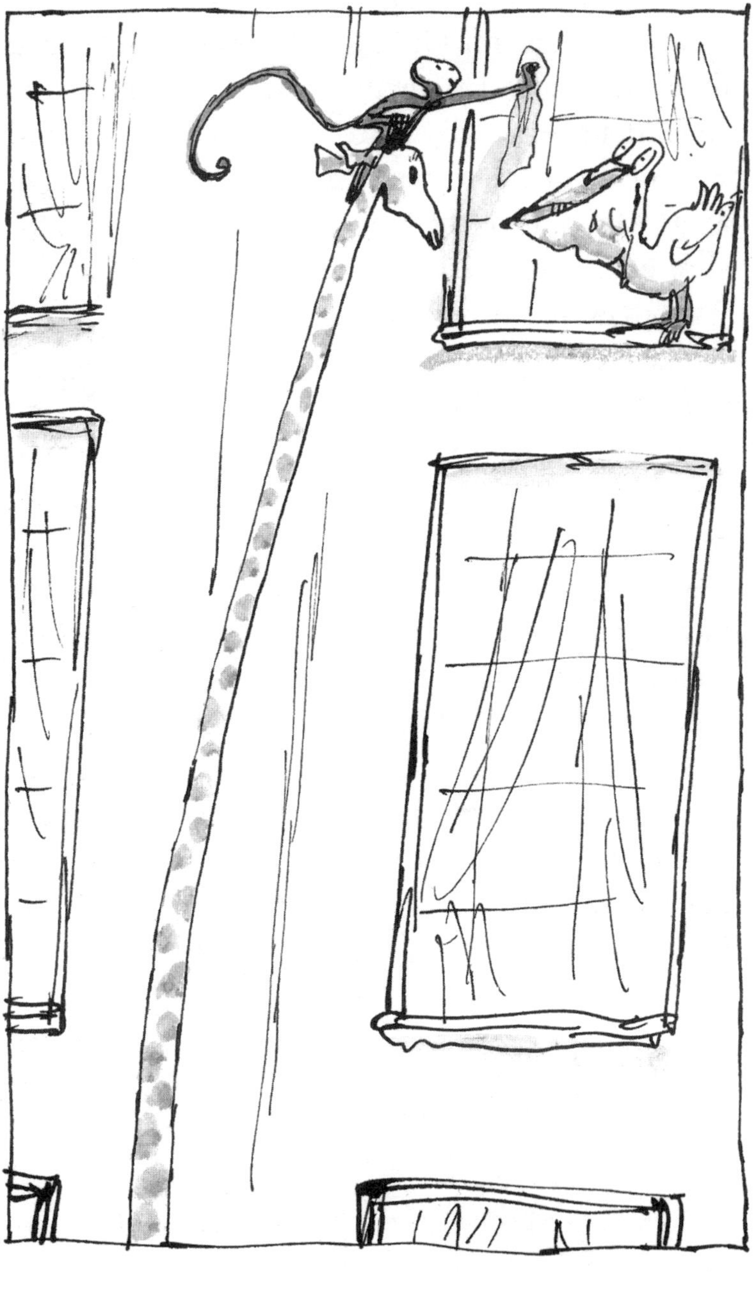

of my windows for forty years! Now I shall be able to sit indoors and enjoy the view!'

Suddenly I saw all three of the Window-Cleaners stop dead in their tracks. They seemed to freeze against the wall of the house. None of them moved.

'What's happened to them?' the Duke asked me. 'What's gone wrong?'

'I don't know,' I answered.

Then the Giraffe, with the Monkey on her head, tiptoed very gingerly away from the house and came towards us. The Pelican flew with them. The Giraffe came up very close to the Duke and whispered, 'Your Grace, there is a man in one of the bedrooms on the third-floor. He is opening all the drawers and taking things out. He's got a pistol!'

The Duke jumped about a foot in the air. 'Which room?' he snapped. 'Show me at once!'

'It's the one on the third-floor where the window is wide open,' the Giraffe whispered.

'By Gad!' cried the Duke. 'That's the Duchess's bedroom! He's after her jewels! Call the police! Summon the army! Bring up the cannon! Charge with the Light Brigade!' But even as he spoke the Pelican was flying up into the air. As he flew, he turned himself upside-down and tipped the window-cleaning water out of his beak. Then I saw the top half of that marvellous patented beak sliding out of his head, ready for action.

'What's that crazy bird up to?' cried the Duke.

'Wait and see,' shouted the Monkey. 'Hold your breath, old man! Hold your nose! Hold your horses and watch the Pelly go!'

Like a bullet the Pelican flew in through the open window, and five seconds later out he came again with his great orange beak firmly closed. He landed on the lawn beside the Duke.

A tremendous banging noise was coming from inside the Pelican's beak. It sounded as though someone was using a sledgehammer against it from the inside.

'He's got him!' cried the Monkey. 'Pelly's got the burglar in his beak!'

'Well done, sir!' shouted the Duke, hopping about with excitement. Suddenly he pulled the handle of his walking-stick upwards, and out of the hollow inside of the stick itself he drew a long thin sharp

shining sword. 'I'll run him through!' he shouted, flourishing the sword like a fencer. 'Open up, Pelican! Let me get at him! I'll run the bounder through before he knows what's happened to him! I'll spike him like a pat of butter! I'll feed his gizzards to my foxhounds!'

But the Pelican did not open his beak. He kept it firmly closed and shook his head at the Duke.

The Giraffe shouted, 'The burglar is armed with a pistol, Your Grace! If Pelly lets him out now he'll shoot us all!'

'He can be armed with a *machine-gun* for all I care!' bellowed the Duke, his massive moustaches bristling like brushwood. 'I'll handle the blighter! Open up, sir! Open up!'

Suddenly there was an ear-splitting BANG and the Pelican leaped twenty feet into the air. So did the Duke.

'Watch out!' the Duke shouted, taking ten rapid paces backwards. 'He's trying to shoot his way out!' And pointing his sword at the Pelican, he bellowed, 'Keep that beak closed, sir! Don't you dare let him out! He'll murder us all!'

'Shake him up, Pelly!' cried the Giraffe. 'Rattle his bones! Teach him not to do it again!'

The Pelican shook his head so fast from side to side that the beak became a blur and the man inside must have felt he was being scrambled like eggs.

'Well done, Pelly!' cried the Giraffe. 'You're doing a great job! Keep on shaking him so he doesn't fire that pistol again!'

At this point, a lady with an enormous chest and flaming orange hair came flying out of the house screaming, 'My jewels! Somebody's stolen my jewels! My diamond tiara! My diamond necklace! My diamond bracelets! My diamond earrings! My diamond rings! They've had the lot! My rooms have been ransacked!'

And then this massive female, who fifty-five years ago had been a world-famous opera-singer, suddenly burst into song.

'My diamonds are over the ocean,
My diamonds are over the sea,
My diamonds were pinched from my bedroom,
Oh, bring back my diamonds to me.'

We were so bowled over by the power of the lady's lungs that all of us, excepting the Pelican, who had to keep his beak closed, joined in the chorus.

'Bring back, bring back,
Oh, bring back my diamonds to me, to me.
Bring back, bring back,
Oh, bring back my diamonds to me!'

'Calm yourself, Henrietta,' said the Duke. He pointed to the Pelican and said, 'This clever bird, this brilliant burglar-catching creature has saved the day! The bounder's in his beak!'

The Duchess stared at the Pelican. The Pelican stared back at the Duchess and gave her a wink.

'If he's in there,' cried the Duchess, 'why don't you let him out! Then you can run him through with that famous sword of yours! I want my diamonds! Open your beak, bird!'

'No, no!' shouted the Duke. 'He's got a pistol! He'll murder us all!'

Someone must have called the police because suddenly no less than four squad cars came racing towards us with their sirens screaming.

Within seconds we were surrounded by six policemen, and the Duke was shouting to them,

'The villain you are after is inside the beak of that bird! Stand by to collar him!' And to the Pelican he said, 'Get ready to open up! Are you ready . . . steady . . . *go*! Open her up!'

The Pelican opened his gigantic beak and immediately the policemen pounced upon the burglar, who was crouching inside. They snatched his pistol away from him and dragged him out and put handcuffs on his wrists.

'Great Scott!' shouted the Chief of Police. 'It's the Cobra himself!'

'The who! The what!' everyone asked. 'Who's the Cobra?'

'The Cobra is the cleverest and most dangerous cat burglar in the world!' said the Chief of Police. 'He must have climbed up the drainpipe. The Cobra can climb up anything!'

'My diamonds!' screamed the Duchess. 'I want my diamonds! Where are my diamonds?'

'Here they are!' cried the Chief of Police, fishing great handfuls of jewellery from the burglar's pockets.

The Duchess was so overcome with relief that she fell to the ground in a faint.

When the police had taken away the fearsome burglar known as the Cobra, and the fainting Duchess had been carried into the house by her servants, the old Duke stood on the lawn with the Giraffe, the Pelican, the Monkey and me.

'Look!' cried the Monkey. 'That rotten burglar's bullet has made a hole in poor Pelly's beak!'

'That's done it,' said the Pelican. 'Now it won't be any use for holding water when we clean the windows.'

'Don't you worry about that, my dear Pelly,' said the Duke, patting him on the beak. 'My chauffeur will soon put a patch over it the same way he mends the tyres on the Rolls. Right now we have

far more important things to talk about than a little hole in a beak.'

We stood there waiting to see what the Duke was going to say next.

'Now listen to me, all of you,' he said. 'Those diamonds were worth millions! Millions and millions! And *you* have saved them!'

The Monkey nodded. The Giraffe smiled. The Pelican blushed.

'No reward is too great for you,' the Duke went on. 'I am therefore going to make you an offer which I hope will give you pleasure. I hereby invite the Giraffe and the Pelican and the Monkey to live on my estate for the rest of their lives.

'I shall give you my best and largest hay-barn as your private house. Central heating, showers, a kitchen and anything else you desire for your comfort will be installed.

'In return, you will keep my windows clean, and pick my cherries and my apples. If the Pelican is willing, perhaps he will also give me a ride in his beak now and again.'

'A pleasure, Your Grace!' cried the Pelican. 'Would you like a ride now?'

'Later,' said the Duke. 'I'll have one after tea.'

At this point, the Giraffe gave a nervous little cough and looked up at the sky.

'Is there a problem?' asked the Duke. 'If there is, do please let me hear it.'

'I don't like to sound ungrateful or pushy,' murmured the Giraffe, 'but we do have one very pressing problem. We are all absolutely famished. We haven't eaten for days.'

'My *dear* Giraffey!' cried the Duke. 'How very thoughtless of me. Food is no problem around here.'

'I'm afraid it is not quite as easy as all that,' said the Giraffe. 'You see, I myself happen to be . . .'

'Don't tell me!' cried the Duke. 'I know it already! I am an expert on the animals of Africa. The moment I saw you I knew you were no ordinary giraffe. You are of the Geraneous variety, are you not?'

'You are absolutely right, Your Grace,' said the Giraffe. 'But the trouble with us is that we only eat . . .'

'You don't have to tell me that either!' cried the Duke. 'I know perfectly well a Geraneous Giraffe can eat only one kind of food. Am I not right in thinking that the pink and purple flowers of the tinkle-tinkle tree are your only diet?'

'Yes,' sighed the Giraffe, 'and that's been my problem ever since I arrived on these shores.'

'That is no problem at all here at Hampshire House,' said the Duke. 'Look over there, my dear Giraffey, and you will see the only plantation of tinkle-tinkle trees in the entire country!'

The Giraffe looked. She gave a gasp of astonishment, and at first she was so overwhelmed she couldn't even speak. Great tears of joy began running down her cheeks.

'Help yourself,' said the Duke. 'Eat all you want.'

'Oh, my sainted souls!' gasped the Giraffe. 'Oh, my naked neck! I cannot *believe* what I am seeing!'

The next moment she was galloping full speed across the lawns and whinnying with excitement and the last we saw of her, she was burying her head in the beautiful pink and purple flowers that blossomed on the tops of the trees all around her.

'As for the Monkey,' the Duke went on, 'I think he also will be pleased with what I have to offer. All over my estate there are thousands of giant nut trees . . .'

'Nuts?' cried the Monkey. 'What kind of nuts?'

'Walnuts, of course,' said the Duke.

'***Walnuts!***' screamed the Monkey. 'Not *walnuts*? You don't really mean *walnuts*? You're pulling my leg! You're joking! You can't be serious! I must have heard wrong!'

'There's a walnut tree right over there,' the Duke said, pointing.

The Monkey took off like an arrow, and a few seconds later he was high up in the branches of the walnut tree, cracking the nuts and guzzling what was inside.

'That leaves only the Pelly,' said the Duke.

'Yes,' said the Pelican nervously, 'but I'm afraid that what I eat does not grow on trees. I only eat fish. Would it be too much trouble, I wonder, if I were to ask you for a reasonably fresh piece of haddock or cod every day?'

'Haddock or cod!' shouted the Duke, spitting out the words as though they made a bad taste in his mouth. 'Cast your eyes, my dear Pelly, over there to the south.'

The Pelican looked across the vast rolling estate and in the distance he saw a great river.

'That is the River Hamp!' cried the Duke. 'The finest salmon river in the whole of Europe!'

'***Salmon!***' screeched the Pelican. 'Not *salmon*? You don't really mean *salmon*?'

'It's *full* of salmon,' the Duke said, 'and I own it. You can help yourself.'

Before he had finished speaking the Pelican was in the air. The Duke and I watched him as he flew full speed towards the river. We saw him circle over the water, then he dived and disappeared. A few moments later, he was in the air again, and he had a gigantic salmon in his beak.

I stood alone with the Duke on the lawn beside his great house. 'Well, Billy,' he said, 'I'm glad they are all happy. But what about you, my lad? I am wondering if you happen to have just one extra special little wish all for yourself. If you do, I'd love you to tell me about it.'

There was a sudden tingling in my toes. It felt as though something tremendous might be going to happen to me any moment.

'Yes,' I murmured nervously. 'I do have one extra special little wish.'

'And what might that be?' said the Duke in a kindly voice.

'There is an old wooden house near where I live,' I said. 'It's called The Grubber and long ago it used to be a sweet-shop. I have wished and wished that one day somebody might come along and make it into a marvellous new sweet-shop all over again.'

'Somebody?' cried the Duke. 'What do you mean, *somebody*? You and I will do that! We'll do it together! We'll make it into the most wonderful sweet-shop in the world! And *you*, my boy, will own it!'

Whenever the old Duke got excited, his enormous moustaches started to bristle and jump about. Right now they were jumping up and down so much it looked as though he had a squirrel on his face. 'By Gad, sir!' he cried, waving his stick, 'I shall buy the place today! Then we'll get to work and have the whole thing ready in no time! You just wait and see what sort of a sweet-shop we are going to make out of this Grubber place of yours!'

It was amazing how quickly things began to happen after that. There was no problem about buying the house because it was owned by the Giraffe and the Pelly and the Monkey, and they insisted upon giving it to the Duke for nothing.

Then builders and carpenters moved in and rebuilt the whole of the inside so that once again it had three floors. On all these floors they put together rows and rows of tall shelves, and there were ladders to climb up to the highest shelves and baskets to carry what you bought.

Then the sweets and chocs and toffees and fudges and nougats began pouring in to fill the shelves. They came by aeroplane from every country in the world, the most wild and wondrous things you could ever imagine.

There were Gumtwizzlers and Fizzwinkles from China, Frothblowers and Spitsizzlers from Africa, Tummyticklers and Gobwangles from the Fiji Islands and Liplickers and Plushnuggets from the Land of the Midnight Sun.

For two whole weeks the flood of boxes and sacks continued to arrive. I could no longer keep track of all the countries they came from, but you can bet your life that as I unpacked each new batch I sampled it carefully. I can remember especially the Giant Wangdoodles from Australia, every one with a huge ripe red strawberry hidden inside its crispy chocolate crust . . . and the Electric

Fizzcocklers that made every hair on your head stand straight up on end as soon as you popped one into your mouth . . . and there were Nishnobblers and Gumglotters and Blue Bubblers and Sherbet Slurpers and Tongue Rakers, and as well as all this, there was a whole lot of splendid stuff from the great Wonka factory itself, for example the famous Willy Wonka Rainbow Drops – suck them and you can spit in seven different colours. And his

Stickjaw for talkative parents. And his Mint Jujubes that will give the boy next door green teeth for a month.

On the Grand Opening Day, I decided to allow all my customers to help themselves for free, and the place was so crowded with children you could hardly move. The television cameras and the newspaper reporters were all there, and the old Duke himself stood outside in the road with my friends the Giraffe and the Pelly and the Monkey watching the marvellous scene. I came out of the shop to join them for a few moments and I brought each of them a bag of extra-special sweets as a present.

To the Duke, because the weather was a little chilly, I gave some Scarlet Scorchdroppers that had been sent to me from Iceland. The label said that they were guaranteed to make the person who sucked them as warm as toast even if he were standing stark naked at the North Pole in midwinter. The moment the Duke popped one into his mouth, thick smoke came gushing out of the old boy's nostrils in such quantities that I thought his moustaches were going up in flames.

'Terrific!' he cried, hopping about. 'Tremendous stuff! I'll take a case of them home with me!'

To the Giraffe I gave a bag of Glumptious Globgobblers. The Globgobbler is an especially delicious sweet that is made somewhere near Mecca, and the moment you bite into it, all the perfumed juices of Arabia go squirting down your gullet one after the other.

'It's wonderful!' cried the Giraffe as a cascade of lovely liquid flavours poured all the way down her long long throat. 'It's even better than my favourite pink and purple flowers!'

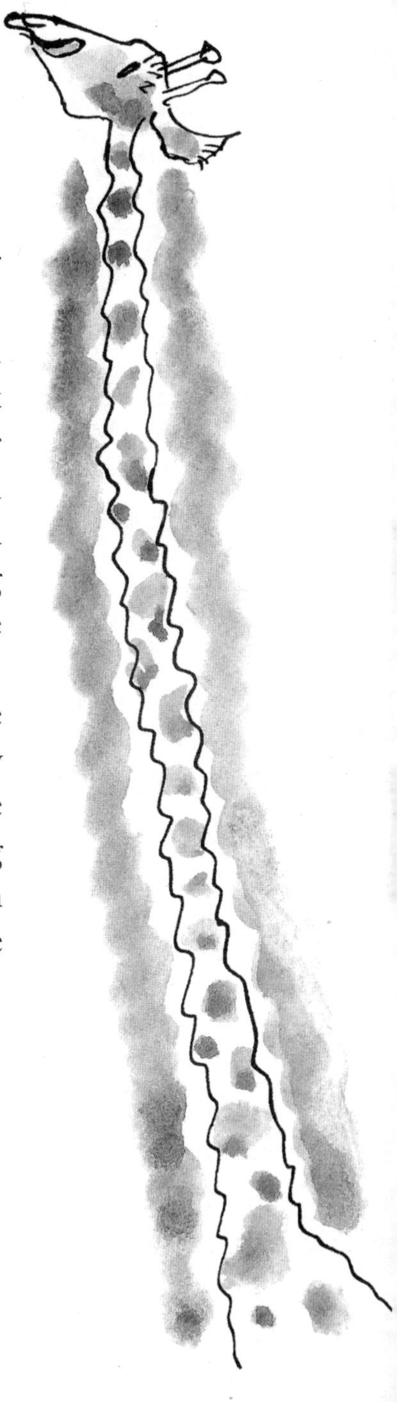

To the Pelican I gave a big bag of Pishlets. Pishlets, as you probably know, are bought by children who are unable to whistle a tune as they walk along the street but long to do so. They had a splendid effect upon the Pelican, for after he had put one of them into his beak and chewed it for a while, he suddenly started singing like a nightingale. This made him wildly excited because Pelicans are not song-birds. No Pelican had ever been known to whistle a tune before.

To the Monkey I gave a bag of Devil's Drenchers, those small fiery black sweets that one is not allowed to sell to children under four years old. When you have sucked a Devil's Drencher for a minute or so, you can set your breath alight and blow a huge column of fire twenty feet into the air. The Duke put a match to the Monkey's breath and shouted, 'Blow, Monkey, blow!' A sheet of orange flame shot up as high as the roof of the Grubber house and it was wonderful.

'I've got to leave you now,' I said. 'I must go and look after my customers in the shop.'

'We must go, too,' said the Giraffe. 'We have one hundred windows to clean before dark.'

I said goodbye to the Duke, and then one by one I said goodbye to the three best friends I had ever had. Suddenly, we all became very quiet and melancholy, and the Monkey looked as though he was about to cry as he sang me a little song of farewell:

'We have tears in our eyes
As we wave our goodbyes,
We so loved being with you, we three.
So do please now and then
Come and see us again,
The Giraffe and the Pelly and me.

All you do is to look
At a page in this book
Because that's where we always will be.
No book ever ends
When it's full of your friends
The Giraffe and the Pelly and me.'

It's time for another tale of unusual animal antics.

Shall we begin?

ESIO TROT

Mr Hoppy lived in a small flat high up in a tall concrete building. He lived alone. He had always been a lonely man and now that he was retired from work he was more lonely than ever.

There were two loves in Mr Hoppy's life. One was the flowers he grew on his balcony. They grew in pots and tubs and baskets, and in summer the little balcony became a riot of colour.

Mr Hoppy's second love was a secret he kept entirely to himself.

The balcony immediately below Mr Hoppy's jutted out a good bit further from the building than his own, so Mr Hoppy always had a fine view of what was going on down there. This balcony belonged to an attractive middle-aged lady called Mrs Silver. Mrs Silver was a widow who also lived alone. And although she didn't know it, it was she who was the object of Mr Hoppy's secret love. He had loved her from his balcony for many years, but he was a very shy man and he had never been able to bring himself to give her even the smallest hint of his love.

Every morning, Mr Hoppy and Mrs Silver exchanged polite conversation, the one looking down from above, the other looking up, but that was as far as it ever went. The distance between their balconies might not have been more than a few yards, but to Mr Hoppy it seemed like a million miles. He longed to invite Mrs Silver up for a cup of tea and a biscuit, but every time he was about to form the words on his lips, his courage failed him. As I said, he was a very very shy man.

Oh, if only, he kept telling himself, if only he could do something tremendous like saving her life or rescuing her from a gang of armed thugs, if only he could perform some great feat that would make him a hero in her eyes. If only . . .

The trouble with Mrs Silver was that she gave all her love to somebody else, and that somebody was a small tortoise called Alfie. Every day, when Mr Hoppy looked over his balcony and saw Mrs Silver whispering endearments to Alfie and stroking his shell, he felt absurdly jealous. He wouldn't even have minded becoming a tortoise himself if it meant Mrs Silver stroking his shell each morning and whispering endearments to him.

Alfie had been with Mrs Silver for years and he lived on her balcony summer and winter. Planks had been placed around the sides of the balcony so that Alfie could walk about without toppling over the edge, and in one corner there was a little house into which Alfie would crawl every night to keep warm.

When the colder weather came along in November, Mrs Silver would fill Alfie's house with dry hay, and the tortoise would crawl in there and bury himself deep under the hay and go to sleep for months on

end without food or water. This is called hibernating.

In early spring, when Alfie felt the warmer weather through his shell, he would wake up and crawl very slowly out of his house on to the balcony. And Mrs Silver would clap her hands with joy and cry out, 'Welcome back, my darling one! Oh, how I have missed you!'

It was at times like these that Mr Hoppy wished more than ever that he could change places with Alfie and become a tortoise.

Now we come to a certain bright morning in May when something happened that changed and indeed electrified Mr Hoppy's life. He was leaning over his balcony-rail watching Mrs Silver serving Alfie his breakfast.

'Here's the heart of the lettuce for you, my lovely,' she was saying. 'And here's a slice of fresh tomato and a piece of crispy celery.'

'Good morning, Mrs Silver,' Mr Hoppy said. 'Alfie's looking well this morning.'

'Isn't he gorgeous!' Mrs Silver said, looking up and beaming at him.

STORIES ARE **GOOD** FOR **YOU.**

Roald Dahl said,
'If you have good thoughts, they will shine out of your face like sunbeams and you will always look lovely.'

We believe in doing good things.
That's why ten per cent of all Roald Dahl income* goes to our charity partners. We have supported causes including: specialist children's nurses, grants for families in need, and educational outreach programmes. Thank you for helping us to sustain this vital work.

Find out more at roalddahl.com

The Roald Dahl Charitable Trust is a registered UK charity (no. 1119330).
* All author payments and royalty income net of third-party commissions.

That's it.
The end of the book.

HERE IS
one LAST **WORD**,
invented by **Roald Dahl**
HIMSELF.
Make sure you KEEP IT SAFE.

BABBLEMENT

Noun: A nice gossipy conversation.

ROALD DAHL